THE EVIL THAT MEN DO

The new Dorothy Martin mystery

Dorothy Martin and her husband, retired Chief Constable Alan Nesbitt, are on holiday in the idyllic English village of Broadway when they stumble across the body of a man who appears to have fallen down a disused quarry. When it is revealed that the man, a local farmer, was probably pushed over the edge, and that the police have failed to find any suspects or motives for the murder, Dorothy can't help but get involved...

*The Dorothy Martin Mysteries
from Jeanne M. Dams*

THE BODY IN THE TRANSEPT
TROUBLE IN THE TOWN HALL
HOLY TERROR IN THE HEBRIDES
MALICE IN MINIATURE
THE VICTIM IN VICTORIA STATION
KILLING CASSIDY
TO PERISH IN PENZANCE
SINS OUT OF SCHOOL
WINTER OF DISCONTENT
A DARK AND STORMY NIGHT *
THE EVIL THAT MEN DO *

* *available from Severn House*

THE EVIL THAT MEN DO

A Dorothy Martin Mystery

Jeanne M. Dams

Severn House Large Print
London & New York

This first large print edition published 2013
in Great Britain and the USA by
SEVERN HOUSE PUBLISHERS LTD of
9-15 High Street, Sutton, Surrey, SM1 1DF.
First world regular print edition published 2011 by
Severn House Publishers Ltd., London and New York.

British Library Cataloguing in Publication Data

Dams, Jeanne M.
  The evil that men do.
  1. Martin, Dorothy (Fictitious character)--Fiction.
  2. Women private investigators--England--Fiction.
  3. Americans--England--Fiction. 4. Vacations--England--
  Broadway--Fiction. 5. Farmers--Crimes against--England--
  Cotswold Hills--Fiction. 6. Detective and mystery stories.
  7. Large type books.
  I. Title
  813.5'4-dc23

  ISBN-13: 978-0-7278-9979-8

Severn House Publishers support The Forest Stewardship Council
[FSC], the leading international forest certification organisation. All
our titles that are printed on Greenpeace-approved FSC-certified paper
carry the FSC logo.

MIX
Paper from
responsible sources
FSC
www.fsc.org
FSC® C018575

Printed and bound in Great Britain by the
MPG Books Group, Bodmin, Cornwall.

To my dedicated readers,
who are very dear to me

ONE

'Will you just *look* at that view!' I pulled my hat down a little farther to shade my eyes, and feasted on the scene before me. A foot or two from where I stood, the drystone wall bordering the footpath boasted flowers growing from every chink. I'm not good at identifying English flowers, but whatever these were, they were gorgeous. In lavish, luxuriant bloom, they ranged in colour from palest blush, through pink and magenta, to lilac and deep purple. The stones themselves, what could be seen of them through their extravagant blanket, were grey, except where they had been covered with lichens in gold and rust. The rich greens of the foliage blended with the paler greens and yellows of the gently rolling fields spread out below us: rye, oilseed and pastureland dotted with the fuzzy balls of sheep and lambs, as yet unshorn on this May day. In the middle distance the square tower of a fifteenth-century church rose serenely towards a misty sky, and in the valley a small river flowed languidly past a dozen or so houses and a pub – the quintessential Cotswold village.

'Happy you came, then, love?' said Alan,

reaching for my hand.

'Happy! I'm ... it's...' Seldom at a loss for words, I couldn't find any to describe my utter bliss.

'It took me that way, too, the first time I saw the Cotswolds,' my husband said, tactfully turning away to look out over the hills, giving me time to blink away the foolish tears that had suddenly welled up. Supreme natural beauty, like perfect music, always makes me cry.

We had decided, some weeks ago in the dreary dregs of February, to take a walking tour come spring. It was something I'd long wanted to do, but had somehow never found the time. I had my eye on the Lake District, or the Yorkshire Dales, but my dear husband, a native Englishman (while I am a transplanted American) had walked those parts of the country before and suggested that for my first time, with my two artificial knees, I might be happier with a less rugged terrain.

He was right. This was our first day out, and I was doing quite well, but after a few hours of walking I realized how badly out of shape I was. Out of breath by the time we got to the top of this rise, I was glad the view gave us a good excuse to stop and pant. At least I panted. Alan is a little older than I, and neither of us is a spring chicken, but he had kept himself fit during his long career in the police force, and still took a lot of exercise even though he was retired.

'Good thing you talked me out of the Lake District,' I said, grinning. 'Next time, maybe. But truly, Alan, I can't imagine anything being more beautiful than this.'

'Not more beautiful, but different. Wilder, perhaps, and more vast. When I visited your American West years ago, parts of it reminded me of the Lake District – such a lot of sky. Here everything is on a smaller scale.'

'Cosier,' I suggested, using one of my favourite words.

'If you like,' said Alan, chuckling. He glanced at his watch. 'And speaking of cosy, it's getting on for teatime. If we hurry a little, and don't get lost, we can make it to Broadway in time for tea at the Lygon Arms.'

'I've heard of the Lygon Arms,' I said, following him obediently down the path. 'Isn't it sort of a fancy place? Will they look down their noses at us, in hiking gear and grubby?'

'It's a bit posh, yes, but every hostelry in the Cotswolds is accustomed to hikers. We'll probably have time to go to our B&B and change, if you want.'

'I want. My shoes are dusty, and I want to get rid of this pack.'

So we set a pretty good pace the last couple of miles, walking as fast as we thought safe. Two miles would be a long way to walk on a twisted ankle, and according to our Ordnance Survey map there were no roads near the footpath until we got to Broadway.

We made it safely to our B&B, the Holly Tree, and took the time for a quick shower before getting into clean clothes and heading to the Lygon Arms for our tea. As we walked up the High Street, I asked Alan about the history of Broadway.

'The name has an odd sound, to an American. Conjures up images of Forty-Second Street and Times Square.'

'Well, I expect your street and our village were given the name for the same reason. The way here – the High Street – is, as you can see, broad. There used to be two streams running right down the middle of the village, on either side of a narrow road. That got to be awkward—'

'I can well imagine,' I said drily.

'Yes, well, particularly as the village was an important coaching stop, being on the main road between London and Worcester. The street was quite narrow for coaches, so eventually the streams were covered and the High Street widened to a boulevard, with grass and trees down the middle. I read somewhere that dip holes were left, so that the villagers could still get water, as they were not on the mains. There are still some here who remember when the holes were filled in. And apparently, when there's a great deal of rain, the streams reclaim their rightful courses.'

'Leading to a great mess. They should build an underground channel and have done with it.'

'Ah, but you're in the Cotswolds, where things move at a leisurely pace. Doubtless the village authorities will get around to something of the kind, one of these centuries.'

Our leisurely stroll took us past houses, small shops, and... 'Alan, tell me that's not a horse farm, right in the middle of the village.'

'Alas, like George Washington, I cannot tell a

lie. That is indeed a horse farm. Fancy a ride, m'dear? I believe one can hire the horses.'

He looked at me blandly, knowing perfectly well that I admire horses only from a distance. The idea of getting on the back of one terrifies me. I was fifty years younger the last time I tried that and discovered how much higher and wider they are than they look. Never again.

'No, thank you,' I said, my tone just as bland as his face. 'I'll just tuck this away in my "There'll always be an England" file.'

'No horse farms in the middle of villages when you were a girl?'

'No villages, period. Small towns, yes, but nothing that in the least resembles an English village. Unless maybe on the east coast ... oh, my!' We had reached the centre of the village, and the building on my right, built of the golden Cotswold stone, looked like a royal palace, or a manor house at the very least. *That* is the Lygon Arms?'

'Indeed. Sixteenth-century coaching inn. Parts of it date to 1532, if I'm not mistaken.'

I drew a deep breath. 'I'm *very* glad we changed clothes.'

We had a splendid tea, sandwiches and scones and all the rest, and when we'd finished I gave a satisfied sigh. 'I feel much better. This is the first time in my life I've walked twelve miles in one day, and my feet are telling me about it.'

'Tired, love? We could go back to the Holly Tree and have a nap.'

'I'm not especially tired, oddly enough. I think the exercise did me good. And now that we're here and I've had my tea, I'd like to explore Broadway a bit. Everyone has told me it's one of the loveliest villages in the Cotswolds. Unless you'd rather rest for a while.'

'Not I. Shall we stroll down to the bottom of the street, since we started at the top?'

The High Street is probably not a mile long from one end to the other. At the top, past our B&B, the street curved gently out of sight into the hills. From the centre of the village, down past the Lygon Arms and pubs and shops, it meandered past the village green, with intriguing little lanes on either side, and then headed between imposing houses, out past an Indian restaurant and into the country. We ambled along, exploring the byways and doing a lot of window shopping. The displays in Broadway's antique shops ranged from authentic, very beautiful and expensive furniture and *objets d'art* to reproduction kitsch, and everything in between. It was a good thing for our budget that the shops were closed by the time we reached them. A small modern shopping area provided a miniature supermarket, where we stopped to buy a bottle of my favourite sherry. One little lane wandered up to the church, where a nearby cottage boasted a splendid thatched roof, the only one I'd seen all day.

'I thought the Cotswolds were supposed to have thatch all over the place.'

'Not here, evidently. Tile and slate tone in better with the Cotswold stone, don't you think?'

'I think it's all perfectly lovely. I also think I'm ravenous. Yes, I know I had a huge tea, but I've

12

walked something like half the circumference of the earth today, and I need a pint, and a meal, and my woolly slippers, in that order.'

'Your wish is my command, my dearest love. Can you walk a few more yards, as far as the Swan, do you think?'

'Just about.'

The Swan was a busy pub, now blessedly free of the smoke that used to blind and smother me. Alan found us a table and went to the bar for our beer. 'I ordered venison for both of us,' he said when he came back with brimming pints. 'And a nice Cabernet to go with it. Will that do for you?'

The beer was excellent, and when our food arrived, it, too, was wonderful. The days when English food was a subject of derision for American tourists are long gone. Our meat was tender and succulent, and the vegetables served with it, both the root vegetables roasted with the venison and the steamed, fresh cauliflower and green peas and beans, were perfectly cooked.

We ate in a comfortable silence. I was very tired. The long day had finally caught up with me and I was happy to eat my meal and drink my wine, and think about what we might do tomorrow.

When I had satisfied my hunger, I looked around at my fellow diners. The pub was noisy, but our particular corner of it was set apart a little from the main room. There were only three other tables, all occupied. The one nearest us held a middle-aged couple, prosperous-looking, running a little to fat (as one tends to do, I

13

thought, wondering guiltily if I should have eaten that last potato). The two young people with them were presumably a son and daughter-in-law, or the reverse. They were having a good time.

I nudged Alan. 'Who's he, do you think?' I said in a low voice, beginning one of our favourite games. 'I think he's the lord mayor. He looks important. Shiny, sort of, and certainly well-to-do.'

'A village of this size probably wouldn't have a lord mayor,' Alan objected. 'I say he's the local MP, paying his duty visit to his constituency.'

'No, he's much too nice to be a politician. And his wife's nice, too. A lawyer, maybe. Solicitor, I mean. A professional man, anyway.'

Just then a large, jovial-looking man came in and stopped at their table. 'George!' he said heartily. 'I hoped I'd run into you.'

'The vicar,' I whispered. 'Going to ask him about a contribution to the Church Roof Fund.'

'How's that mare coming along? My wife's birthday's next week, remember, and I promised her a nice surprise.'

'In splendid form, Sam. As nice a ride for a lady as anyone could want. If you'll come around Sunday morning, I can let you have a look at her.'

Alan and I looked at each other and burst into laughter.

We took our time walking home. I was developing some blisters, I thought, but it had been a lovely day, a perfect day. As we passed the horse farm Alan gave me a look.

'Solicitor, eh?'

'And the vicar. As a character analyst I make a good schoolmistress.'

'Hmm. And speaking of mistresses...'

The end of the day was very pleasant, too.

TWO

One might gather, from looking at me, that I enjoy my food. One would be correct. I tucked into our splendid breakfast next morning with an appetite undiminished by two large meals the day before.

'Mrs Littlewood, you're a marvellous cook,' I said as our hostess stopped by our table. 'Do you bake like this every morning?' She had made three different varieties of breakfast bread to go with our eggs and bacon and sausage and potatoes and grilled mushrooms and tomatoes and juice and toast and marmalade, and there was cereal and porridge on offer, as well as fruit smoothies for the health-conscious.

'I love to bake,' she said with a brilliant smile. 'And do call me Pam. We're not formal here. You're staying several days in Broadway, I believe?'

'Yes, and we're so glad we booked in here. But if I eat like this every morning you'll have to roll me out.'

'We'll walk it off, my dear,' Alan said.

'Do you know Broadway at all, then?' Pam asked Alan.

'Not to say know it. I visited once or twice, many years ago, but it's changed a good deal.'

Pam sighed. 'Much more commercial, isn't it? It's all good for business, but I'm not sure I like what it's done to the village.'

'You seem to have a full house,' I said, glancing around the room. The tables were beginning to empty, but they had all been occupied a few minutes ago. 'Are any of your other guests staying long?'

'Oh, yes. The two Irish ladies in the corner, Mrs O'Hanlon and Mrs McGath, are here for three weeks. I'm sure they'd love to meet you. And the young man who just went out – I don't know if you noticed him – has been here for a week, and plans to stay for several more days.'

'The one with the scruffy beard?' I asked, my voice lowered. 'He seems an odd type for a B&B. More the youth hostel sort. If they still have youth hostels. Goodness, I'm dating myself. Maybe those went out with the end of the hippy era.'

Pam laughed. 'Oh, no, they still exist. Every summer they swarm with earnest German students carrying huge rucksacks. This boy is English, though. Well, I say boy. He's probably in his twenties, but he seems very young. A trifle unkempt, perhaps, but he has very nice manners.' She glanced at her watch. 'Oh, dear, I must fly. So nice to talk to you!'

'What a dear,' I said when she'd whisked herself back to the kitchen.

16

'And a beauty, too,' said my loving husband with what he fondly imagined to be a leer.

I ignored him. 'I'm going to introduce myself to the Irish ladies. Would that be proper, do you think?' I've lived in England for years now, but I'm still unsure of myself in some situations. The rules are different here, and I haven't absorbed all the subtleties.

Alan was amused. 'Perfectly proper, love. Though I can't imagine why you're bothered. You do rather make your own rules, don't you?'

I made a face at him and went to the table in the corner, where the Irish ladies were just getting ready to leave. 'Good morning,' I said in my cheeriest tones. 'I don't mean to intrude, but our hostess happened to mention that you're staying here for a couple of weeks, and my husband and I will be here for a while, too, so I thought I'd introduce myself. My name is Dorothy Martin, and—'

'Yes, well, we were just going, weren't we, Eileen?' said the younger of the two women. Her accent was the lovely soft lilt of the Irish, but there was nothing lovely or soft about her manner. 'We'll not be spending our time here. We've come to walk. Good morning.'

'Well, you called that one wrong,' I said, sliding back into my chair, my face burning. 'They obviously thought I was being rude and intrusive. What an unpleasant start to the day!'

'Don't worry. You did nothing wrong. The woman got up on the wrong side of the bed, that's all. Are you ready?'

We had decided that we would spend the

17

morning wandering around Broadway, having got only a taste of it the day before, so we first headed up the High Street to its end. I kept pausing to take pictures. 'I'm going to run out of space on the disk, or whatever they call it,' I said, zooming in on an idyllic view. 'I don't think this scene has changed a bit in the past three hundred years.'

'Take away the lamp post and the motorcycle, and I'm inclined to agree with you,' said Alan.

I began to frame another shot, and then lowered my camera. 'Look, Alan. Isn't that the bearded wonder from the Holly Tree?' The young man had come out of one of the houses and was climbing aboard the motorcycle.

'Looks like him.'

'I wonder what he was doing at that house. It is just a house, isn't it, not a shop?'

Alan shook his head. 'There's no sign, but I suppose it could be an antiques shop. Some of them are oddly reserved about their trade. Hours by appointment only, that sort of thing.'

'If he's an antique hound I'll eat his motorcycle. More likely visiting a relative, or a girlfriend. That might explain why he's staying at the Holly Tree. It's at the right end of town.'

'Hmm. It's a trifle expensive for someone like him, though, and the distances in Broadway are not so great as to make that a consideration, especially for a motorbike.'

'All right, what's your explanation, then?'

'I haven't one, and speculation on no data is futile. We'll probably find he's an art student in search of culture in the Cotswolds. Remember the lord mayor and the vicar?'

'I don't care.' I linked my arm through his. 'It's just a game, and it's fun. Wot's the h'odds, so long as you're 'appy?'

Alan winced. 'You'd never make a Cockney, Dorothy. Shall we turn around and go down to the end of the town?'

So of course I began reciting 'James James Morrison Morrison Weatherby George Dupree,' and Alan joined in, and neither of us paid the least attention to the amused stares of passers-by.

Broadway is a biggish village, as villages go, but we'd pretty well seen what there was to be seen by noon. 'Right,' said Alan, as we collapsed on to a bench on the village green. 'Lunch. Then we'll rest for a little, and then climb up to the Broadway Tower?'

'Agreed. Where shall we lunch?'

The only question was which pub, since Broadway, long a tourist destination, boasts several. Having experienced the Swan, we decided to try out another one, the Hunting Dog. That turned out to be a mistake.

We finally found a table, but it took Alan for ever to get our beer, and when he came back with it, I had already begun to cough. 'Someone is smoking in here,' I said when a gulp or two of beer had cleared my throat for a moment. 'Several someones. I thought that was illegal now.'

'It is,' said Alan morosely. 'The law isn't always enforced. I didn't order anything to eat. The selection was sparse and not terribly tempt-

19

ing. Drink your beer and let's go.'

I took another swallow. 'It's not very good, is it? Watery and sour. More like American beer. I've had enough.'

We left half our pints and threaded our way to the door. As we stepped into the welcome fresh air and started up the sidewalk (pavement, I reminded myself), Alan pulled me back sharply. There was a screech of tyres, a clattering crash, and the smell of burned rubber.

'Bloody fool!' Alan roared.

I took a shaky breath. 'It's all right, Alan. He never touched me. No harm done.'

'It is bloody well not all right! The idiot doesn't belong on the pavement! I should—'

'Look, I'm really sorry!' The bearded lad from the Holly Tree stood before us. 'There was a patch of mud or something, and I lost control. I didn't hurt you, did I?'

His motorcycle lay forlornly on its side, fluid seeping slowly from somewhere in its middle. He was white and shaking, and covered with mud. His jeans were torn and his brow was bleeding profusely, staining his shirt and the hands with which he was trying to stanch the flow.

'I'm sorry, truly,' he kept repeating.

I found my voice. 'You're the one who's hurt. You're staying at the Holly Tree, aren't you?'

'Ye-es.' He sounded a little wary. Was he afraid I was getting an address to give to the police?

'So are we, my husband and I. My name is Dorothy Martin, and this is Alan Nesbitt.'

20

He put out a hand, and then quickly withdrew it. 'Sorry. Not fit to touch anyone. Paul Jones.'

'All right, Paul, I think we'd all better go back to our B&B. That cut on your cheek needs seeing to, and then we could all do with a drink, I imagine.'

Alan had been remarkably silent through all this. His face was closed, and I thought, with a little glint of amusement, that a man was never too old or too happily married for a spot of jealousy. Mr Paul Jones was, despite his torn and ragged clothes, beard, and blood, a very handsome young man.

'I'll go and clean up, but you don't have to go with me, Mrs Martin. I can fend for myself. I'm quite used to it.'

Was there a touch of bitterness in that last remark? None of your business, Dorothy, I chided myself. But I found myself intrigued by Paul Jones, and welcomed the chance to get to know him better. 'Well, we'll walk with you as far as the Swan, anyway. At least I suppose you'll have to walk. Your bike doesn't look as if it's going anywhere for a while.'

He looked at it. 'No,' he said briefly. 'And it's borrowed.'

Oh, dear. The boy didn't look as though he had two pennies to scrape together, much less enough for expensive repairs to a friend's motorbike.

And yet, I thought, he's staying at the Holly Tree, which runs to nearly seventy pounds a night for one person. A real bargain for what it is, a lot cheaper than a hotel of the same quality, but

21

still...

Not your problem, I told myself firmly as the three of us walked up the street, Alan slipping my hand over his arm and holding me close.

When we got to the Swan, Paul stopped. 'I'll leave you here,' he said, a little awkwardly. 'And thank you for being so understanding.'

'No,' I said. 'You're coming in with us, and we'll treat you to a beer. Just to show there are no hard feelings.'

'But...' He gestured at his torn jeans, his dirty and bleeding face.

'Then we'll eat outside. It's a lovely day, and I can bring you a paper towel to mop up your face. I insist.'

Alan had still not spoken a word, but now, to my surprise, he seconded my invitation. 'You need to sit, Jones. You're still shaking. My wife is quite right. I'll fetch us some beer and a ploughman's apiece. Stilton all right for you?'

'No, I couldn't. I mean, yes, Stilton is great, but...'

He was talking to the air. Alan had disappeared into the pub.

He came back in a remarkably short time with three brimming pints and a fistful of damp paper towels.

'Lunch is on its way,' he said, distributing the beer without spilling a drop. 'And this should make you look a trifle less disreputable.' He smiled and handed Paul the towels. 'Careful. That's hand sanitizer, not water. It'll sting a bit.'

Paul dabbed at his face, hissing as the alcohol hit the raw patches.

'Here, let me.' I took the towels from him. 'You're just smearing everything around.' He set his jaw and allowed me to torture him. 'There. More or less clean and sanitary. There's not much we can do about your clothes, I'm afraid.'

''S'all right. I can patch the jeans. I told you, I can look after myself. But thanks.' He lifted his beer in a salute, and drank deeply.

I raised my eyebrows at Alan, who gave a tiny shrug and addressed himself to his beer. I persisted in trying to make conversation. 'You have a Welsh name, but not the accent. Are you Welsh, then?'

'No.' He would have left it at that, but I fixed him with a bright, inquisitive look, and he was, after all, drinking our beer. 'I'm ... I was adopted. When I was a baby. Jones isn't my real name. And no, I don't know what my real name is.'

That, I thought, could explain quite a lot. If he'd been legally adopted, Jones was in fact his real name, but apparently he didn't lay claim to it. A troubled family? Abandoned at some point? *I can fend for myself*, he'd said. The defensive attitude, the penniless appearance ... but I still couldn't figure out why he was staying at the Holly Tree. Was there a way I could find out, without prying?

Well, no, not really. And it was, I told myself for the third or fourth time, none of my business.

I am involved in mankind, said John Donne in my head. And there was something about this boy...

Our meals arrived just then, so for a little while we were occupied with crusty bread and creamy,

23

tangy cheese, and chutney, and salad, and I confined myself to comments about the food. Paul responded only with the occasional nod. He was picking at his food, when I'd expected him to have the hearty appetite of the young. Ah, well, he was upset, and of course he'd partaken of, or at least had been offered, the same enormous breakfast we'd had ourselves.

When I had popped the last pickled onion into my mouth, and taken a last swallow of beer, I began, 'Are you enjoying the Holly Tree, Paul? We think it's the nicest B&B we've ever stayed in.'

'It's great, yeah. And I'd better get back there and change, and then see what I can do about the bike. Look, this'll pay for part of my lunch, anyway. Thanks a lot.' He pulled a fistful of change out of his pocket, plunked it on the table, and was gone.

'What is eating that child?' I demanded when he was out of earshot. 'I'll swear it's more than just embarrassment about the accident.'

'I don't know,' said Alan, running his hand down the back of his head in the familiar gesture that meant he was thinking furiously. 'I agree, it's more than just embarrassment. He couldn't wait to get away from us.'

'And why? We were being nice to him. We fed him, didn't fuss about him nearly running me down, doctored his injuries. I tried to draw him out, but he wasn't talking. Pam Littlewood is right; there's nothing really wrong with his manners, but his *manner* is peculiar.'

'That's just the thing. His manner. You realize

24

we've spent an hour or so with the boy, and we know nothing whatever about him except his name – and he told us himself that it isn't really his.'

'I usually manage to do better than that with new acquaintances.'

'Indeed. Inside of fifteen minutes you know their name, address, occupation, favourite brand of tea, and number and breed of pets. If the police had you on staff, they wouldn't need a database.'

'So why wouldn't Paul talk to me?'

'I think the answer to that question might prove very interesting.'

THREE

When we got back to the Holly Tree there was no sign of Paul Jones, or whatever his name was. I considered asking Pam if he was registered under that name, but she was nowhere to be found, and anyway I hated to bother the poor woman. With her house so full, she must be run off her feet, even with her husband and a small staff to help.

'Let's stick to the original plan, shall we?' said Alan. 'I've never seen the Broadway Tower, and it's only a short walk.'

'Uphill all the way,' I said, a little dubiously.

'Ah, but then it's downhill all the way back.

Come on, love. Onward and upward.'

I found my stick, with the nice sharp point for negotiating slippery slopes, and we set out.

I was panting and lagging at the end of ten minutes. 'Alan, exactly how far away is this thing?'

'Mile and a quarter, according to the little village map.'

'And how far *up*?'

He had to get out the OS map for that one, and when he'd unfolded the thing to the proper panel I got a look at the contour lines, which were very, very close together in the direction we were going. I let out a little squeak. 'For Pete's sake, how high is this thing? Nosebleed territory? Are we going to need oxygen?'

'Not according to my Sherpa guide,' he said. 'It's only about three hundred metres.'

'And we were starting from what?'

'A hundred, roughly. And we've already climbed forty or thereabouts.' He consulted the map again. 'So a hundred and sixty to go, perhaps. I do believe it will be worth it.'

'One hundred sixty metres,' I said grimly. 'That's ... let's see ... Alan, that's almost five hundred feet!'

'Yes, dear.' And he forged ahead.

It took us an hour to walk that mile and a quarter, and at the end of it I would have wanted to do nothing but throw myself down on the grass and lie there for another hour, except...

'The view, Alan! I've never seen anything ... those are mountains over there!'

'The mountains of Wales,' he said in that

deprecatory, throwaway tone the English use when they're extraordinarily proud of something. 'It's a trifle misty today, but on a truly clear day I'm told one can see ten counties.'

One would have thought he'd invented the view himself.

'OK.' I grinned and held out a hand. 'You were right. It was worth it. But I flatly refuse to climb any stairs to the top of the tower. The view is just fine from right here. And do you suppose we can find a different way down, that's not quite so steep? Because down is still harder than up for me, even with the nice new knees.'

'Hmm.' He unfolded the map, which he had put away. 'Well,' he said after studying it for a little, 'there are other footpaths. They're a bit out of our way, but they take the grade rather more gradually. I don't know how well they'll be marked.'

'How far wrong can we go? My stick has the compass, and as long as we keep heading downhill, we're bound to end up in Broadway somewhere.'

That probably falls into the category of 'Famous Last Words'. When we were rested, and sated with the view, we started down. The footpath set off to the south at first, away from Broadway for perhaps a quarter of a mile, almost on the level, and then turned more or less west and sharply downhill.

At least that's what it did on the map. We were all right until it came to the point where we should head west. This was not one of the named paths like the Cotswold Way, but simply a track

27

used for the last several centuries by countrymen and women who wanted to get from here to there and had no horse or wheeled conveyance. And although landowners are supposed to keep the paths cleared and open, either this landowner had abandoned the responsibility, or we had missed the turn. We headed out confidently, walked a few steps and realized this couldn't be the path, doubled back, tried another promising lead, and in five minutes were hopelessly lost in a steep, wooded area with rocks. Lots of rocks.

I tripped over one and would have fallen without Alan's sustaining arm. 'This is ridiculous!' I said angrily. 'How can we be lost, so close to Broadway and just a few hundred feet from a landmark like the Tower?' I was tired and hot and cross, and I wanted my tea.

'We're not exactly lost,' said Alan, with a calm equanimity that made me want to spit. 'We've simply strayed from the path. It's broad daylight in a civilized, well-populated part of the country, and all we need do is make our way downhill, as you said earlier. We'll have to watch our step, though. The trees make it hard to see very far ahead, and the map says there are abandoned quarries hereabouts. I shouldn't like either of us to fall in.'

'No?' I meant it to be sarcastic, but it came out sounding a bit forlorn.

'Buck up, old girl. You'll have your tea in no time. Meanwhile, I planned ahead.' He pulled a bar of dark chocolate out of his pocket. It was soft from the heat of the sun and of Alan, and the paper stuck to it, but it tasted wonderful.

28

I smiled shamefacedly. 'Prescription for chasing the nasties away, right? It works. Let's find the way home.'

'That's my girl. Here, take my arm. That blasted yellow Cotswold stone makes beautiful buildings, but it's foul underfoot.'

Inch by inch, it seemed, we made our way through the dense wood. It was, I suppose, lovely, but I was in no mood to appreciate it. There were clouds of tiny flies, for one thing, not the sort that bite, but the sort that get in your face and hair. I was afraid to open my mouth, afraid almost to breathe lest I inhale them. There were gorse bushes, heavy with blossom and scratchy with briars. There were other bushes that would, presumably, be thick with blackberries later in the season, but now were thick only with blossoms and thorns sharp as tiny knives. I clung tightly to Alan's arm and tried to avoid the treacherous rocks that seemed to be everywhere.

The undergrowth became so dense and the path, if path it was, so narrow I was forced to step behind Alan and follow him. We were moving at the pace of a couple of elderly, arthritic turtles, but I still bumped into him when he stopped abruptly. 'What? Have you found the edge of the quarry?' I couldn't see more than a few inches ahead.

'Yes. Stay where you are, Dorothy. Don't move an inch. I'm going to take a look.'

He sounded odd. I wanted to move to see what he was looking at, but he so seldom issued a direct order, I thought I'd better wait.

He rustled through the bushes. I heard him

pause for a moment before he returned.

'I wish to blazes I knew exactly where we are,' he said, pulling out his mobile.

'What is it, Alan?' I was suddenly cold.

'There's someone down in the quarry, and I'm very much afraid he's dead.'

It took a while for the police to get there. We had wandered farther to the south than we should have, and were on the edge of a different quarry than the one Alan had seen on the map, but Alan stayed on his phone until he could hear the Land Rover approaching, and then directed them as near to us as they could manage.

While we waited, Alan allowed me to lean against a tree, but said not to move more than a few inches from where he had stopped me. 'I've already contaminated the scene by moving to the edge, but I had to make sure of what I saw. I wish I could let you sit down, but I don't want to mess anything up further.'

'I understand. And it's almost impossible to get up from sitting on the ground, anyway. I'll be all right. I don't suppose you have any more chocolate?'

'Alas.' He turned his pockets out, but there was nothing more interesting than the slightly stale pack of gum he kept for clearing our ears when we fly. I turned that down and shifted my weight to the other foot.

Once the scene of crime officers arrived, we were questioned thoroughly, but very politely. Alan didn't know any of the police authorities in this part of the country, but they knew his name and reputation, and were careful to step on no toes. A chief constable, even though retired, was to be treated with respect and deference. After they had examined the rim of the quarry, they put paper bootees on both of us and allowed us, one at a time, to peer over the edge at what lay below.

It lay about halfway down, on a ledge created by the quarrying. The exposed rock, the ubiquitous yellow Cotswold stone, looked well-weathered. I supposed the quarry had been in disuse for a very long time.

The body was identifiable as human only by the clothes. It was clad in dark trousers and a dark shirt, with a scarf or something around the neck. When asked if I recognized the person, I could make no intelligent reply. To me, it seemed impossible at this distance even to tell if it was a man or a woman.

At last we were allowed to go on our way. One of the policemen showed us the quickest way back to Broadway, by way of a narrow lane. We found it in minutes and were sitting down to our tea half an hour later in the pleasant garden at Tisanes Tea Shop.

'Poor soul,' I said when I'd finished my first cup of hot, strong tea with lots of milk and sugar. 'I suppose he – she – whoever, stumbled over the edge and couldn't get a handhold to keep from falling.'

'Maybe,' said Alan, his hand once more moving down his neck, 'but there was no sign of scuff marks in the weeds on the edge. It was quite clean.'

'Yes, but if one tripped over a rock, one could go flying headlong. I nearly did exactly that back there. Would have, if you hadn't been there to catch me.' I poured more tea for both of us. 'You're suggesting suicide, aren't you?'

'I don't know. Probably not. Just an accident, I suppose. There ought to be a fence just there. It's a sheer drop.'

I laid my hand on his. 'Don't go making mysteries, Alan. You're retired, and on holiday, and the weather is perfect for once. Drink your tea and count your blessings.'

'Yes, Mummy.' He leaned back in his chair, stretched out his long legs, and smiled at me.

I wasn't fooled. He wouldn't be happy until he was certain that the person in the quarry had got there accidentally.

FOUR

We took the walk back to the Holly Tree slowly. We were both tired and occupied with troubling thoughts. 'I hope it really was an accident,' I said as we neared our temporary home. 'I hate to think of the pain that would drive someone to suicide. In a beautiful place like this, on a beautiful day...'

'"Though every prospect pleases, and only man is vile".'

'I've never liked that verse. For that matter,

32

I've never much liked the hymn. Since when did missionaries trek over Greenland's icy mountains? Who do you suppose it was?'

Alan knew I was no longer talking about the hymn. 'The police will find out. May already know, if the victim carried identification.'

'And how long dead, do you think?'

'My dear, I don't know. And it's no longer any of my business, thank God.'

Which was a not so subtle hint that it wasn't my business, either.

We were utterly exhausted by the time we'd climbed the stairs to our room, or at least I was. I fell on the bed, pausing only to take my shoes off, and was asleep in minutes.

I was awakened by voices. Loud voices, in the hallway outside our room.

I sat up, muzzy and disoriented. 'What time is it? What's happening?'

'Getting on for seven, and my guess is, the word has spread.'

'Word?' I still wasn't quite back on the scene.

'About the body in the quarry. You might as well get up, love. It's nearly dinner time, and we can't sleep with all that hubbub.'

Hubbub was certainly the word. When I'd pulled myself together and opened the door, the two Irish ladies were still going at it, at full volume.

'And they'll be finding out he did it, sure as the sun rises,' said one of them. I still hadn't figured out which was which.

'I'm thinking you're right, Barbara,' said the

33

other. 'Or why would he run off like that, without a word to anybody? You always said he was up to no good.'

Alan and I exchanged a look, then I shrugged and opened the door.

Far from being embarrassed about being overheard, the taller of the two women pounced. 'Ah, there you are. Mrs Martin, I believe? Mrs Littlewood was telling us you found the man in the quarry.'

'My husband did,' I replied shortly. I really didn't want to talk about it, and tried to get past. The woman didn't move, but rounded on Alan. 'Mr Martin, we haven't met. My name is Barbara McGath, and this is my friend Eileen O'Hanlon. Do tell us—'

'I'm delighted to meet you, ladies, but my name is Nesbitt. And I fear I can tell you very little. Dorothy and I lost our way this afternoon and barely escaped falling into one of the disused quarries. Someone else was apparently not so fortunate.'

'Oh, then you hadn't heard.' Mrs McGath lowered her voice to the register appropriate for imparting superbly dreadful news. 'The man was murdered! And that Paul Jones, as he calls himself, has disappeared. Now what do you think of that?'

Alan grasped my arm firmly. 'How very unfortunate,' he said mildly. 'I know you won't mind if we don't talk about it. My wife is very sensitive to such matters. Good evening, ladies.'

And he piloted me down the stairs.

'Alan!' I said as soon as we were out of the

34

house and on our way down the High Street.

'Yes. Quite upsetting.'

'That poor boy! Surely he couldn't really ... could he?'

'We have no data, love. We don't even know it really was murder. Those two silly women are just repeating gossip.'

'And they don't like Paul, for some reason.'

'He has a beard, and dresses casually, and has a Welsh name. That might be sufficient for a Barbara McGath.'

'But if he's really disappeared...'

'We don't know that, either.' Alan sounded a trifle weary. 'And may I remind you that we're on holiday? Whatever has happened, it's nothing to do with us. And I devoutly hope we can keep it that way.'

I sighed. 'You're right, of course. I just wish...'

'Look.' Alan pointed. We were passing the horse farm, and the low evening sun shone across the pasture, gilding each blade of grass and giving each mane a halo. Somewhere a dove cooed softly.

I smiled at him and tucked my hand into his arm. It *was* beautiful.

All the same, I found myself humming the hymn tune as we sought our dinner, and I didn't seem to have much appetite when we found it.

I had a hard time getting to sleep that night. It was partly the quiet. Our home in Sherebury is right next to the Cathedral, and even at night there's a certain amount of coming and going. Then of course there are the bells. There was at one time a question of silencing the clock

35

chimes during the small hours of the night. Some of the hotel-keepers claimed the noise kept their patrons awake. But a public outcry from the townspeople stopped the idea. I scarcely hear them any more, but I miss them when I'm away from their reassuring clamour.

And of course I'd had a long nap, which always leaves me wakeful at night. But the real problem was the boy. Paul Jones, or whatever his name was.

He'd been extremely upset when we saw him at lunchtime. Upset – and covered in blood. True, he had face and scalp wounds, and scalps, especially, bleed copiously. But was that enough to account for all the blood on his clothes?

What if he'd staged that accident with the motorbike? It seemed a little odd, now that I came to think about it. He said he'd slipped in a patch of mud. But Broadway's streets were kept clean, and anyway there'd been no rain for at least a week. Where had there been mud? And surely he'd have had to be going really fast to lose control like that.

Had there been blood on the body?

I had no idea. It had been too far away, down near the bottom of the quarry. I turned over and gave my pillow a vicious poke. I travel with my own, having learned that hotel pillows in England are quite variable, and I'm old enough to value my small comforts. Tonight, I couldn't get it moulded to my liking.

Alan grunted and turned over.

He was right, of course, I repeated to myself. It was none of our affair. I seemed to have been

36

reminding myself of that a lot lately. Was I really turning into an unregenerate snoop? I should forget about it and enjoy this magical place.

And meanwhile, Paul Jones was on the run from something.

I got up, went to the bathroom, poured myself a glass of water, stubbed my toe on a suitcase that had no right to be in my way, bit back what I wanted to say, poured a little more water and took a sleeping pill, and crawled wearily back into bed.

Of course I was completely dopey in the morning. Alan turned on the kettle and made me a cup of instant coffee. Vile stuff, but the caffeine brought me to some semblance of responsiveness.

'I'm hungry,' I said after a while.

'Of course you are. You didn't eat your dinner. Get dressed, woman, and let's go down and have some breakfast and plan our day.'

We were the last down to the breakfast room. The Irish ladies, thank heaven, weren't there, nor were any of the other guests. I began to apologize to Pam Littlewood.

'Don't worry, it's no trouble. The house wasn't quite so full last night, so things were easy this morning.'

'Is it true, then, that Paul Jones has gone?'

'Without a word. He left all his things, so he'll be back, but it's a bit worrying.'

'I hope his bill is paid!' I didn't like any part of this, but I certainly couldn't see Paul as the kind who would skip out.

'He paid in advance, for two weeks. That's not

37

the problem. I suppose it's silly of me, but I'm worrying about him. He's such an intense boy. There's something on his mind.'

'I'm sure you're right about that. We talked to him yesterday, briefly, but he wasn't very forthcoming.' For some reason I didn't want to tell her about the near-accident, the blood on his clothes, his manner of barely controlled panic. 'I'm surprised he paid in advance. He doesn't look as though he has much money.'

'No. But that's the way kids look these days, you know. He's been properly brought up, I'd swear. Holds the door for one, that sort of thing. And he's so good with Zulu! She misses him already.'

'Zulu?' asked Alan.

'The dog. She's not allowed in here, or I'd introduce you.'

'What sort of dog?' I asked with some trepidation. I like some dogs, but not large rambunctious ones. I've lived with cats too long to want to be jumped on and licked.

'She's a German shepherd. She's very gentle and sweet, and she fell in love with Paul the first time he walked through the door. She's been looking for him since yesterday. Now, what would you like for your breakfasts?'

We ate our enormous, cholesterol-laden breakfasts without a qualm, or at least with very few. We never ate like this at home, so surely we could have a few days off the leash. Besides, filling my stomach could sometimes keep my mind off unwanted thoughts. Like where Paul had gone. And why.

38

Alan had brought the maps down so we could spread them out in the lounge. 'We could walk to Chipping Campden,' he said, pointing. 'It's only about five miles. Less, if we follow the road instead of taking the footpath.'

'Hmm.' I studied the map and its contour lines. 'A lot of it looks like it's straight up.'

'There's a bit of that at first,' he admitted. 'Then it levels off. And Chipping Campden is one of the beauty spots of the Cotswolds.'

'What's in the other direction?' I got out the big road atlas we took everywhere.

'There's Cheltenham. It's too far to walk, about twenty-five miles, but we could probably get a bus.'

'What's in Cheltenham? Is it a pretty village?'

Alan chortled. 'It isn't a village at all, but a bustling city, built around a spa.'

'Like Bath?'

'Very like Bath in some ways. Both were always tourist attractions, because of the spas. Bath is very much older, of course. Cheltenham doesn't have the Roman history, but like Bath, it's almost entirely Regency in style. Lots of museums and churches, at least one with windows by Burne-Jones or some of that lot, if I remember correctly. Lots of gardens. A famous racecourse. Lashings of shops, if you're in the mood for shopping.'

'Actually I'm not, if you can believe it, and I'm never in the mood for a horse race. I'm in the mood for sightseeing.'

'And it's a beautiful day. I'll go find Pam and ask her for a bus schedule.'

'Was it stupid not to bring the car?'

'Not unless you think so. You can see a good deal more of the country from a little local bus. And a lot more local colour; you're fond of that sort of thing, my dear.'

I was. Even after living in England for years, I would never think of myself as English. I was too old, too many years an American to be really assimilated. But I adored the people of my adopted country, and delighted in every opportunity to get acquainted with more of them. A local bus sounded just the ticket.

I remembered the first time I'd ridden one, many years ago in Scotland. I was by myself for some reason I'd now forgotten. My first husband, Frank, had been off on some ploy of his own. So I decided to visit Kirkcudbright, a village made famous by a Dorothy Sayers novel. I could no longer recall the details of the journey, not even the route, but I would never forget the brief delay in some tiny village along the way, while the bus driver waited for a magnificent white Persian cat to decide to get up from its nap in the middle of the road. All the passengers knew the name of the cat, and where she lived, and freely expressed their opinions about whether she should be home nursing her sixth or seventh litter of kittens.

Alan came back with Pam and a large, dignified dog. 'This is Zulu,' said our hostess. 'Zulu, say hello to our guests.'

Zulu nodded her head gravely in our direction, then gave each of us a paw to be shaken. I was enchanted.

40

'What a lovely dog! She's beautiful, and so well-behaved.'

'She's a good girl,' said Pam in that foolish, fond tone dog owners use for their darlings. 'Now, I've brought you a bus schedule, but you might also want to think about the train.'

'I thought Broadway didn't have rail service any longer,' said Alan, confused.

'We don't, not regular service. That's been gone since, oh, the sixties, I suppose. But we're very excited about the new steam line. Well, it's an old line, really. The GWR – that's the Gloucestershire Warwickshire Railway – used to run from Oxford to Cheltenham, and they've been rebuilding the line for pleasure trips. And just this spring they finished the Broadway station. It's great fun, the trip from here to Cheltenham. Here, I've brought a brochure.'

Alan and I love old, traditional places and events. We took one look at the brochure, with its glossy pictures of shiny locomotives and flower-bedecked Victorian stations and sweeping vistas, and were sold. 'Let's see – how long does it take?'

'Ages,' said Pam, laughing. 'Steam trains are not about getting places, but it's such a pleasant journey. I think you've just time to get to the station, if you hurry. Or no, look, I can run you there, if you'd like. I have to go out anyway. That'll give you ten minutes to get organized.'

We didn't need to think twice. While I brushed my teeth, Alan pulled out a backpack and put in a few things. 'What's that all about?' I asked through a mouthful of toothpaste.

41

'In case we decide to stay the night. Here, love, rinse off that toothbrush and toss it in.'

On the way to the station, Alan asked Pam to hold our room. 'If it works out that way, we might spend the night in Cheltenham. Would that be a problem?'

'Not at all. It's only a worry when someone doesn't tell me.'

Someone like Paul. None of us said his name, but he was in everyone's mind.

The day was straight out of a Visit England brochure. Blue skies, balmy air; more like June than May. Our charming little train chugged along through a landscape I wanted to clasp to my heart. Oilseed, rye, oilseed again, a little wood here and there. Pastures dotted with fluffy white balls, big ones and small, frolicking ones. Farmhouses. More pastureland, with cows, this time, lovely big black and white cows. Every now and then the train would utter a cheerful whistle.

'I half expect to look out and see a farmer walking behind a horse and plough,' I said to Alan. 'We've stepped right into the nineteenth century.'

Alan's reply was a contented murmur.

We visited dollhouse stations, bright with fresh paint and hanging baskets of flowers, bought coffee and postcards at miniature cafés, and finally arrived at the last station, Cheltenham Racecourse.

'We're not going to a race, are we?' I asked in some dismay, looking at the milling crowds.

'Not if you don't want to. This is the station for

42

Cheltenham. The steam trains don't go into the main rail station. Different gauge, you see.'

'Oh, of course! I don't suppose they have a platform nine and three quarters.'

Alan grinned. We both adore the Harry Potter books.

Getting into town looked to be a bit of a hassle. We could have walked, of course, but the traffic made the prospect unappealing. All the cars seemed to be coming to the track, and none of them seemed to be taxis. We finally found a minicab willing to take us to the city centre, at an exorbitant price. I must have looked shocked, because Alan shrugged and said, 'We're on holiday. Blow the expense.'

So we squeezed in. Alan is a bit tall and bulky for a small back seat, but I pulled my feet out of the way, and we managed. 'Where to, guv?' asked the driver.

'I really don't know. Where would you recommend we start a tour of Cheltenham?'

The driver guffawed. 'The racecourse. That's where I'd be if it wasn't for earnin' me keep. D'you want shoppin', or churches and that, or what?'

I opted for 'churches and that', and our driver headed off at a brisk pace.

Too brisk. I was watching the passing scene when I was thrown violently against Alan. Alan cried out, the brakes screeched, the car slewed sideways and stopped up against the kerb.

'Bloody hell!' screamed the driver. 'Did you see that? The bastard never looked. I could have killed him!'

'What happened?' I asked, once my breathing was back in order.

'Idiot crossed the road right in front of me!' The driver was still shaking with shock and fury. 'Never even looked, just steps right out, a foot away from my tyres. And then walked off, cool as you please! He's lucky he's alive. And what about my tyre?'

The car was certainly listing, now that I noticed. I supposed the accident had caused the tyre to blow out. The driver got out to look, swearing under his breath.

We had nearly reached the centre of town. A small crowd had gathered to gawk, and a policeman approached. As the driver began to tell his story, with excited gestures, Alan turned to me. 'All right, love?'

'I'm fine. I was just shaken up a little.'

'Then why don't we walk from here? It's not far, and this chap's going to be tied up for a bit.'

'Fine with me.'

We got out, with difficulty, and Alan caught the driver's attention long enough to pay him.

'Here, mate! I never got you where you was goin'!'

'It's all right. Not your fault.'

'Straight ahead, then, and the first big church is on your right, about half a mile.'

Alan tucked my arm through his. I was actually a little unsteady, and glad of the support. 'Did you see what happened?' I asked. 'I was looking at the houses and never saw a thing.'

'I saw,' he said.

'What? You sound peculiar.'

44

'Do I? I was just contemplating our young friend's capacity for trouble.'

I stopped and looked at him.

'The pedestrian who behaved so thoughtlessly back there was Paul Jones.'

FIVE

'Alan, are you sure?'

'Quite sure. His face is distinctive, with that beard. And I recognized his walk.'

'He was on foot, then. Not with his motorbike, I mean.'

'On foot. I doubt he'd have had time to get the bike repaired. And Dorothy...' He paused.

I waited, with the feeling I didn't want to hear what he was about to say.

'He recognized me, too. I think that was why he ran.'

'To talk to us, before we got too far away?'

'No.'

I looked up to see if a cloud had come over the sun. There was no cloud in the sky. Why did the day suddenly seem so dark?

'He really is on the run, then,' I said drearily.

'It looks that way.'

We walked on in silence.

'Why would he come here, though? And how did he get here? It's too far to walk.'

45

'Not for a young man in good physical condition. Or he could have hitched a ride, though that would be risky. Someone might remember him, and tell the police. As for why he came to Cheltenham, perhaps because it's the nearest mainline rail station. From here he could get to London easily enough, and London is the best place in the world to get lost.'

'Won't the police be watching the stations?'

'If Paul really is suspected of involvement in the murder. If it really was a murder. But even given those conditions, Paddington is an enormous station, and the police can't be everywhere at once. He could probably slip through.'

'Then why hasn't he?' I stopped in the middle of the pavement, causing annoyed pedestrians to jostle around us. 'If he left yesterday after lunch, that's nearly twenty-four hours he's had to get here and get on a train to London. Plenty of time. So why is he still here?'

Alan propelled me into the doorway of a shop, out of the stream of traffic. 'Dorothy, we don't know. We don't know anything. And yes, I can understand your concern. I rather like the boy, too, and I agree it's frustrating not to be able to help him.'

'You could find out about the case. They'd tell you, of all people, whether it was murder, and whether they suspect Paul – all that.'

'Perhaps. But don't you see our position? Or mine, at any rate? I have no right to go poking about in a case that would be well out of my jurisdiction even if I had any authority anywhere, which I no longer do. The police are

46

jealous of their prerogatives, Dorothy, and they don't like superannuated bigwigs trying to throw their weight around.'

'But...' But what? But he's only a child? That was no argument. Paul was plainly in his early twenties, and however childlike that might appear to me, he was an adult. But he was in trouble. That didn't need saying.

I could understand what Alan was saying, and why he felt he couldn't get involved. We had gone a-sleuthing together several times, most recently at a country house where we were spending a long weekend. But that was different. We were isolated by an epic storm, and there had been no other police presence to look into the strange things that were happening.

This time there were plenty of official toes to be stepped on.

I took a deep breath. 'Alan, I do understand. But is there any reason why I shouldn't do a little nosing around? Strictly unofficially, and without your trying to get any information from anybody?'

He looked at me and shook his head, but with affection. 'And can I stop you, my dear? I've never known you to see another human being in distress and not try to do something about it. All I ask is that you leave me out of it.'

'But we can talk about it, can't we? Of course we can. Reason things out together. I go off at tangents, you know, and I need you to do a reality check for me now and then.'

He hugged my shoulders. It was as overt a demonstration as he would allow himself in a public place, and it made me feel warm all over. 'Nor have I ever been able to stop you talking. Hold off the fire in your eyes, woman! I suggest we defer any talk until we are in a place where we can hear ourselves think. Meantime, shall we enjoy the beauties of Cheltenham?'

I'm afraid I remember very little of the beauties of Cheltenham, though I've seen pictures since, and regretted what I missed. Alan tells me we saw a good deal of Regency architecture, walked through some lovely gardens, saw buskers advertising the performing arts festival being held in the city.

It was mid-afternoon when we walked, weary and footsore, into the cool and quiet oasis of a church.

'This is the famous All Saints', with the Burne-Jones windows,' said Alan, looking not at the windows but at me.

'Oh. Oh! Yes, they're lovely,' I said, glancing at a window presumably by Burne-Jones.

'Dorothy.' Alan's tone drew my attention. 'My dear, you don't like the Pre-Raphaelites.'

Well, no, I didn't like them much. They were a group of English painters and decorative artists – Edward Burne-Jones, Dante Gabriel Rossetti, William Morris, others I'd forgotten – in the mid-1800s who believed that painting was at its best and highest level before the time of the painter Raphael, and went about working in a consciously archaic style. They accomplished some outstanding art, granted, especially the William Morris designs for wallpaper and the like, but also an awful lot of what I considered

48

mediocre, and for the most part I didn't like their style.

'You don't care much for fake classical arte-facts, either,' Alan went on, 'but you've been putting up with those ghastly caryatids all day.'

'Caryatids?' I said vaguely, thinking for some reason of katydids.

'Those imitation Greek things all over the shopping area. Inappropriately dressed women carrying the weight of the world on their squared-off heads.'

'Oh, those. I'd forgotten what they were called. No, I've never liked them, even in Greece. In pictures, I mean. I've never been to Greece...' I tailed off.

'You're still worried about Paul, aren't you?'

It wasn't really a question. I sighed. 'I'm sorry, Alan. I haven't been exactly "with it" for a while, I realize. I guess I'm just not in the mood for sightseeing, after all. I keep thinking about him, and seeing that poor man in the quarry. I suppose it was a man. I never got a good enough look to know for sure.'

'I watched the news for a bit this morning, while you were still asleep. It was a man. A local farmer.'

'And it really was murder?'

'I'm sorry, love. It really was murder.'

I waited.

Alan shook his head. 'There were no details given, Dorothy. Naturally not. You know we always try to give the media no more than they need to know. "Foul play" was all they said.'

'So – no idea whether there was a lot ...

whether he was shot, or...?'

'No, to what you're really asking. We don't know – *I* don't know whether there was any blood at all. And no pictures of the body, thank God.'

'I've never understood how they can do that to the family. How horrible to see your murdered husband or father or brother in living colour ... or rather...'

Alan didn't laugh, bless him. 'Indeed. The sensitivity of the media often leaves something to be desired.'

'Alan, do you honestly think that boy could have had anything to do with it?'

'Speaking as a human being, I hope not. I rather liked him. Speaking as a policeman, and knowing virtually nothing about the evidence, I have to say there seems to be reason enough to ask him some questions.'

'I like him too. Well, you already figured that out. But...' I spread one hand and began to tick off points on my fingers. 'One, he was bleeding quite a lot when he almost ran into me. Or at any rate, there was blood all over the place.'

'Scalp wounds bleed profusely,' Alan observed, slipping into the role of devil's advocate.

'But all that fresh blood could easily cover up some that was a little older. Did the TV report give any idea of when the man died?'

'Certainly not. That's one piece of information we like to keep to ourselves.'

We, I noted. He'd used the word more than once. Alan could say as much as he liked about not being a policeman any more, but he still considered himself part of the force, whether he realized it consciously or not. I passed on to the next point. 'Two. He was extremely upset when we made him have lunch with us. He couldn't wait to get away.'

'Not feeling well after the accident,' Alan offered half-heartedly. 'Worried about his friend's motorbike.'

'I don't buy that for a moment, and neither do you. There was something serious wrong, something ... some crisis.'

'You don't know the boy well enough to make that judgement.'

'I don't know him at all,' I retorted. 'But I knew enough boys in forty years of teaching to be able to read emotions pretty well. Paul Jones was ... was afraid, Alan. Afraid, that's it! He was terrified, even.'

'You could be right,' Alan admitted. 'That would explain—'

'Excuse me.' A woman had come up the aisle to where we were sitting. 'Do forgive me for interrupting, but I overheard you talking about someone named Paul Jones.'

Uh-oh! I had meant to keep my voice down, but I suppose stress had lifted it. Was this a policewoman, tracking him down? She was squarely built, stocky, a no-nonsense, middle-aged person with a shock of short, untidy grey hair, who looked quite a lot like my neighbour, Jane Langland. Or to put it another way, like Winston Churchill.

While I tried to think what to say, the woman went on, 'It's a common name, of course, but as

51

it happens I'm trying to find someone by that name, whom I expected to meet today. My name is Jo Carter. I'm ... connected with his family, and a bit annoyed that he hasn't turned up. You wouldn't happen to know where he is, would you?'

SIX

I was still struck dumb, unable to make up my mind about this woman. Alan picked up the conversation so smoothly I'm not sure the woman even noticed my hesitation.

'No, as a matter of fact we were rather wondering about him ourselves. Not that we know the lad, really. We happened to run into him in Broadway yesterday, and exchanged a few words.'

I had opened my mouth to chime in, but I choked on the 'run into him' line. *'Au contraire,'* I whispered to Alan, who frowned at me.

'In Broadway?' the woman asked sharply.

'Yes, we're staying there for a few days,' I said, in as broad an American accent as I could muster. After living in England for years, I sometimes find it hard to produce Midwestern vowels, but some instinct told me a spot of disguise might not hurt anything. 'A beautiful little town, isn't it? I'm just wild about it.'

52

A husbandly elbow to my ribs told me I was laying it on a bit thick. He clasped my hand in a firm 'keep still' grip and said, 'Yes, we're finding it most restful.'

'Indeed,' said Jo Carter drily. 'You haven't heard, then, about yesterday's murder?'

'I ... we...' Alan's grasp became almost painful and effectively shut me up.

'Would that be the man found in the quarry?' Alan asked, allowing the tiniest tremor of unease into his voice.

'Yes.' Jo Carter was watching him carefully.

'Oh, dear. Murder, you say?'

'Yes.' The single monosyllable again.

'But that's most ... distressing. You see, I was actually the one who found the poor man.'

'Really.' The woman's voice was drier than ever. 'I understood that discovery was made by a police officer.'

Alan took a deep breath and released my hand. I rubbed it to restore the circulation.

'I *am* a police officer, Ms Carter. Or I was. Alan Nesbitt, Chief Constable of Belleshire, retired. This is my wife, Dorothy Martin. As I see you know something of the matter, we can stop playing games. Do you work with the police here in Cheltenham?'

'How do you do, Mr Nesbitt, Ms Martin. I do in fact work with the police, quite closely, but I am not employed by them. I work with social services. And I would very much like to know more about your connection with Paul Jones.'

I finally stood up and spoke. 'Why?' I asked bluntly.

'Excuse me?'

'Why do you want to know about Paul?'

She looked me up and down, a searching look that made me feel as if I were being X-rayed. I stood my ground, giving her much the same look, the look I used, years ago, to quell a roomful of fourth-graders.

'Why do you object to telling me?' she finally asked, in a much milder tone.

'Because I like the boy. Oh, young man, I suppose, but he's a boy to me. I think he's in some sort of trouble, and I'd like to help him. But if telling you anything at all about him is going to ... to betray him in some way, I have nothing to say.'

Slowly she smiled. You know, sometimes the clichés are true. It really was like watching the sun come out after a storm. Her face, which had been stern, almost sullen, relaxed into kindness and good humour. 'You speak your mind, Ms Martin.'

'It's Mrs Martin, please. And yes, I suppose I do, at least when I feel strongly about something. Or someone.'

The choir began to practise. I wondered why on earth they were working on Handel's *Messiah* in May. It was beautiful, but the organ was extremely loud.

'It looks,' said Alan, 'as though we're going to continue this conversation. Might I suggest we repair to someplace where we will not have to conduct it in competition with "Hallelujah"?'

'You sound exactly like Peter Wimsey,' I said. 'Or Jeeves. Come off it.'

'As you wish, madam. To put it another way, shall we go down the pub?'

'Now you're talkin'!'

Ms Carter (who told me that was her preferred form of address) knew a nice quiet pub just around the corner. When we were seated with our pints, and Alan had ordered sandwiches for the two of us by way of a very belated lunch, she began to tell us a little of her story, choosing her words carefully.

'I've been a friend of Paul's family for a very long time,' she said. 'I've watched him grow up. His path ... has not always been smooth.'

'That could be said of most people, I suspect,' said Alan. 'Especially young people today. There are so many pitfalls.'

'Some of their own choosing, of course,' Ms Carter agreed. 'At any rate, Paul has settled down quite nicely of recent years, quite nicely indeed. He has a good job.' She smiled, glanced at both of us, and went on. 'He's doing very well for himself. I'm pleased.'

I looked at Alan. He shrugged. 'That wasn't quite the impression we'd formed. In fact, we ... well, we treated him to lunch yesterday because we thought he looked hard up.'

'He does dress casually,' said Ms Carter, 'but I assure you he can buy his own meals.'

'He's driving a borrowed motorcycle,' I said. 'And he damaged it pretty badly yesterday, and looked worried about it.'

'I see.' She looked thoughtful. 'How did he do that?'

'Nearly running my wife down,' said Alan

calmly.

'Oh, dear!'

So we explained. 'And he was really a bit of a mess, mud and blood everywhere. We took him into the pub to clean him up, and then gave him lunch, although he didn't eat much of it,' I concluded. 'He did give Alan a little money for it. A few pounds. We thought it was all he had.'

'We all run short of cash from time to time,' said Ms Carter. 'And then what?'

'Then he left, and we went back to our B&B, and then climbed up to the Broadway Tower, and on the way back...'

'Ah, yes. And when did you next see Paul?'

'We didn't,' said Alan before I could speak. 'As you may have gathered, he's staying at the same B&B as we are, the Holly Tree. But he left without a word to Mrs Littlewood, and so far as we know, he hasn't been back.'

I kept my mouth shut.

'I see.' She gave us a thoughtful look, but said only, 'If you should see him, I'd be grateful it you'd tell him I'm a bit concerned about him. He knows where to find me here in Cheltenham, but I may go back to Broadway tomorrow to see if he's returned.'

With that she sketched a wave and was gone. I turned to Alan. 'You didn't want to mention we'd seen him here in Cheltenham.'

'She told us very little about herself, and almost nothing about Paul ... did you notice?'

'Actually, I did. I'm inclined to trust her, Alan.'

'I suppose I am too, but I often make it a policy

to tell a little less than I know. Once a thing is said, it can't be retracted.'

'Hmmm. The cautious policeman. I guess you're right, though I can't see what it would have hurt. Wherever Paul is now, it isn't at that corner where we nearly ran over him.'

'What do you think he was doing there in the first place?'

'Is it too far-fetched to think he was looking for Ms Carter? She mentioned something about social services. Could she be ... his parole officer, or something?'

'That wouldn't come under the heading of social services, unless she was using the term very loosely. Some sort of counsellor, would be my guess. She has that trick of eliciting confidences while saying very little herself.'

'I noticed,' I said, in a tone almost as dry as hers. 'I really spilled my guts, didn't I?'

'What a revolting expression, my dear! You demonstrated that you trusted her, and also that you're firmly in Paul's corner if it comes to a battle. I doubt you told her very much that she didn't already know.'

'Except about the motorcycle, and almost knocking me down. I don't think she knew that.'

'You may be right. She didn't seem terribly disturbed about it, though, did you think?'

I pondered. 'No, not really. Interested, but not alarmed. Now why, do you suppose?'

'Who knows? Maybe it's exactly as she said, or implied. She's an old family friend, slightly worried about the boy because he's gone missing.'

I yawned. 'Maybe. Anyway, what are we going to do with the rest of the day? I'm ashamed to admit it, but I need a nap.'

'I could do with one myself. Why don't we find a good B&B and stay the night? If we feel like it, we could take in a play tonight. I think I saw *The Importance of Being Earnest* on a poster somewhere.'

We took an early bus back to Broadway the next morning. It wasn't as much fun as the steam train, but it was faster, even with the several stops it made. We found the village in a ferment of activity. 'What's going on?' I asked Pam. We had arrived just in time for a late breakfast, to which she had graciously invited us, even though we'd spent the night away.

'Oh, it's the arts festival,' she said. 'Hadn't you seen the posters? They're all over town.'

'Goodness, is this festival heaven? There was a performing arts festival going on in Cheltenham yesterday. We saw a great performance last night at the Everyman Theatre.'

'Oh, *The Importance of Being Earnest*! I saw it last week. It never palls, does it? I didn't know the Lady Bracknell, but wasn't she superb?'

We discussed the play for a little while. Then I asked, 'But about this arts festival?'

'Oh, it's really rather exciting. This is the first time we've tried it, but we hope to make it a biennial event. A great many artists have lived here at one time or another, you know.'

'I didn't know, actually.'

'Oh, yes. It was a coaching stop originally –

you know about that?'

'Alan told me.'

'Well, then. But then the railways came along, and Broadway became a backwater. But the wealth was still here, and the big houses, and all the lovely shops and so on that had sprung up for the coaching trade. So the village was beautiful, and very peaceful. And the artists came, and the writers and composers. Barrie lived here—'

'The Peter Pan man?'

'The very same. And Henry James, and Edward Elgar. And you may be surprised to know that John Singer Sargent painted one of his most famous paintings right here in Broadway.'

'Sargent! But he was American, surely. I know he painted a portrait of Mrs Astor, and Isabella Gardner...'

'He was certainly born of American parents, but in Florence, and he lived all over the place. I doubt if there are many beautiful women of his time that he didn't paint ... beautiful, wealthy women at least! The point is, he painted *Carnation, Lily, Lily, Rose* here in Broadway, and he and it are the focus of our festival this year. It's at the Tate Britain, of course, but one of the galleries will have a full-scale copy.'

'That's the one with the little girls, isn't it? And the Japanese lanterns?'

'Of course. That's why there are Japanese lanterns all over town. You must go to the festival, if you're at all interested in art. It promises to be quite splendid!'

'Where does it take place?'

'Almost everywhere. Most of the galleries in

59

town are participating. It doesn't open until tomorrow, but you can get brochures anywhere and plan what you want to see and do.'

She went away to tend to her duties in the kitchen and we sat finishing our coffee. 'Shall we?' I asked Alan.

'Might as well. I rather like Sargent, and we haven't visited the galleries yet.'

'And there's nothing more we can do about Paul unless ... no, until he comes back.'

Alan grinned. 'The eternal optimist! That's the reason I love you.'

'That and my great beauty,' I said, pushing back my chair with some difficulty. 'And it's going to be even greater unless I stop eating these incredible breakfasts.'

My tastes in art are rather specialized. I like almost all the Impressionists, French, English, and American. I don't, as I've said before, care for the Pre-Raphaelites. I'm picky about the Old Masters, and I refuse to look at just about anything created after, say, 1910. So Alan and I have never done a lot of gallery-hopping, where much of the work is likely to be either contemporary or amateur, or both. I am, in short, both an old fogy and an art snob, neither trait being attractive.

But I truly do admire Sargent's work, and there was a piquancy to discovering him in an English village. I was happy enough to wander the village on Alan's arm, looking in windows and deciding where we wanted to go when the festival opened the next day.

Most of the galleries were closed in preparation for the festival, but one of the big ones on the High Street had its door standing wide. We sauntered across the street and walked in.

Two women stood in the far corner, in such intense conversation that neither noticed us. Paintings and drawings hung on the walls. There were a good many bare spots, and under them other works stood leaning against the wall, apparently just taken down or ready to be hung. Alan, drawn to a lovely piece of sculpture in one corner, brushed one of the frames on the floor with his foot and stopped immediately with an exclamation.

The two women looked up. One of them hurried towards us, looking worried.

'Sir! Madam! The gallery is not open. I'm sorry, but I must ask you to leave. Our insurance...'

The other woman fixed us with steady scrutiny. 'Mr Nesbitt, Mrs Martin, good morning.'

It was Jo Carter.

SEVEN

She promptly made introductions. 'Sarah, this is Alan Nesbitt and his wife Dorothy Martin. Mr Nesbitt is a retired policeman. We met yesterday in Cheltenham.' She turned to us. 'My friend, Sarah Robinson. I hope I got your names right.'

Everyone made the appropriate noises. 'I'm so sorry for intruding,' I said, 'but the door was open. We didn't know...'

'Of course not.' Ms Robinson had recovered her manners. She was a woman in her forties, not beautiful, but extremely tidy and well-groomed. She pushed her glasses back on her nose. 'Not your fault in the least. There's another big painting coming in, so we left the door open. But I do have to ask you to leave. The security system isn't ... that is, the insurance...'

Alan came to her rescue. 'We understand. And I'm terribly sorry I stumbled over the painting, but I don't believe I've done any damage. You might want to take a look to be certain...' He stopped speaking. Neither Ms Robinson nor Ms Carter was paying him any attention.

They were staring out the front door of the shop, apparently at a group of people walking down the street. Ms Robinson's face was ashen, and she was gripping Ms Carter's arm so hard I was sure she'd leave bruises.

The group moved past. Ms Carter gently loosed her friend's fingers and moved forward to shut the front door with a solid little click. 'I think, Sarah, it might be better if the painting came in the back door, don't you? And if our guests wouldn't mind leaving that way...'

We were politely but very efficiently shepherded out and the door pulled shut behind us. We found ourselves in a narrow passageway with a couple of rubbish bins and a distinct reek of tomcat.

'Not the best way to bring in a big painting,' I observed after a moment.

Alan looked at the small door through which we had just passed, and the foot or so of clearance between the wall of the building and the rubbish bins. 'No,' he said in a voice devoid of expression. His nose wrinkled. 'Nor the most salubrious. Shall we?' He gave me his arm and we edged our way out to a larger alleyway, and thence to the street.

It was too early for lunch, but we'd lost our taste for art. It was a perfect day, sunny but not too warm, so we strolled to the green and sat on one of the benches to rest and watch the world go by.

At least that was the excuse I made to myself.

'And what,' I finally demanded, 'was that all about?'

Alan shook his head. 'It was not about our wandering into a closed gallery by mistake.'

'No. It wasn't about us, or not entirely. But they were definitely disturbed that we were there.'

'Disturbed that anyone was there?' Alan suggested.

I frowned. 'Well, that, too, but I got the feeling that there was something about us, specifically, that made the situation worse. I can't imagine what.'

'Nor can I. We barely know Ms Carter, and the other one ... Robinson, is it? ... we don't know at all. Do you suppose she owns the gallery?'

'Robinson, do you mean? I don't think so. Along with everything else, she was nervous about letting someone come in when the alarms were off. Nervous the way an employee is nervous, afraid she'll get chewed out.'

'I do sometimes wonder, my dear, if you'll ever learn to speak the Queen's English.' He shook his head in mock dismay.

'Garn!' I said in my best Eliza Doolittle imitation. 'But seriously, something's badly wrong in there. Alan!' I was struck with such a dreadful thought I stood up in my agitation. 'You don't suppose we interrupted a robbery in progress? Some of those Sargents must be worth an awful lot of money. Should we go back and—'

'No.' Alan was quite definite. 'You're letting your imagination run away with you. That is a circumstance I would recognize. You keep forgetting, my dear, how long I was a policeman. I have been involved in bank robberies, hostage situations, abductions, the whole gamut, and I would lay any odds you care to propose that no one but the four of us was in that gallery.'

'Then where was the owner? Because I'm sure

that Robinson woman is an employee.'

'Who knows? Perhaps off fetching that large painting, or escorting it. Escorting it, most likely. And I sincerely hope that their insurers never find out about that open door or the disabled alarm, because the painting would be whisked back to its home before you could say Sarah Robinson.'

'You don't think...'

'Why not? There was a prominent blank wall, right in the middle of the room. Just about the proper size, if I'm any judge, and certainly the proper position for the star of the show. Even a copy can be quite valuable, you know.'

I stuck my tongue out at him. 'Nonsense. Nobody would be that careless with a painting of value. Anyway, whatever was going on in that gallery, it didn't have very much to do with the art; I'm reasonably sure of that. It was ... I don't know what it was, but I can't get that woman's face out of my mind. Ms Robinson, I mean. I thought she was going to faint.'

'When we came in?' Alan sounded dubious.

'No, in that odd little moment when everything froze. You were a few steps behind me, so maybe you couldn't see her face, but it was white. Not pale, not what everyone means when they say that about a face, but white, like ... like paper, or a blank canvas. Alan, that's the second time in twenty-four hours that I've seen naked fear on someone's face.'

'And Ms Carter was there with her.' Alan's voice was very thoughtful.

'And she was very careful to let Ms Robinson

65

know you were a policeman,' I added. 'Why?'

Alan ran his hand down the back of his neck. 'Lots of questions. I could do with a few answers.'

'Ms Carter has most of the answers. I'm sure of that.'

He shifted on his bench. 'What did they see, the two women, when they reacted so strongly?'

I made a frustrated gesture with my hands. 'That's just it! I have no idea. When I looked where they were looking, all I saw was a group of people passing by, laughing and talking. They looked like perfectly normal tourists, some of them Japanese, maybe. Anyway there were a bunch of cameras in evidence. Nobody was doing anything in the least threatening, nobody was lurking, nobody was doing anything at all out of the ordinary. And they were gone in seconds.'

We sat in silence for a while. Two children were playing ball with a black and white dog of uncertain ancestry, probably mostly terrier. A fat man sat solemnly chewing on a sandwich. A coach stopped in front of the Lygon Arms and discharged its load of tourists, Americans by their accents and rather vivid shirts.

I sighed and stood up. 'I have no useful ideas at all, and I'm hungry. The Swan?'

We went off in search of sustenance.

After lunch, of course, we took a nap. One of the lovely things about ageing is that one need not apologize for afternoon naps. I lay down sure that I wouldn't sleep a wink for worrying about

our problem, and woke two hours later chuckling.

'What's funny?' asked Alan, sitting up with a
yawn.

'Oh, just a silly dream. I dreamt I was a little
girl, and staying with Aunt Maude. She was
really a great-great aunt or something of the sort.
I was too young to get the relationships quite
straight. I thought she was ancient, and I didn't
like her very much. She lived in a big, dark,
gloomy house in Chicago that smelled of dust
and old lady, and once for some reason I had to
spend a day or two with her, without my parents.
She served me some sort of tasteless lunch, and
made me eat every bite of it, too, and then sent
me to bed for a nap. I thought I was too old for
naps, and I hated that big, dark bedroom. I don't
know why it was so dark in the middle of the
afternoon, but I tried desperately not to go to
sleep, afraid of what might be lurking in the
shadows.

'So anyway, I dreamt about that, and relived
how much I hated having to take that nap, and
the nightmares I had afterwards about being
abandoned at her house for ever.'

'And that made you laugh.' Alan spoke in the
careful voice of a man who hopes he will at
some point understand what his wife is talking
about.

'Only when I woke up. I told you it was silly.
I just started thinking about how much I hated
that nap all those years ago, and how much I
love them now, that's all.' I stretched luxuri-
ously. 'Alan, let's get out of town this afternoon.

Go for a walk. I'd like to forget about everything for a little while and just enjoy ourselves.'

'Fine with me. Where shall we go?'

'You choose. So long as it's not too far away, and the way there is reasonably horizontal, I don't care.'

He got out the OS map, which by now was beginning to show definite signs of wear, and pondered. 'Well, we could go north-east to a village called Willersley. It's not far, and there don't seem to be any hills to speak of, but there's no footpath. We'd have to go by the road. Or we could go about the same distance south-west to a hamlet, scarcely a village, called Buckland. There's a footpath, one of the national ones, so it should be well-marked. Some hills are involved, but there's a nursery and something called the Buckland Manor Hotel. We could probably get tea.'

'You said the magic word. And I think I've seen a brochure about that hotel. It's supposed to be the last word in luxury. Buckland it is.'

It was a beautiful walk on a perfect afternoon. Amazingly, we didn't get lost once, and the views were spectacular. We had a wonderful tea at the storied hotel, though I nearly choked on my scone when I happened to see the bill.

'We only live once, love,' said Alan in an undertone.

'And at those prices it's a good thing!' But I lingered over my tea, to enjoy every gold-plated bite.

After tea we poked around the church. I found it much more to my taste than the nineteenth-

68

century concoctions in Cheltenham. Then, pleasantly tired, we wandered back to Broadway, watching the cows going home to be milked. Somewhere a church bell sounded.

'"The curfew tolls the knell of parting day,"' began Alan, and of course I chimed in. We recited as much as we could remember, which was shamefully little, and I suddenly felt my eyes stinging.

Alan took my hand and questioned me with a tilted head.

'Nothing,' I said, brushing away the single tear that had rolled down my cheek. 'It's just that the "Elegy" was one of my father's favourites. The first time I ever visited England was with my parents, and we saw that country churchyard. My father could recite almost the whole poem.'

'Happy tears, then.'

'Happy memories. Another of the blessings of old age.'

We walked along hand in hand, each with our own thoughts.

'Are you hungry?' said Alan as we walked up Broadway High Street.

I dragged my mind back from my childhood. 'Not particularly. That was an incredible tea.'

'Why don't we see if we can find some snacks, then, and stay in tonight?'

Some of the shops were still open, so we bought some cheese and biscuits and a bottle of wine and took them back to the Holly Tree.

We found a mindless comedy on the small television in our room, and stretched out on the bed, heads propped up with pillows, drinking

69

wine out of coffee cups and spilling crumbs on the bedspread and giggling at the silly jokes.

'I feel like a kid,' I said when we finally turned off the TV and called it a night. 'I haven't done anything like that in years.'

'Nor have I. Ridiculous programme, wasn't it?'

'Idiotic. My face hurts from laughing.'

'Must be the wine. Goodnight, darling.'

'Goodnight. I love you.'

EIGHT

We both slept late next morning, so late we missed breakfast. 'I think I'm finally in holiday mode,' I said as I ran my fingers through my hair, yawning. 'I can't seem to get moving.'

'Doesn't matter. There's nothing we need do today.'

'I suppose not. But ... you're not going to believe this, I'm starving.' I leaned over, looking for my slippers.

'You're spoiled, that's what you are.' He gave me a swat on the backside I was so obligingly presenting. 'Get moving, woman, and we'll go out in search of some coffee and pastries.'

I took my time over my shower, but it still wasn't too long before we were out in the High Street. I didn't bother with a hat. My hair was still damp, and it was going to be too warm for one, anyway.

'Lots of activity this morning,' Alan commented.

'Mmm. Where do you suppose we can get that coffee?' I am not at my best and brightest until I've ingested some caffeine.

'Take my arm, and I'll be your leader dog.'

'It's not fair. You've had coffee.'

I felt a good deal better once we were seated in a little bakery, with the scents of coffee and yeast and cinnamon all around us, and better still when the scents materialized in front of us and I had that first lovely hot, fragrant swallow.

'I don't know,' I said when I had downed the first cup and was putting sugar into the second, 'who it was who first figured out that those red berries from the coffee plant could be processed six ways from Sunday and end up as this magical fluid, but here's to whoever it was.'

Alan raised his cup to mine and smiled. 'Good morning, my dear. You seem to be with us again.'

I just grinned and looked around. 'Goodness, it's crowded.'

'Yes, dear. I believe I said something like that a while ago, when you were still semi-conscious. It must be the arts festival, don't you think?'

'Of course! How stupid of me. Senility setting in, I expect. What are we going to do about it? The festival, I mean.'

Alan sipped his coffee. 'My vote is, we wait until tomorrow to do anything much. If we spend today getting the feel of the festival, what's worth seeing and what isn't, then tomor-

71

row we can make better choices.'

'Tomorrow's Saturday. Won't the crowds be even worse?'

'Possibly. But opening day often draws the real aficionados, the ones who will linger. Tomorrow's crowd might be the thirty-seconds-per-picture sort. In any case, if tomorrow won't do, we can wait for another day. The festival runs through next week.'

He was leaving something unsaid. I waited.

'Oh, very well, I don't want you going back to that gallery until whatever it is has died down. Don't glare at me! You know quite well you have a talent amounting to genius for getting into trouble...' He held his hand up. 'Through no fault of your own, granted. Usually.'

'And you feel obliged to defend your honour as an English gentleman and protect me.' I sighed. It was an old issue between us. I often fought for my independence, but today I was feeling relaxed and peaceable. 'Very well. I will bow to your wishes with my usual sweet docility and wait until tomorrow to pose as an art lover. Today ... I know! Today I'll go shopping!'

It was said with malice aforethought, I admit. Alan hates to shop. It's not usually my favourite occupation, either, but on a beautiful day in an enchanting village, it seemed like a good idea. And it was a mild assertion of my right to choose my own activities.

My husband sighed elaborately, then grinned. 'A draw, I believe. Very well. You do your shopping, my dear. Do try to remember that Bill Gates has not yet given us that grant.'

'I'll do my best. And what are you going to do, meanwhile?'

'I haven't decided. Perhaps I'll gamble away what pittance you leave me, at the Cheltenham racecourse.'

'You go right ahead. Who knows, you might win, and then I could shop some more.' Alan had been known to place a small wager on a political contest from time to time. He had never, in the years I'd known him, bet on a horse. I had no idea how he planned to spend the day, but my attitude, unlike his about me, was that he was in no need of supervision. Alan is tall, broad-shouldered, and fit, despite his seventy years. He is also both intelligent and sensible. He could look after himself. As, I firmly told myself, could I. 'Back at Tisanes for tea?'

We amiably went our separate ways. I had very little cash with me, but a visit to the nearest ATM soon remedied that. Anyway, in today's society cash is almost unnecessary. Almost. If I decided to hop a bus for Chipping Campden, I'd need some actual money.

I didn't think I'd do that, though. That was the sort of excursion that would be more fun with Alan. No, I would confine myself to Broadway. Certainly it had enough shops to keep me busy as long as I could stand it.

My first stop was the Edinburgh Woollen Mills. Some people, I know, shun the chain outlets. Not me. Their clothes are inexpensive and very often to my taste, and there's always something on sale. This time they were offering very attractive tee shirts, decorated with embroidery and lace and other delectable trimmings, at an excellent price. I bought three, left, and went back and bought three more, a little guiltily. It wasn't the price, but the bulk. We were travelling on foot, and backpacks will hold only so much. We could always ship them home, though, and I liked the way I looked in them.

After browsing in a couple of antique shops and finding much of interest, but nothing I wanted to buy, I was in need of a place to sit and a little sustenance. I'd had a pretty skimpy breakfast, after all. I had wandered freely and wasn't sure of my bearings, so I looked around for a sustenance provider.

I couldn't see anything that looked like a tea shop, but a small and attractive pub stood on one corner. I could get a cup of coffee there, and perhaps a snack, and I could sit. One hates to admit it, but as age creeps up, sitting becomes more and more desirable.

There was only one other patron inside, though a few people were drinking beer under attractive umbrellas in the garden. I got my coffee and one of those odd buns the English call doughnuts, and found a comfortably padded chair in front of the fireplace. It was unlit on this bright, warm day, but its warmth might be welcome when night fell.

The other man in the room looked vaguely familiar, but I couldn't think where I'd seen him until he was joined by another man, also striking a chord in my memory. Then they began to talk, and I recognized the horse farmer I'd mistaken the other night for the lord mayor, and his eager

74

customer.

'Sam,' said the farmer, nodding on his way to the bar.

'George,' responded the other. The typical effusive greeting between two Englishmen. I smiled into my coffee.

They said no more until George had settled down with his pint. At (I looked at my watch) 11:15 in the morning. Ah, well.

'Lucy's in splendid form, Sam,' said George after he'd taken a healthy swig. 'I'm sure you'll be pleased.'

'Lucy?'

'The mare you're thinking of for your wife.'

'Oh. Oh, yes. Well, the fact is, George, Mavis isn't feeling so well. She can't seem to shake that last bout of the flu.'

'Oh? I hadn't known she was ill. Matter of fact, I've never met the lady. I hope she's better by next week.'

'Next week? Well, I'm not so sure. She's had a bad go.'

'What a pity if she's ill on her birthday.'

'Yes. That's why I'm thinking of taking her abroad. Spain, south of France, someplace warm.'

'I see.' George was not pleased. His sale of an expensive horse had just evaporated. 'I'm sorry, Sam. I hope when you're ready to consider a horse for Mrs Smith, I'll have as nice a mount as Lucy.'

Sam frowned. 'I'd hoped you could keep Lucy for me. For Mavis, that is. It shouldn't be more than a few weeks.'

75

'Can't do it, Sam. I have another buyer for her. Of course you had first refusal, since you spoke to me first, but the other gentleman will be delighted to get her. His daughter's just out of university, a fine horsewoman, and wants to show Lucy. Good morning, sir.'

With a brisk nod, he was gone, leaving Sam open-mouthed at the table. After a moment he gulped down his beer, scraped his chair back, and left without a word.

'Well,' said the barman. 'Gentleman in a hurry, it would seem. A bit hot for that, I'd say, myself.'

Have you ever noticed that when an unusual word or phrase comes to your attention, you seem to hear and see it over and over again in the next few days? Someone will mention Tuscaloosa, Alabama, for instance, and you don't even know exactly where it is, but everywhere you turn for a week, someone's talking about Tuscaloosa, or it's in the library book you check out, or in an old note you unearth in your desk.

I had the same feeling as I continued my shopping spree. Everywhere I went, there was Sam, the man from the pub. He was leaving a gift shop as I entered it to find a gift for my godson. He was sitting on the green as I approached it, watching people pass by with an attention that seemed entirely out of proportion to the interest of the scene. I love to people-watch, myself, but he seemed to be getting no enjoyment out of it, judging by his fixed frown.

I walked down to the bottom of the High Street, bent on getting some Indian takeout for my lunch. Sam was just entering the restaurant

76

as I neared it. I turned away and settled for a rather dry sandwich from a grocery store. I looked in the window of one of the art galleries to decide whether I wanted to go inside tomorrow, and there was his reflection, coming up behind me.

I did finally manage to lose him when I went in a shop to look at handbags. I needed a new one, and found several attractive ones at bargain prices, but I lost my heart to a beautifully crafted bag in green leather. It would, I knew, not go with a single outfit I owned. Nevertheless, I walked out of the shop with it on my arm, idiotically pleased with my purchase.

Weary and footsore, I found myself near the church, St Michael and All Angels, and went in seeking peace and quiet.

I had forgotten they were to have a flower festival starting tomorrow. The church was swarming with ladies, and a few men, moving great tubs of flowers around, arranging them in various nooks and crannies, discussing details (arguing would be perhaps too strong a word). And there in the middle of it all was the man called Sam Smith, trying to talk to the poor distracted rector.

'No, really, I'm sorry I can't help you, but I don't know the woman. Never seen her here. We contribute to the shelter, of course, but ... no, I've never visited it. I do assure you ... yes, if I see her, I'll tell her you're looking for her, but ... oh. Very well.'

A small woman in a very wet apron approached apologetically. 'Mr Venables, I'm sorry, but we can't find the small altar vases anywhere. Could you just...?'

'Sir, you see I really must attend to matters here. If I see the woman I'll try to let you know. Well, yes, check back if you wish, but I'm quite frightfully busy at the moment ... yes, Mrs Freebody, I believe I know where they are. Excuse me, Mr ... oh, dear.' The man was gone, and the rector scurried off to find the missing vases.

I gave up. I staggered with my purchases back to the High Street and Tisanes, where Alan and a generous tea awaited me.

NINE

'You seem to have been remarkably restrained in your shopping,' he said as he helped me stow my parcels around our table in the garden. 'It seems I will not, after all, have to declare bankruptcy, unless you dropped off some of the booty at the Holly Tree.'

'No, this is all, unless you count the bespoke ball gown for the Royal Wedding, and the two cases of Dom Pérignon; they're being shipped. Ahhh!' The tea was almost too hot to drink, but it was marvellously refreshing.

'The Royal Wedding was almost a month ago.'

'Oh, dear, then they must have forgotten our invitation. I'll have to cancel that order. Actually it works out to several summer tops, a few gifts

78

– I bought Nigel Peter a lovely stuffed airplane, see? – and the new handbag. Isn't it gorgeous?'

He duly admired it, in his male fashion, having no idea why it was so special, but content that I should be happy with it. I devoured a couple of sandwiches. 'Of course, had I been fitted for a gown and splurged on champagne, it would have been in expectation of your winnings on the ponies,' I added when I had swallowed a scone and more tea. 'What did you do all day?'

He was looking at the flowers. 'Just look at those peonies, will you? They should have bloomed and gone by now, but they're still spectacular.'

'Mmm. Did you spend the whole day in town?'

His knee jogged the table, which was a bit teetery on the flagstones. The plate of jam tarts skidded dangerously close to the edge. He caught it, but at the expense of soaking his sleeve in his tea.

'Alan.'

He looked at me just a trifle sheepishly.

'You're not usually clumsy. What have you been up to?'

He removed his jacket, dabbed at the sleeve, gave it up as a bad job, and hung it over an extra chair. I waited.

'I've been talking to the police.'

'Alan Nesbitt! And without me!'

He looked both guilty and relieved. 'I thought you were going to scold me for betraying all those high-flown principles I've been spouting.'

'Yes, yes, take that as read. What made you

79

decide to go, after all?'

'I didn't like that little scene at the gallery yesterday, Dorothy.' He was serious again. 'I didn't like it at all. On the surface it couldn't have anything to do with the body in the quarry. I do wish that didn't sound so much like the title of a thriller,' he said in an irritated aside. 'But the more I thought about it, the more I wondered. You know our favourite theory is that when a good many odd things are happening in the same place at the same time, they're likely to have something to do with each other.'

Well, it was my theory, and not even mine originally, but cribbed from some of the mysteries I read constantly. But never mind. I nodded. 'Go on.'

'Well, you can say I thought it was dangerous not to know a little more. Or you can say my curiosity got the better of me. I do miss being in the thick of things, you know.'

'Of course you do. Go *on*, before my curiosity gets the better of me. What did you find out?'

'That's the worst of it, Dorothy. I learned almost nothing, except that there's almost nothing to learn.'

'What *do* you mean?'

'They're at a dead end, Dorothy. They know the name of the man who was killed. William Symonds, farmer. In his sixties. Stone deaf, poor man. Lived alone with two dogs and a good many cats. Paid his bills on time. Sidesman at St Michael's, Buckland. No family, never married. Lived comfortably but not lavishly. Owned nothing worth stealing, and in fact his person was not robbed, nor was his house apparently entered. Full stop.'

'In short,' I said bitterly, 'that rare being: a man with no enemies and no earthly reason to get himself killed.'

'Exactly. Which means the police have no place to look.'

'Who inherits his farm?'

'The Crown, presumably. He died intestate.'

I took another jam tart. 'There must be something. Weapon? How did he die?'

'He died,' said Alan precisely, 'as a result of a fall of some forty feet on to a stone ledge. A large bruise on his back suggests that he was pushed, as does the fact that there are no signs of his trying to save himself.'

'I thought bruises took a little while to develop, while the person is still alive, I mean.'

'They do, normally. Mr Symonds had very thin skin, however, and bruised easily and quickly, according to his doctor.'

'Still, though ... oh, dear! That poor man could not have died instantly, then. Imagine lying there in pain, helpless...'

'Don't give yourself nightmares, love. He was unconscious from the moment of impact. The doctor's certain of that. Yes, he might have lived an hour or two, but he felt nothing.'

'So the time of death was...?'

'You know they're never willing to pin themselves down about that. He was last seen about eight thirty in the morning, heading out to look for a strayed calf. We found him at three thirty-seven, and the police got there about half an hour later. The best guess is he died between three and six hours before that. They'll know more when they've done a full autopsy.'

Stomach contents, insect activity, other indicators. I put down my jam tart, no longer hungry. 'And I suppose no one saw anything, heard anything, saw anyone leaving.'

'You've been there, Dorothy. It's a very lonely spot. We were there only because we lost our way.'

'And the weather's been dry. So no footprints.'

Alan raised his hand and let it fall. 'As I say. Nothing to get hold of. The superintendent is quite discouraged.'

A tiny suspicion was fluttering around, trying to get my attention. 'Alan ... why did they tell you all this? I mean, courtesy to a retired VIP is one thing, but details about the man's finances, the medical report ... that's pretty unusual.'

Alan shrugged.

The suspicion settled and flaunted itself. 'They want your help, don't they?'

'Well ... I wouldn't put it quite as high as that. Let's just say they might turn a blind eye if I happened to go about asking questions.'

'Did they ... did you get the impression they have suspicions of Paul Jones?'

'They'd like to know more about him. Anyone who disappears immediately after a crime attracts police interest. But since nobody has any apparent reason to have killed poor Symonds, and they have no evidence pointing in Paul's direction, or anyone else's, I doubt he's first on their list to be questioned.'

I picked up my tea cup and took a sip. 'Well, he is on mine,' I said when I could speak. 'I want to know all about that young man, and I know where to find out. As soon as I can track her down, I intend to have a good long talk with Jo Carter.'

Alan smiled. 'And where do you intend to start? Seeing as we don't know where she works, or where she lives, or anything about her, really?'

'I'm going to start with that woman at the art gallery. What was her name ... Robinson? Goodness, we do seem to be running into a lot of people with conventional names. Jones, Robinson, Smith ... we need a Brown to complete the list.'

'Smith? Who's named Smith?'

'That man who wanted the horse. Only now he doesn't.'

Alan looked completely confused, so I explained. 'I nearly forgot to tell you, actually. It was almost funny, in the end. I just couldn't get rid of the man.'

'You mean he followed you?'

'No, actually it was more as if I was following him. I don't think he ever even noticed me.'

'Only because you aren't wearing one of your noticeable hats.'

'I have been neglecting them lately, haven't I?' Alan knew very well that a backpack doesn't have a lot of room for hats. Not my kind of hats, anyway. 'But back to Ms Robinson. We know where to find her, and I'm sure we can find out about Ms Carter from her. Now.' I looked at the last crumb of salmon sandwich on my plate and decided with some regret to leave it. 'I don't know about you, but I'm more than ready for my nap.'

Saturday dawned bright, sunny, and warm, another perfect day in the Cotswolds. 'Surely this weather can't last, Alan,' I said as we dressed. I took some care with my appearance and even donned a hat. If we were going to be Art Patrons today, I wanted to look the part. 'I don't think I've ever seen such a long dry spell in this part of the world. Back home, we would have been well overdue for a rip-roaring thunderstorm by now.'

'You're quite right. If it doesn't rain soon, some of the crops and a great deal of wildlife will be facing serious trouble. It's lovely weather for a holiday, but I hope we're not in for another drought.'

'Maybe it'll rain tomorrow, and we'll have a good excuse for staying in. I think I'm just about ready for a day or two as a couch potato. There's a lovely fireplace in the lounge, and a decanter of sherry we haven't sampled yet.'

'Indeed. Ready, my dear?'

I was very good at breakfast, passing up the bacon and sausage in favour of scrambled eggs and toast, and nothing else except coffee. Alan raised his eyebrows at my order. 'Slimming, darling?'

'Sort of. The fact is, this skirt is very nearly too small for me. If I stuff too much food in, the button's going to pop.'

84

'I prescribe another shopping trip. I do like you just the way you are, you know. Never did care for Twiggy.'

I chuckled, nearly choking on my coffee. If I lost fifty pounds I still wouldn't approach the emaciated look of the waif-like model so popular in the sixties. 'Whatever happened to her, anyway, I wonder?'

'I believe she's involved with one of those American "reality" shows on television. Eat up, love. We'll find you another skirt.'

So I changed my mind about bacon and mushrooms and tomatoes, and got up, panting slightly, to brush my teeth before we sallied forth to appreciate Art. I stepped out of Pam's way as she darted out of the kitchen.

'Oh, by the way,' she said, 'I meant to tell both of you, but I've been busy. Paul turned up yesterday. I know you've been wondering about him.'

I stopped dead in my tracks. 'Turned up! Here?'

'Yes, just briefly, to get some of his things and let me know he'll be gone for a few days, but back early next week. I thought you'd be relieved.'

'Relieved! Of course, but where in the world has he been? Why did he go off like that, without a word to anybody?'

'I don't know. He didn't say. But he did tell me a secret. I promised not to say anything to anybody, but ... well, I can tell you tomorrow. If you don't already know by then.'

She was gone with a flourish of her apron strings and Alan and I were left staring at each

85

other.

'So much for our runaway,' he said. 'Seems he can take care of himself.'

'Ye-es. Maybe. But in that case, why was Jo Carter so worried about him?'

I still wanted to talk to Jo. There were too many unanswered questions about Paul, and about that strange little episode in the gallery. But it was going to be a while before I could get my questions asked.

We had vastly underestimated the numbers of people who might want to come to a beautiful village on a beautiful day to look at art. It wasn't easy to walk down the street, much less get into the galleries.

I stepped aside, out of the stream of chattering tourists, and pulled my festival brochure out of my pocket. 'Look, Alan. It says there's a tour of Broadway, featuring places where the artists and writers and composers lived and worked. It starts every day at ... let's see ... at ten thirty, from Trinity Gallery. And it's nearly that now. Let's do that first, and go to the galleries later when they're not so crowded.'

Alan looked across the street to the crowd gathering in front of the big gallery. 'You go, love. I'm not fond of being herded, and I do actually know some of the sites. I'll just wander on my own, and perhaps join you later.'

He kissed me on the nose and walked away, and I crossed the street.

The tour was interesting, and informative. The guide was an artist himself, and knew so much about the Broadway artists, past and present, that he soon lost me. A few of the names were familiar, but many more were not, so I trailed along, happy just to see the houses and gardens and watch the other people on the tour. They were a mixed lot: young, old, and from several different countries. The Japanese family was unmistakable, even though their English was very good. I sometimes think Japanese boys, in particular, are born with cameras hanging round their necks. There were quite a few English, of course, a good many Americans, and a handful of Canadians just recognizable by their accents.

I looked more closely at one of the Canadian women. 'Penny!' I cried. 'It is you, isn't it? What on earth are you doing here?' Penny Brannigan was a delightful woman I'd met on a quick trip to Wales, when a friend insisted I needed a manicure and steered me to Penny's recently opened spa.

'Same as you, I expect,' she said, 'playing tourist. Wales isn't all that far away, and I've always enjoyed British arts festivals. You never know what you're going to find, and I thought I might pick up something for my new cottage, but the prices!'

I nodded sympathetically. 'You must have champagne taste and a beer budget, just like Alan and me.'

'That about sums it up. So I decided to do the tour of Broadway. I've never been here before. What a gorgeous place!'

'Isn't it? I do love English villages.'

'Then you must visit more of Wales. The

87

villages there are different, but just as charming. Plus, we have the hills and valleys. Now tell me, have you managed to get yourself mixed up in another crime?'

'Well ... not exactly.' For some reason I didn't feel like telling her about the body we'd found.

'You're holding out on me, Mrs Martin. You're up to something. Just try to keep out of trouble, will you? And,' as she glanced at my hands, 'try to schedule a manicure one of these days, OK?' With a friendly wave, she turned to follow the guide and, cheered by the encounter but beginning to flag, I looked around for a place to sit and spotted Alan. 'Learn anything, darling?' he asked as he slipped my arm through his.

'Lots. Too much to digest all at once.'

'Were you nearly finished?'

'I am entirely finished. I'm hot, and this hat isn't doing much to keep the sun off.' Alan suppressed a grin at my hat, a large floppy straw with one huge pink rose. 'I think the tour is finished, too, or almost. Where are we? I've been down so many lanes and through so many gates I've lost my sense of direction.'

Alan kindly did not remark that I'd never really had one. 'We're nearly at the end of town. How about lunch at the Indian place?'

He didn't need to ask twice. I'd been hankering for Indian food ever since we'd first seen the restaurant.

There may be better aromas than the warm, spicy smell of Indian food, but I couldn't think of too many. My mouth was watering before we sat down, and Alan was quick to order cold lagers for both of us and a basket of garlic naan bread before we decided on anything else.

'So you know how I spent my morning, absorbing culture. What did you do with yours?'

'I thought I'd smooth your path a bit, so I went looking for Jo Carter.'

'Oh, well done! Any luck?'

'Not in Broadway. She's likely to work out of Cheltenham, I suppose, though she was here just yesterday. But I learned something interesting.'

'What's that?' I swallowed a chunk of the lovely flatbread and washed it down with beer.

'Someone else is looking for her, too. In three or four of the places where I asked, someone had been there before me. And no one so much as admitted knowing who she was.'

'Alan, that's downright peculiar! First, it's odd that in a village, even a largish one like Broadway, she can be unknown to everybody. And it's certainly odd that more than one person is looking for her. Who on earth is she?'

'Ah! Our food. Tuck in, love, and when we've satisfied the inner man, we'll go and try to find out.'

TEN

We had lunched early, so when we got back to the cluster of galleries on the High Street, the crowd had thinned considerably, most of them apparently seeking out food. We had no trouble getting into the gallery where Ms Robinson worked.

And we were lucky. There were only a few customers inside, there to look at the special displays or, possibly, to buy some of the works that were for sale. My eyes swerved immediately to the large, central wall that had been bare before. And there, sure enough, was a large, beautiful painting, but not the one I'd been expecting. It was a full-length portrait of a lovely woman whose name I did not recognize.

'Exquisite, isn't it?' The voice was behind us, and I turned around to see Ms Robinson. She recognized me, too, and stepped back, her hand at her throat in the classic gesture of dismay or fear.

Alan was right behind her; she trod on his foot and stumbled. 'Oh, I'm ... forgive me, I...'

'We startled you,' said Alan. 'But in fact we wanted to talk to you, Ms Robinson, if you have a moment.'

The woman at the desk by the corner, in pearls

and possessing that indefinable air of wealth, could only be the gallery owner. 'Goodness, Sarah,' she said, 'it's well past time for your lunch. Do go with your friends, and don't hurry back. You've worked like a demon these past couple of weeks. I can manage until Jack gets back, and I think the big rush may be over for the day.'

'But...'

Ms Robinson might well have protested that we were not her friends, that she barely knew us, and that she wasn't eager to pursue the acquaintance. All of that trembled on her lips, but a couple came in just then, obviously old and valued customers, for the owner cooed at them and exchanged air-kisses.

'Colin! Lesley! How lovely to see you! You came in at just the right time. One can move about at the moment. Now you must see...'

She had no attention to spare for her assistant. Ms Robinson said, 'I really don't need lunch just now. And I'm quite busy, so...'

'Ms Robinson,' said Alan quietly, 'I realize you know nothing about us, but we wish only a moment or two of your time. If you prefer not to leave the shop, is there a quiet corner somewhere?'

'Nonsense,' I said briskly. 'The woman needs tea. Goodness, Ms Robinson, you're so tired your face is grey. Alan, do you still carry your identification?'

Without a word he pulled out the card that identified him as a very senior member of the police indeed.

'Retired,' he added.

'Yes, so this is nothing official,' I said. 'I just wanted you to be sure we weren't white slavers or Bonnie and Clyde or whatever you seem to be so afraid of. Now, will you come with us and have a cup of tea and something to eat?'

'I ... oh, very well. But I can't imagine why you need to talk to me, or think you do.'

'That's all right,' I said meaninglessly, as we went out the door.

'Where?' asked Alan. It was a reasonable question. Any tea shop or café or restaurant or pub would be full, with a line of people waiting.

'Well – if you're not particular, Ms Robinson, we could give you tea at our B&B. I don't think there's anything in particular to eat except some biscuits...'

'Cheese,' said Alan. 'We've quite a lot of that left. And a little wine.'

Ms Robinson obviously didn't care one way or the other. She sighed and followed us.

When we got to the Holly Tree, though, she hesitated at the door.

'Look, what is it?' I asked, trying to sound patient. 'We really are not planning to do you any harm.'

'No. No, of course not. It's just ... never mind.'

We went in and up to our room. It was a bit cramped for three, but I preferred that this conversation be private. Alan busied himself making tea and setting out our comestibles, such as they were, while I pulled off my hat and tried to think how to begin.

'I guess I need, first, to explain how Alan and

92

I met Ms Carter.'

'She told me,' said our reluctant guest. 'She overheard you talking about Paul ... Paul Jones.'

'Yes, and she was apparently looking for him. A lot of people were looking for him at that point.'

'Jo said he was suspected of some crime?' Her voice was casual, but her hands were clenched. If you ever need to lie convincingly, learn to keep your hands relaxed.

'He was, at the time, but he isn't now.' Alan handed her a cup of tea as he spoke, and I thought she was going to drop it as every muscle in her body sagged. 'I added sugar. I hope you don't mind, but you look as though you could do with some energy.'

'I ... yes, it's all right. Thank you.' She sipped. 'But you still haven't told me what it is you wanted of me. It isn't about this Jones boy, is it? Because I know almost nothing about him. Only what Jo told me.' The tension was back.

'Well, actually, that's what we did want to ask you. Have a biscuit, and some cheese.'

Alan offered a plate of assorted snacks. She took a minute piece of cheese, placed it on the edge of her saucer, and ignored it. She looked at me, a look far too intense for the ordinary conversation we appeared to be having.

'We wondered if you know where we might find Jo – Ms Carter. We've been asking around town, but no one seems to know her.'

'She doesn't live in Broadway.' Ms Robinson relaxed a trifle.

'Cheltenham?'

'Outside Cheltenham. I'm afraid I don't know the address. You know how it is when you know where someone lives; there's no need to remember the address.'

'You've known her for some time, then?'

'She's my best friend in the world.' That was, I thought, the first statement of pure truth that she had uttered.

'Then you would have her phone number.' Alan picked up a pad and pen.

'Actually, no. That is, I don't remember it. It's programmed into my mobile, which I left at home. Mrs Clarendon doesn't like us to have them at the gallery. Why are you so eager to find her?' She was slowly crumbling a biscuit.

'Mostly,' I said, 'to get to know her better. She's an interesting person, don't you think? A professional woman, I gathered. What is her occupation?'

'Social service. Yes, she's an interesting woman. So interesting, apparently, that you felt you needed to virtually abduct me in order to find out more about her.' She stood, scattering crumbs. 'I'm sorry. I have no idea what your interest is in Jo, or in me, but I have no wish to pursue this acquaintance. Thank you for the tea.'

She was out the door before I could say a word.

'Not one of my more successful efforts.' I began to tidy up the remains of our totally un-necessary picnic.

'No. The woman's terrified of something, Dorothy. What, do you suppose?'

'It has to do with Paul Jones, I'm sure.' I made

94

an attempt to clean up the crumbs on the floor.

'Leave it. Pam and her staff will cope. She was certainly lying when she said she didn't know him, did you notice?'

'Give me some credit, husband of mine. I haven't been married to you for all these years without learning a little something about liars.'

'Most of which you knew already. Teaching those wretched children, and reading every detective novel ever written.'

'Only the cosies,' I said absently. 'Sayers and Christie and that crowd. Alan, whatever is wrong with the women?'

'Something to do with Jones, I agree. And Pam said we'll get a surprise about him this evening. Or something like that.'

'Meantime, I've given up on sleuthing for the moment. We're getting nowhere, and it's nap time.'

'And the house is apparently deserted,' said my husband, with a certain tone in his voice.

We did nap, eventually.

It was late afternoon when I woke. The sun streaming in our window had a honeyed look, the waning of a gorgeous summer day. I yawned and stretched, and smiled at Alan, who had been up for long enough to make tea. I had a cup, showered and dressed, and then we wandered the village for a little while, had an early dinner, and came back to the Holly Tree.

'What now?' I asked Alan, sitting on the bed. I was beginning to get a trifle homesick. Doing exactly what one likes can actually pall after a while. I wanted my cats, my home, even my housewifely duties.

'A bit restive?' Alan asked. The man nearly always knows what I'm thinking. 'Perhaps we should find Pam and ask her what her big secret is. She seemed to think we might know by now, but I haven't a clue.'

'I guess there's nothing better to do. I've been wondering why I even care about Paul. He doesn't seem to be in trouble any more.'

'You care because you like the boy, and there's some mystery about him. Perhaps if we find Pam, the mystery will be solved.'

So we went downstairs. No one seemed to be in the kitchen or Pam's private suite, but voices were coming from the lounge, so we followed them.

'Ah, there you are,' said Pam. 'I hoped you would see this. It's almost time. Sit down and have some sherry.'

Most of the guests seemed to be in the lounge, as puzzled as we. Barbara McGath and Eileen O'Hanlon shared a small couch, looking as disapproving as ever. The television was on, end credits rolling for some programme I didn't recognize. Pam found chairs for Alan and me and poured us sherry, and we sat and waited.

When the next programme started, we all looked at each other in some dismay. Eileen O'Hanlon said 'Preposterous,' and she and Barbara tried to get up to leave, but the small room was too tightly packed with people and furniture to make escape easy.

I understood the impulse, though. For once I was in agreement with the two Irish ladies. What we were about to watch was, apparently, a rock concert. For someone like me, whose taste runs from Bach to Gilbert and Sullivan, it would be a form of torture.

'Excuse us,' said Barbara, steel in her voice. 'Could you let us through, please ... excuse us...'

'Sshh!' said Pam. 'They're about to begin.'

Barbara and Eileen sat down again, perforce. Barbara folded her arms and picked up a magazine from the table in front of her. It was a golfing magazine, and there was too little light to read, but she effectively demonstrated her distaste for her situation.

'And now, for the very first time on television, ladies and gentlemen, we are proud to present ... Peter James!'

The end of the emcee's announcement was swallowed up in cheers and screams and applause. The backup group began playing and singing immediately, though they were inaudible to us over the crowd noise, and I suspected to those in the crowd, as well.

'Can they hear anything at all?' I murmured to Alan.

'Probably not. They're all partially deaf, anyway, from listening to this rubbish since they were babies.'

The boom of the bass cut through the general riot of sound, and the camera panned the group and then zoomed in on the soloist caressing the mike.

Alan was the first to react. He slapped his knee with a sharp crack that I felt but couldn't hear. 'So that's it,' he mouthed in my ear.

'What's what ... oh!'

Heads came up throughout the room. Barbara's mouth dropped open; Eileen clutched her arm.

Pam, her hand on the remote, turned the volume down and beamed at us all. 'And that is the secret Paul Jones confided to me yesterday! He is Peter James!'

ELEVEN

'So that's that,' I said rather flatly as we were reading in our room before bed. 'Shave off the beard, and he's a famous pop star. At least I suppose he's famous. I'm not up on that kind of music.'

'Oh, he's famous, all right. And probably ten, twenty, forty times richer than we are.'

'And we felt sorry for him and bought him lunch.'

Alan grunted. It struck me as funny, for some reason. I chuckled.

'Mmm?'

'You're disgruntled. You grunted. Never mind.'

He smiled, giving the remark more credit than it deserved. 'I am, a bit. We've been wasting a good deal of sympathy on that lad, and spoiling our holiday. Let's hire a car tomorrow and get ourselves to St Michael's, Buckland, for church. And then we can take off in whatever direction suits our fancy.'

'What a good idea. That's a beautiful church, and I'm getting a bit claustrophobic here. Shall we keep our room?'

'We're booked in for a week, and tomorrow night would be the last night of that. Let's leave our things here, and decide on Monday what's next on the agenda.'

'Did you check on service times?'

'Service time, singular. It's a very small village, you know, and the parish must be tiny. Holy Communion at nine thirty, *and* with the 1662 Prayer Book.'

'Not only tiny, but conservative as well. This is a very good idea, Alan. Only, can we hire a car on a Sunday morning?'

'I'll go down and ask Pam. I need to tell her we won't be in for breakfast, anyway.'

He was a little longer than I had hoped, and when he got back the news wasn't great.

'There's no regular car hire in the village,' he reported. 'Bourbon, love?' He held out the bottle of Jack Daniel's and, when I nodded, poured a tot into a tea cup and passed it to me. 'Pam thinks we might be able to talk one of her friends into some sort of unofficial arrangement, but I'd actually rather not, because of insurance complications.'

'Oh, shoot. I was beginning to look forward to a service in that beautiful church.'

'All is not lost. There's one chap in Broadway who will drive us anywhere we want to go, even on a Sunday. If he's free, we can go to church, then have him drive us back to Winchcombe where we left our car. Then we're mobile again and can go where we like – on foot when we want, in decadent comfort when we don't.'

'Perfect,' I said, and lifted my cup in a toast to pleasant plans.

We got up early the next day, to the sweet sound of church bells, and everything went like clockwork. Pam had phoned the driver, and yes, he was free, and yes, he would be happy to take us anywhere we liked. Our hostess had also kindly packaged up a portable breakfast, so on the brief drive to Buckland we nibbled on fruit and oatmeal bread and drank excellent coffee.

I marvelled, as we drove, over how different the countryside looked from a car. I had never given much thought to how much one misses when being whisked along at highway speeds. The small flowers, the strange and beautiful beetles, the lovely, fresh smell of the moist earth, the movement of the clouds – all of these are overlooked. 'We've lost something,' I said to Alan.

He smiled, knowing what I was thinking. 'We'll walk more, I promise. There's good walking near home, too, you know.'

'They all used to walk. Everyone. These paths were made by people going someplace, hundreds and hundreds of years ago.'

'Yes, but don't forget that some of them rode, the wealthy ones who had horses or mules. And if they had a long way to go, they had to contend with rain and wind and even snow sometimes, and predatory animals – and humans. We've lost the closeness to the earth, but we've gained safety and comfort. And of course speed. We could be in Edinburgh by teatime.'

'I don't want to be in Edinburgh by teatime. I want to be right here, doing exactly what I'm doing. And later I want to walk and walk.'

'Hmm,' was all Alan said.

The church service was lovely, simple and dignified. There was no choir, which was possibly just as well. We were used to the acclaimed Cathedral choir at Sherebury, and the efforts of a small group of village singers wouldn't have been quite the same. But the organ was good, and the organist acceptable, and the congregation sang the hymns with vigour.

After the service we explored the church more thoroughly than we had on our previous visit. The oldest bits of it were thirteenth-century, and there were some remarkable works of art, extremely old and very well preserved. One of the sidesmen (I called them ushers until somebody, years ago, told me the proper English usage) showed us around, with a good deal of expert knowledge and not a little pride. 'One of the finest parish churches in all of England,' he said, and we couldn't disagree. Of course we would not have, anyway, but it was easy in this case to say the right thing.

'In Broadway for the festival, are you?'

'In a way,' I said. 'We're enjoying it, although we didn't know it was happening till we got there. We live in Sherebury.'

'You're American, though, aren't you?'

'By birth. I've lived in England for a good many years, now, but I guess I'll never quite lose the accent.'

'It isn't just the accent, you know, love,' put in my husband, with an amused smile.

'Well, I don't see what else it is! I buy all my clothes here, for heaven's sake. I know how to pronounce Gloucester and Worcester and Leicester, and I think it's a mean trick that Cirencester is pronounced with every single letter given its full value. I watch English television and read English books. I love fish and chips and steak and kidney pie. *Why* am I instantly spotted as an American?'

Alan and the sidesman looked at each other and shook their heads. 'Can't put it in words, ma'am, but you just *look* American. Something about the way you walk?'

I rolled my eyes. 'And I suppose we just *look* as if we've come from Broadway this morning.'

'Well, maybe. I happen to know Fred, your driver.'

He said it without the hint of a smile, and Alan replied as gravely, 'Ah, well, that would help.'

I swear I'll never know for sure when an Englishman intends to be funny. Maybe that's one of those indefinable things marking me for ever as American.

'Terrible thing that was, poor Bill Symonds getting killed the other day,' said the sidesman, now certainly serious. 'You'll have heard about that, I expect?'

Alan took my arm and pinched me, rather hard. 'We did hear something about it, yes. Did

102

you know him?'

'Sixty years and more. Went to school together, been sidesmen here long as I can remember. I stood up at his wedding.'

'I thought—' I began, and Alan's pinch grew stronger.

'He was married, then?' he said mildly.

'Widower. His wife died years ago, trying to have their baby. He's lived alone all these years, but for his friends.' The man took a handkerchief out of his pocket and blew his nose fiercely. 'A good man, he was, and coped wonderful well, for all he was deaf as a post. You'd never have known it, talking to him. He could read lips as well as you and I can read a book.' He paused, and then said, with a dark intensity more convincing than a shout, 'Whoever did that to him is a devil from hell, and if I find out who he is, that's where he's going.'

'Why didn't you want to talk about it?' I asked Alan as we got back into the car. 'And did you need to pinch quite so hard? I'll be black and blue.'

'Sorry, love.' He pulled me over to him and kissed the spot. 'There. That'll make it better. And in answer to your question, I don't quite know. Old policeman's habit, I suppose. Ask more than you tell. It probably wouldn't have mattered at all, and I'm truly sorry I hurt you.'

'I'll mend. But goodness, he was upset, wasn't he?'

Alan ran his hand down the back of his neck. 'The man Symonds was well-loved, they told me in Broadway. Of course everybody knows

103

everybody in a place like this. It's unusual, when someone has died, to find no one with an axe to grind, but in this case all the clichés seem to hold true.'

'Not even some ill-natured gossip at the Post Office about goings-on with the widow next door, or a deal gone wrong over pigs, or anything?'

'Not a thing. They'll be proposing him for canonization any day now.'

'Oh, dear.' Like all policemen, Alan hated cases that were not only unsolved, but apparently incapable of solution. This looked like being one of those, and even though it wasn't his, he was going to brood about it.

It was nearly lunchtime when we got to Winchcombe, so we found a pleasant pub and treated our driver to lunch before sending him on his way with thanks.

'Now, where shall we go?' We had reclaimed our car from the station car park, and Alan was at the wheel.

'How about back to Broadway? Then maybe we can figure out a way to walk to Chipping Campden without climbing too many hills.'

The old saying about the best-laid plans is irritatingly true. We had reached the Holly Tree and found a place to park just up the street when the rain started. I found a rain hat in the back of the car and put it on, but it wasn't even real rain at first, just mizzle. Then the drops got bigger, and came faster, and we were really wet by the time we got in the door.

'Alan.'

'Yes? Would you mind not shaking your hat quite so fervently? It's showering me like a wet dog.'

I shook it in the other direction. 'Is this rain what you meant back awhile when you said "Hmm"?'

'Hmm?'

There was still plenty of water left on the hat.

I have quite a lot in common with cats. I possess a lively curiosity, and I love my comfort. One of my favourite precepts is: 'When in doubt, nap.' So after we got out of our wet clothes, it seemed only natural to crawl under the covers and get warm. And I didn't wake until teatime.

'You know,' I said with a yawn, 'other than eating and drinking and spending money, there isn't actually an awful lot to *do* in Broadway.'

'Lots of pictures.'

'I think the galleries are all closed by now. Anyway, I'm getting sort of tired of pictures. And...'

'And they're getting tired of us. At least there's one gallery where I feel we might not be welcomed back with great hosannas.'

I made a face. 'I wish I knew what was eating that woman. We really were just trying to help.'

'Perhaps she doesn't like our faces.'

'Or my hats. Alan, is it still raining?'

He peered out of the window. 'Looks like it's settled in for the night. Not hard, but steady and determined.'

'Too bad to drive?'

'Where did you have in mind?'

'Just Cheltenham. I want to see another play, and there are lots of good ones on. Shaw, and Shakespeare, and I think I saw that somebody was doing some Gilbert and Sullivan.'

'Lead on, Macduff.'

'And no, I do *not* want to see *Macbeth*, thank you very much.'

So we went to Cheltenham and had our tea, and then found a rollicking performance of *HMS Pinafore*, and then a late supper, and so back to Broadway and to bed.

But I woke up in the middle of the night wondering, again, what was so badly wrong with Sarah Robinson.

TWELVE

In the morning, at breakfast, all the guests were still bubbling over the revelation that a celebrity had stayed in our midst.

Well, perhaps *bubbling* isn't quite the word. The English don't bubble a whole lot. I was reminded of a joke going around a while back among my American friends, about the contrast between the English and American 'security alert' levels, in which the highest English level was reported to be 'really rather cross'.

So the English guests were really rather pleased, in a quiet way, though I suspected they, like

Alan and me, would have been somewhat more enthusiastic had Paul turned out to be a minor royal, or a Shakespearean actor. Most of us were a bit too old to go into raptures over rock stars.

The Irish ladies were more effusive. 'I knew he was something out of the ordinary,' said Mrs McGath to Mrs O'Hanlon, but at a volume that included the whole room. 'I was telling you, wasn't I? That boy will go far, I said.'

I choked on a bit of bacon. 'Easy, love,' said Alan in an undertone. 'I know, but we can't talk about it here.'

'She never uttered one good word about Paul until she found out he was famous!' I fumed when we were back in our room. 'Now she acts like she invented him!'

'Yes, dear. By evening she'll believe she really did think and say what she claims. Her type used to be the bane of my existence. She doesn't lie deliberately. She is simply sure that whatever she wants to believe is true. As a witness, the family cat was more reliable.'

I nodded. 'I've known some like that, too. If they possess a memory at all, it's infinitely malleable to the shape they want. Alan, let's get out of here. If I have to stay in the same house with that woman much longer, I'm going to say something I'll regret.'

'It's time we moved on, in any case. New worlds to conquer.'

'Or something.'

We packed quickly. Having the car made everything much easier. 'No more walking tours, don't you think? Day trips, there and back. And

107

if we want to go farther afield, we can take the car.'

'What happened to your new-found love of the earth, walking the paths trod for hundreds, nay thousands of years?'

'I think it got rained out. Where shall we go?'

'I've been looking at the map. There's a town called Upper Pinnock just about in the middle of where we intended to walk, roughly equidistant from here, Winchcombe, Bourton-on-the-Water, and Moreton-in-Marsh. And there's a highly recommended holiday cottage just outside the town, within easy walking distance of two stately homes you'll love, Sezincote and Stanway. Shall I see if we can book it? Oh, I should warn you, it's self-catering.'

'That means I cook.'

'That means we cook. Or eat out.'

'Show me.' I leaned over the map as Alan unfolded it on the bed.

'See? Here's Sezincote – you'll love that, it's incredible, quite a lot like Brighton Pavilion – and here's Stanway. And right at this crossroads is the cottage.'

I looked at the many inches between the indicated crossroads and the two little symbols that meant stately homes. 'That's easy walking distance?'

'Less than four miles to either. You're forgetting the scale of the map. The whole map, both sides, covers only about a twenty by twenty-five mile area. A good walker could cover the whole perimeter in less than a week.'

'Well, I don't propose to find out. But, yes, see

if the cottage is available. It sounds ideal.'

We said goodbye to Pam with real regret, and to the Irish ladies with considerable relief, which I hope we managed to disguise, and headed out. We stopped at one of Broadway's excellent shops to pick up a hamper and a selection of delicacies to fill it, and then concentrated on finding our way down roads charitably described on the map as 'generally less than 4m wide'. In some cases, considerably less. Blind corners abounded, and the rain didn't help. If I'd been driving I would have been reduced to a quivering jelly in about ten minutes – just as we encountered the first flock of sheep.

Alan, however, is used to this sort of thing, and managed to keep the car on the road and off the sheep, and found our destination with no more than a few words we wouldn't have wanted our clergy friends to hear.

The owner, Mrs Bostock, was waiting for us. 'So sorry about the rain,' she said, as we stood in the front hallway dripping. 'Don't worry at all about tracking in. It can't be helped, and the rugs are all washable. I've turned the heaters on, to take the chill off, and there's plenty of wood for a fire if you'd like one later. The larder's stocked with the basics, and you'll find milk and eggs in the fridge. All right?'

'Splendid,' said Alan. 'And the key?'

'Oh, we never bother about keys, I'm afraid. The area isn't teeming with desperadoes. If you really want one, I could ask my husband. He might know what we've done with it.'

'Oh ... well ... I wouldn't want you to go to the

trouble. It's your house, after all, and if you're comfortable leaving it unlocked...' I left the sentence unfinished, and she nodded briskly.

'The doors do bolt from the inside if you'll feel safer locked in at night. Actually it might be a good idea, because we do have the occasional marauder.'

'I thought you said...' Alan began.

Mrs Bostock grinned. 'Not your usual thieves. Goats. We try to keep them penned up, but they're clever rascals, and curious as cats. And of course they'll eat anything. So...'

She smiled, and we laughed. 'We'll keep a sharp eye out for criminally minded goats,' Alan assured her.

'I'll leave you to get settled, then. If you need anything at all, we're just down the lane, and our phone number's posted in the kitchen. Enjoy yourselves, and I do hope the rain stops for you.'

'Why do the English keep apologizing for the weather?' I asked idly as I found tea things and turned on the kettle.

'Don't Americans?' asked Alan in surprise.

'I don't think so.' I tried to remember. 'I think we complain about it, constantly. Or brag about it, in a sort of reverse snobbery. "You think this is bad. You should have seen the Blizzard of Seventy-Eight!" That sort of thing. And actually, American weather can be far worse than English. Tornadoes, hurricanes, blistering heat, frigid cold, not to mention earthquakes. A little summer rain is nothing.'

'Then shall we go for a nice walk before lunch?' he said wickedly, looking out the win-

110

dow at the rain splashing in the puddles.

'Certainly. As far as the car.'

We had our tea, and then unpacked. The cottage was roomy and pleasantly appointed, with all the necessities of life for a few days. Big bathroom, fluffy towels. Comfortable bed. Dishes and glassware and cutlery, and a modest selection of pots and pans – and the all-important dishwasher. Tea, coffee, sugar, milk, eggs, breakfast cereal, bread, butter, biscuits. The basics, as Mrs Bostock had said. We'd brought ham, various cheeses, smoked salmon, marmalade, and salad makings, along with fruit and an utterly sinful and delectable chocolate cake I could not leave in the shop.

We did in fact take a stroll before lunch, just to get our bearings. The rain wasn't overpowering, though it was deceptively wet, making its way into any possible gap in one's rain gear. We could see well enough, though, and the view almost made up for the rain.

We were situated on the top of a hill, the land before us rolling in typical Cotswold fashion. It's a gentle sort of country, content with the quiet beauty of fields and woods, streams and hedges, crops and sheep and cattle.

My native country is huge, with so many different kinds of scenery that it's impossible to pick one and say 'This is America.' But for me, growing up in the Midwest, Indiana cornfields were America. England, on its much smaller scale, is also quite varied. At that moment, looking out over the Cotswold hills, I was quite sure this was the essence of England.

Our home from home was just outside the town of Upper Pinnock, which stretched out below us. 'Upper', Alan explained, referred not so much to the elevation, but to the fact that the town lay upstream from, and was also much more important than, the companion Pinnock.

'So where is Pinnock?'

'Vanished completely. It was a medieval village, over more or less that way, I think. All that's left of it is a few depressions in the earth where houses and barns used to be.'

'Good grief, what happened to it?' Visions of fire, of plague and pestilence, of internecine warfare flashed across my brain.

'I have no idea. You're free to use your lurid imagination.'

'And what's in Upper Pinnock?'

'Again, no idea. It's good-sized on the map, looks to be nearly the size of Cheltenham, so presumably there will be all the amenities of a Cotswold market town.'

'Well, the amenities I'm concerned with right now are first, towels, and second, food.'

We lunched on smoked salmon, salad, and crusty bread. Simple and very satisfying. I virtuously topped off my meal with a handful of grapes, saving the cake for dinner. Alan helped with the dishes, no great chore.

It was still raining.

'No walk to Sezincote today,' said Alan. We were sitting in the lounge, in seductively comfortable chairs. 'I don't even care to walk into the town.'

I shivered, quite unnecessarily. The room was

112

warm. 'Nap time?'

Alan just looked at me.

'Well, no, I'm not actually sleepy, either.'

There was a little silence. Then Alan said, 'There's no point in trying to run away from it.'

'Is that what we were doing?'

That look again.

I sat up a little straighter. It took some effort. 'All right. What are we going to do?'

'We're going to be methodical about it. Do you suppose there's anything to write on in this establishment?'

'Have you ever known me to be without a notebook?' I am addicted to spiral notebooks, and carry one everywhere I go. I struggled out of my chair, nipped into the bedroom, and found the small one I'd brought along. 'Now.'

Alan tented his hands in a gesture that made him look more like Alistair Cooke than ever. 'First: what do we want to know?'

I headed a page 'Queries' and created a sub-head, 'Paul'. 'There's a lot we want to know about Paul. Why was he staying in Broadway – or why is he staying there? He may have come back, after all.'

'Right. And why was he incognito?'

'Oh, but that's an easy one. He—'

'No, let's get the questions down first, and then see if we have any answers. There's quite a lot more about Paul. What is his real name, Paul Jones or Peter James, or maybe something else entirely?'

I got that down. 'Why did he disappear, and where did he go?'

'We know part of the answer to that one, but the most puzzling one is, why was he so upset when he nearly ran into you?'

'Yes, and where did all that blood come from?' I paused. 'Any more about Paul?'

'Not that I can think of at the moment. Oh, yes, there's one, but we might as well make it a query about Jo Carter. Why is she, or was she, trying to find Paul?'

'Or in general, what's she up to? What's her relationship with Sarah? Where is she, Jo, I mean, where is she now?'

Alan thought for a moment. 'Well, as we've got to Sarah, what is it that's troubling her so badly?'

'And to that one I haven't a clue.' I looked at my list. 'Goodness, there's a lot we don't know.'

'And you've forgotten the matter that really should have come first,' said Alan, looking very sober.

'What's that?'

'Who killed William Symonds, and why? That's where this all started, you know.'

'Or at least where we came into it. Alan, I have the feeling we've waded into something that goes a long way back. There was a novel I read once, by Mary Stewart, I think, that talked about entering a situation in the middle of the third act, with no idea what the play was about or even who the characters were. That's the way I feel now.'

'That's nearly always the way it was in police work, Dorothy. Or at least, no. Most of the time it was boring routine. Wife throws pot at hus-

114

band, husband stabs wife. Thieves fall out. Drug deals go bad. A crowd of bored, stupid teenagers decides to go on a rampage.'

I shuddered. 'I'm very glad you're out of all that.'

'Not half as glad as I am. But in the odd case when the solution wasn't obvious, we always had to go back. It was almost never a matter of where John Doe was at ten thirty on the night of the fifteenth. Oh, it came to that in the end, of course, when we knew who the villain was and had to find the evidence to prove it. But in order to come to that assurance, we had to look into the relationships of everyone concerned, what someone stood to gain, or to lose. It was almost never pretty.'

'No. Crime isn't, is it? But Alan, that's exactly the problem with the death of the farmer. There's nothing in his background that could lead to murder. And yet he's dead. I suppose the police in Broadway really did their job?'

'Oh, yes. It's easier in a village. In a city a man can be anonymous. Not in a village. Believe me, if Bill Symonds had any secrets in his life, past or present, they would have been discovered instantly. There was *no* reason for him to be killed.'

'Well, then, logically, he's still alive.'

'Which he is not. Therefore the logic has a flaw. And as we have no idea what it is, perhaps we'd be more productive exploring some of our other questions. What do you suggest?'

I looked again at my list. 'I've numbered them. How about Paul, question two: why was he incognito? I think the answer to that one is obvious.'

'Do you? And what is your answer?'

'He's a rock star. He didn't want to be recognized. Hence the beard and the false name.'

'Ah, but that answer raises more questions. Why didn't he want to be recognized?'

'His fans. He didn't want to be mobbed.'

'You're forgetting a couple of things, love. One: Saturday night was his first appearance on television. That means the number of people who knew what he looked like is limited.'

I grinned, happy to be one-up for a change. *'You* are forgetting the Internet, and YouTube, and Facebook, and all the other ways teenagers trade information these days. Half the world could know what he looked like, and we old fogies would be the only ones left in the dark.'

'All right. I'll grant you that one. Do you think that's why he came to the Holly Tree? He must be making a fortune. He could have stayed anywhere.'

'Well ... it does seem an unlikely place for him. And you know, you've raised some questions in my mind, actually. Most rising young stars revel in publicity. They wallow in it. I suspect their agents insist. And here he is, just on the verge of his big television debut, choosing to hole up, incognito, in a small B&B in a Cotswold village. It doesn't make a whole lot of sense.'

'Which gets us back to ... would it be Paul, question one, on your list? Why he was in Broadway at all?'

'It would be, and that's been one of the big

116

questions all along. Even before the death of the farmer.'

'He was there for a private reason, something that had nothing to do with his career. I'll swear to that. His whole demeanour was that of a private individual. When he ran you down—'

'Nearly. Not quite.'

'—nearly ran you down, he was terribly shaken, but it wasn't the fear that he would be exposed, the great Peter James, as a reckless driver. He was concerned about you.'

'And about something else. His anxiety was out of all proportion to the minor damage he'd done to me, or to himself, for that matter. Alan, that child was terrified.'

'I agree. So let's put a few facts together. First, where was he coming from?'

I looked blank. 'I haven't the slightest idea. I wasn't paying attention. We were leaving the pub. I don't remember the name. It wasn't very nice.'

'The Hunting Dog. Near the bottom of the High Street. We had turned to go back to the Holly Tree, or in that direction, anyway. He came from behind us. Therefore from the west.'

'If you say so,' said I, the geographically challenged.

'Second, what was the time?'

'Around lunchtime. We had stopped in the pub to get some lunch.'

'So, say around one, or a little past. Now, do you remember when William Symonds was presumed to have died?'

I felt a distinct chill. 'No.'

117

'Latest time, around one. Earliest, about ten that morning.'

'Alan, you're not saying Paul killed him? I thought we disposed of that long ago.'

'I think so, too. I'm saying, as a hypothesis, that he saw him killed.'

'But...' I stopped talking and thought about that. 'Why would he not go to the police?'

'Because he knew the killer.'

THIRTEEN

That one silenced me. 'How do you work that out?' I said, finally.

'I said it was only a hypothesis. I can't come within miles of producing evidence, but it fits the few facts we know.'

'Such as?'

'Fact: William Symonds was killed sometime between ten and one on Tuesday. Fact: Paul Jones – we'll call him that for now – was going somewhere at a hell of a clip just before one. Fact: he was coming from the west.'

'That's an inference, not a fact,' I argued. 'We didn't see him coming. And even if he was, how would that mean he was coming from that quarry? Isn't it more or less south of here? Of Broadway, I mean?'

He looked at me in some surprise. 'Your

118

geography has improved.'

'No, it hasn't. I've been studying that miserable OS map until I'm nearly blind, and even I know that down, on a map, is south.'

'Yes. Well. The point is, yes, you're right about the direction. But remember that Paul was on a motorbike. He couldn't have ridden that to the quarry, or back. Even the Land Rover had to stop some distance away, you remember. And if you can bear to look at the map once more, I think you'll see that he would have had to go west from the quarry to get to anything like a road.'

'All right, but why would he have been to the quarry at all? I wouldn't have said he was the outdoor type.'

'I have no idea, at least not yet. But you will have to admit that he was in a state of near collapse when we saw him in front of the Hunting Dog.'

'No argument about that. But any number of things could have caused that.'

'For instance?'

'Well ... he had a fight with someone. That would explain the blood, too.'

'With whom?'

'*I* don't know! I know nothing about him, really. Maybe with the person he came to Broadway to see. And that would explain why he left town right away, too. He was fed up with the situation and wanted to get away.'

'It's possible. I don't think so, though. Dorothy, you're better than I at reading people's reactions, but at the time we both thought Paul was struggling with fear, not anger.'

I cast my mind back to the boy's face, ashy white where it wasn't covered with blood and mud. I saw again his frantic haste, his reluctance to talk, his desperate effort at courtesy in spite of everything. 'Yes, you're right,' I said slowly. 'He was afraid. All right. Your theory is full of holes, but all right. For the sake of the argument, he saw the murder done. I repeat, why didn't he then go to the police? He seems to me to be a law-abiding sort.'

'And I repeat, he knows the murderer. And is terrified of him, or her.'

'Terrified of him? Or *for* him?' A new idea was trying to surface in my brain.

Alan leaned forward, or tried to. 'Blast it, this furniture is demoralizing! Comfortable, but not conducive to escape. Dorothy, you may have something there. Afraid *for* the murderer. I like it. That seems to capture the sense we had, or at least I had, of his condition at the time. Afraid, yes, but afraid something worse was going to happen to someone he loved.'

'Which implies that the murderer...'

'Is someone very close to him. Dorothy, have you heard anything about his family?'

'I don't even know if he has one. No, wait! Jo said something ... when we first met her, remember? Something about being a friend of his family. She would know.'

'Then the first thing we need to do is talk to Jo.'

'We have to find her first.'

'That shouldn't be too hard. She works in social services, presumably in Cheltenham. We

120

will go to Cheltenham.'

It was a short trip, even in the rain, which by now had become a downpour. We finally found a car park with a few empty spots, paid-and-displayed, and then huddled in the car trying to decide where to go.

'It might have been simpler to call,' I said. 'Drier, anyway.'

'Perhaps, but bureaucracies are difficult enough to navigate in person. On the phone they can be impossible. Do you have any idea how many agencies could come under the general heading of "social services"?'

I was about to find out.

Alan has a mobile phone that does everything but dance the can-can, which he used to locate the main office of the Gloucestershire County Council. It was a long way from our car park, and our umbrellas didn't help much. A receptionist in a skimpy stretch top asked if she could help us, quite obviously hoping she couldn't.

Alan gave me his 'Let me handle this' look and said, 'We're looking for Ms Carter, Jo Carter. Can you tell me where we might find her office?'

'And what agency is she with?'

'I'm afraid I can't quite remember. Foolish of me. Can you look her up?'

The woman, already bored with us, looked at her computer screen and then shook her head. 'Not unless you know the agency. What kind of help were you wanting?'

I drew breath. Alan stepped on my foot. Gently, but unmistakably.

'Actually, we're simply visiting from out of town and wanted to call on her for a few minutes. Do you not have a directory by name?'

'Can't divulge personal information. Here, this might help.' She handed us a brochure listing various agencies and turned her attention firmly back to the computer screen where, I saw as I took a deliberate look, she was playing a card game.

'Blood pressure, darling!' whispered Alan. We retired to a quiet corner and Alan tried all the agencies' phone numbers, one after another. He spent enough time on hold, or being told by a computerized voice how important his business was and how privileged the voice was to serve him, that I wished I had a computer game to amuse me. I was sorely tempted to take over the receptionist's desk.

And none of it was any use at all. Alan did, finally, get to talk to someone at almost every agency. Some were coldly polite, some actively stupid, and some genuinely interested in helping, but no one would admit to ever having heard of Jo Carter.

Even though I had surmised, from his end of the conversations, what he was going to say, my shoulders still sagged when he told me. 'So that's that.'

'Oh, no, that is very far from that. Buck up, my dear. We've exhausted only the governmental agencies. Now we must try the private ones.'

'Oh. And how many of those might there be?'

'Dozens, I should imagine. There are almost unlimited numbers of well-meaning souls setting out to do good in some sphere or other. Churches, twelve-step programmes, women's centres, homeless shelters, even police-sponsored charities.'

I took a deep breath. 'We can't cover all those in what's left of the afternoon. It's almost tea-time. Let's go find some tea and a telephone directory, and do what we can by phone. I'll spell you.'

There was a tea shop nearby, though not the sort we usually favour. I like atmosphere with my tea and cakes. This place had once been starkly modern, with pale wood tables and angular steel chairs. Now it simply looked tired. Perhaps not surprisingly, it wasn't well patronized, which was fine for our purposes. We secured a table in the corner; Alan went to the counter and bought a pot of tea and some shopworn buns.

We consumed our tea, and a great deal of time, with no more luck than before. Oh, there was a lot less waiting time until we were connected to real live human beings, and the people we talked to were nicer, on the whole, than the bureaucratic lot. Amateurs are often full of enthusiasm for what they do. Perhaps that's their reward. But for all their eagerness to help, no one knew where we might find Jo Carter.

I was ready to give up, at least for the day, when Alan found one more number. 'It's a women's shelter. You'd probably have more luck than I.'

'I've stopped believing in luck.' But I punched in the number. There was a long wait before a

123

woman answered in a weary voice.

'Eight-three-oh-five-two-seven, good afternoon.'

'Good afternoon. I wonder if I might speak to Jo Carter, please.'

Silence.

'Excuse me, I can't hear you.'

More silence, or nearly. I could hear the cry of a baby in the background, so I knew I hadn't lost the signal.

'Hello? Are you still there?'

'Yes, madam.' A different voice, harder, crisper. 'Who is calling, please?'

'I'm a friend of Jo Carter's. My husband and I are in town and hoped to see her for a few minutes.'

'And your name?'

This hadn't come up before. 'Name?' I mouthed at Alan, with raised eyebrows.

He nodded.

'My name is Dorothy Martin.'

'I see. One moment, please.'

Silence again, but this time real silence. The phone had been muted. 'They're checking, I think,' I whispered to Alan.

The woman came back on the line and cleared her throat. 'I'm sorry, Ms Martin. There is no one here by the name of Carter. Good afternoon.'

'Wait! Wait, I—' But the connection was broken.

'More tea?' asked Alan, watching my face.

'No. Definitely no more tea. A pint is what I need. Or better yet, a glass of wine.' I looked at

124

the clock on the wall. 'Alan, it's too late for us to accomplish any more here, and I'd like to get back to the cottage before nightfall. Driving those lanes in the dark, and in the rain, is a challenge even for you.'

We didn't talk on the way back. I was trying to sort my thoughts, and Alan needed no distractions. But when we got back to the cottage, and Alan had built a fire and I had assembled a snack supper, I told him my thoughts about the last phone call.

'They were lying, Alan. That was perfectly obvious. They know who Jo Carter is, and almost certainly where she is, but they wouldn't tell me.'

'Then why did they ask your name? If they weren't willing to talk about the woman – and God knows why that might be – why didn't they just say straight off that they'd never heard of her?'

I sipped at my wine. 'Beats me. I'm beginning to think there must be something peculiar about Ms Carter. Nobody knows who she is or what she does or where she is. I suppose we really did see her, talk to her? She isn't just a figment of our imaginations?'

'My imagination is not that vivid, my dear. Nor is she a ... what did they used to call an odd phenomenon ... a mass hallucination.'

'She's the Sphinx,' I said, and giggled.

Alan raised his eyebrows. 'Either you've had too much wine, which seems unlikely at half a glass, or you're too tired to think properly. Why the Sphinx?'

'A riddle wrapped in a mystery inside an enigma. Didn't somebody say that about the Sphinx?'

'The phrase is Winston Churchill's, and if I remember correctly, he said it about Russia. We are going to stop thinking about our problem tonight, Dorothy. Perhaps tomorrow our minds will be working more clearly.'

FOURTEEN

'I figured it out,' I said calmly over coffee the next morning. The rain had gone. The sky was beautifully clear and so were my thought processes.

'Congratulations.' It was a growl. For once Alan hadn't been up as long as I had, and he was only midway through his first cup of coffee. One of the things I adore about him is that he is seldom cheery first thing in the morning. I don't think I could stand waking up to a merry little ray of sunshine on the next pillow.

I was pining to share my brilliant idea, but I saw it would be better to wait. I poured myself more coffee, made more toast, and fidgeted.

'All right, darling,' he said at last with a husbandly sigh. 'I'm more or less present. What did you figure out?'

'It's a women's shelter!'

126

He didn't roll his eyes. Quite. 'Yes, I know. I believe I told you that. That's why you called. I thought a male voice might put them off.'

'Exactly. So what they got was a female voice. But on a phone belonging to a man. And a man with a different last name. You don't have your ID blocked, do you?'

'No, but ... why should that make a difference? People use each other's mobiles all the time. And you don't even know that they can check.'

'I should think they'd have to, wouldn't you? Think about it, Alan. This is a place where battered women go to escape their abusers. It's a safe house for women and children, until they can straighten out their lives. They have to have a published phone number, but it's essential that the abusers don't find them. So they screen phone calls. Mine was suspicious, because of the difference in names, so they hung up. And I'll bet you anything that if I call again on that same phone, no one will answer.'

He handed the phone to me. I punched redial and let it ring until it terminated the call.

'So, what do we know, besides the fact that they are admirably careful about protecting their clients?'

'We know Jo Carter is there, or at least they know where she is.'

'And how are we going to use that information?' Alan was still a trifle grumpy. I thought he had slept badly, as in fact I had, too.

'I've figured that out, as well.' I had in fact gone for an early-morning walk and done a lot of thinking. I thought perhaps I'd better not mention that. 'I think the best thing to do is go to a clergyman in Cheltenham, someone who will certainly know the women's shelter, and get him to make the call.'

'Or,' said Alan, smiling as the brilliant morning sunshine reached his back and bathed him in warmth, 'we can simply ask the priest how to get in touch with Jo. If he knows the shelter and she's associated with it, he'll know. And I think we'll start with All Saints', since we met first met Jo there.'

I hit myself on the forehead. 'And why on earth didn't we go there to begin with?'

'Beats me.' He tried to say it with an American accent. I tried hard not to laugh.

There is something about sunshine that absolutely makes the world turn more smoothly, I'll swear to it. We had no trouble getting to Cheltenham, no trouble finding a place to park. It was even free. The rector of All Saints' was happy to put himself at our disposal. Alan explained our mission, this time with scrupulous truth.

'Jo Carter? Certainly I know her. She has done fine work with those poor women. Of course I can't tell you where to find her at this instant. She's extremely busy and travels a great deal.'

'Travels?'

'Oh, in a very small circuit, only Gloucestershire and environs, but she wears out her little cars with some regularity. At any rate, you need to find her. Let me call the shelter for you and explain. I'm sure they'll help you once they know who you are. If you'll just excuse me ... I haven't yet resigned myself to a mobile. I'll go to my office.'

We waited. The Burne-Jones windows, this morning, looked far lovelier than I had expected. I actually had only the vaguest memory of seeing them before. After a third study, however, their charm began to pall.

The rector returned, and the peaceful friendliness of his face had turned to a mask of worry. 'It's really most disquieting. Mrs Bryant, at the shelter, has not heard from Ms Carter since early yesterday morning. She said then she'd be in by noon at the latest. They've tried to reach her, but her mobile is out of service. She ... really, it sounds terribly melodramatic, but she seems to have disappeared.'

Alan went straight to the police in Cheltenham, while I waited in the car. The time for amateur detection was over; the authorities had to become involved. In a few words he explained the possible connections with the 'Broadway Tower murder', as the tabloids were inaccurately calling it. If just anyone had put the matter to them, they might have paid little attention. Members of the public are always annoying the police with cockeyed theories. But Chief Constable Alan Nesbitt, retired, had a reputation as an unusually competent, even a brilliant policeman. They listened, and they acted.

'Would you like to come with us to the shelter, sir?' asked Superintendent Davids, an attractive woman of about fifty. 'They're not always that keen on male visitors, as you might understand, but you have all the details at your fingertips. I think they should hear what you have to say.'

'I would be happy to, on the condition that my wife accompany me. She knows just as much as I about the facts, and may be able to contribute some insights of her own.'

'Certainly, sir.'

The car we took didn't look like a conventional police car. No blue lights, no chequerboard pattern. It was, however, so anonymous and discreet that I felt it must scream 'Police' to any intelligent criminal who happened to see it. One hoped that the homes neighbouring the shelter didn't house criminals, because the point, presumably, was to make our visit as discreet as possible.

We were met at the door by Mrs Bryant, the matron or housemother or whatever she was called. She spoke a few words, and I recognized the voice of the woman who had hung up on me.

The superintendent introduced Alan and me. Mrs Bryant looked at us sharply. 'Mrs Martin. And Mr Nesbitt. It was you...'

'It was. And I understand completely. You have to be careful.'

'Yes. Will you come in?'

Her office was spartan. She offered us no tea, nor any apologies. This was a no-frills operation, existing, I suspected, always on the edge of disaster. There was no room here for waste of either time or money. Her desk was innocent of any stray papers, or indeed of anything except a virgin writing pad. There was no phone, even. Presumably she used only a mobile. I shivered.

The atmosphere was anything but warm and cosy.

'You think something untoward has happened to Jo,' she said without preamble.

'I fear it might have done,' said Alan.

'Why?'

He had whittled the story down to its essentials to present to the Cheltenham police. He repeated it now for Mrs Bryant.

'Our acquaintance with Ms Carter is very slight. We know she has some connection with a young man called Paul Jones, though that may not be his real name. He also uses the name Peter James, again perhaps a pseudonym. We have reason to believe that this young man witnessed a murder—'

Mrs Bryant made a small sound that might have been the beginning of a gasp. 'Sorry,' she said. 'Go on.'

'—witnessed a murder last week. The last time we saw him, he seemed to be very much afraid of something. If we are correct in our surmises, and if Ms Carter is in the young man's confidence, they could both be in danger. And you say she is not here, where you expected her to be. You can understand our concern.'

'Yes, I see.' She paused. 'You say you know Jo only slightly. May I have the details, please?'

'We met in Cheltenham. She overheard us talking about Paul Jones and asked if we knew his whereabouts, as he had missed an appointment with her. Later we saw her in Broadway, where we were staying. We are on holiday.'

'And how do you know Paul Jones?'

131

I could no longer contain my impatience. 'Mrs Bryant, I realize you have to be careful with what information you release to strangers, but we're dealing with a critical situation! We don't know Paul well, either. He was staying at our B&B in Broadway, and we liked him. Now he's in some sort of trouble, and we think Jo might be, too. Can you tell us anything that might help us find them?'

She sat looking at a picture on the wall. It was a cheap reproduction of one of the Renaissance Madonnas. I doubt if she saw it. After what seemed an eternity she spoke.

'I wish I could help you, but I don't think I can. The last time I talked to Jo, she said she planned to be here yesterday, as usual. I was disturbed when she didn't turn up, but not unduly. Her work sometimes takes her far afield.'

'What exactly is her work, Mrs Bryant?'

'She is one of our social workers. She acts as advocate for individual clients, helping them to escape the cycle of violence. It can mean working with them to obtain job training and financial understanding, helping them to find permanent homes, getting them into treatment programmes if they are addicted to drugs or alcohol ... any number of things. It is a difficult job that requires patience, compassion, clear thinking, and boundless energy. There is a high rate of burnout, as you can imagine. Jo has been doing it for over ten years, and is the best worker I've ever had. Please find her, Superintendent.'

'We'll try, Mrs Bryant. It will help if you can tell us more about Paul Jones and his connection with Ms Carter.'

'I know nothing of anyone called Paul Jones. You say it may not be his real name?'

'His real name might be Peter James.'

Mrs Bryant shook her head. 'Nor is that name familiar. Have you a picture?'

I was opening my mouth to say no, when the superintendent produced one. 'It's not very good, I'm afraid, only a printout from the Internet.'

'But this ... this is some sort of performer!'

'Peter James is the newest pop music phenomenon, my children tell me,' said the superintendent with a smile. 'He made his television debut on Saturday.'

'He didn't look like that when he was using the name of Paul Jones,' I put in. 'He had a beard and wore really scruffy clothes.'

Mrs Bryant handed the picture back. 'I'm sorry. I can tell you nothing about him. If he ever passed through these doors, it would have been years ago, and children are often unrecognizable when they grow up.'

'Your records, perhaps?' Alan suggested.

'We do not keep photographic records. Surely you can understand why. And in any case, all records are destroyed after a period of time. It is a security measure, Mr Nesbitt.' She leaned forward. 'You have, in your career with the police, encountered many violent criminals, I'm sure.'

Alan nodded.

'And you know that they can be utterly determined to achieve their goals, utterly ruthless, utterly without moral restraint.'

'That is largely what makes them crimin-als.'

'Of course. You can understand, then, that we are dealing with men of that sort. They have beaten their women, often also their children, sometimes nearly to death. They are outraged when those women and children escape, and are determined to find them. Our mission here, our purpose overriding all else, is to make sure they don't succeed. It is quite literally a matter of life and death. Therefore we keep as few records as possible, guard them with great care, and destroy them when the clients have moved on.'

'Do they never come back?'

A look of great pain passed across Mrs Bryant's face. 'Often. Many of them go back to their abusers, you know. They have little sense of self-worth when they come to us, and if we are not able to help them learn to value them-selves, they will go back, and the man will promise never to hurt them again. He always does, of course.'

I was sitting next to Alan. I let my hand touch his, in a gesture of love and gratitude. I had been so fortunate. My first husband, Frank Martin, had been a kind and considerate man. His death had devastated me, but then I'd had the supreme good fortune to meet Alan. Just as kind, just as considerate, and happy to stay by my side for the rest of our lives.

'Just one last question, Mrs Bryant. Or perhaps two. Can you tell me what, specifically, Ms Carter was working on when you last spoke with her?'

'She was taking a little holiday. Her clients here had no urgent needs. Yesterday she was to begin work with a new client who badly needs a job.'

'I see. And do you know where she was calling from?'

'No. She was using her mobile. She could have been anywhere.'

The superintendent thanked her, and we left, not much wiser than when we came. When Alan and I had been taken to our own car, though, and were on our way back to the cottage, he said, 'There was at least one interesting thing in that conversation.'

'She lied.'

'Yes. She recognized that picture.'

'She almost said so, and then thought better of it and made some remark about an entertainer.'

'She knows who Paul is, or Peter, or whatever we want to call him.'

'Let's stick to Paul, for the sake of simplicity, shall we? I think if she were certain, she might have told us,' I said. 'She's the sort of person who wants everything nailed down, everything precise and tidy. Did you notice how painfully neat her desk was?'

'It's understandable. She lives in a world of violence, an untidy world of emotions, of actions without thought. She needs to control what she can.'

'And we need to find Jo Carter and Paul Jones. Do you think if we went back...?'

'I doubt we'd get much further. She has to decide what she can reveal without harm to her

135

present clients, or to Ms Carter, and she's going to decide that on her own time.'

'Well, she'd better hurry up about it.' I was cross. 'I have a bad feeling about this.'

FIFTEEN

'What are we doing to do about it?' We had finished our breakfast. It was another glorious day. 'Shall we go back to the shelter and try to get some more information out of the head clam?'

'It's worth a try, I suppose. Do keep in mind, love, that the police are doing their best to find Ms Carter, and their best is very good indeed. They'll talk to all her known associates and put out bulletins. They have many dedicated men and women who know their jobs.'

'Of course they do. But Alan, they don't have a personal interest in finding Jo. We do.'

'You specialize in personal interests, don't you, my dear? And your real interest is in Paul.'

'He's only a boy, Alan. He's mixed up in something awful.'

'He is also a wealthy young man with a raft of agents, fans, hangers-on. I'm not sure he needs our protection.'

'It's not so much a matter of protection. It's just ... do you think any of these people really

136

care about Paul?'

There is a look Alan gives me occasionally that always brings tears to my eyes, a look of love and understanding, of compassion and warmth that no words could express. He kissed me and said, 'Get a move on, my girl. We need to get to Cheltenham.'

I never can find a place to which I've only been driven, rather than driving there myself, but Alan, with his far superior bump of direction, found the shelter with no trouble. The front door was, of course, locked. He rang the buzzer and waited. Eventually an automated voice sounded from a speaker above the buzzer. 'Please state your name and business.'

'Alan Nesbitt, to speak briefly to Mrs Bryant.'

We waited some more. Another voice, human this time, said, 'Mrs Bryant is not able to see you.' A click sounded, with finality. Alan rolled his eyes and pressed the buzzer again. We waited for a long time before there was any response at all, and then the door opened a crack and a young woman looked out. 'Mrs Bryant can't see you now,' she said, sounding scared.

I could imagine that she had spent a good deal of her life sounding scared.

She started to close the door, but Alan hadn't been a policeman all those years for nothing. Somehow his foot was in the way. 'I understand that she's busy, and I don't mean to take more than a moment of her time. Would it be possible for us to wait?'

'I'll ask.' The door closed.

'It's a good thing it's a nice day.' I leaned

against the wall. 'We may be here for some time.'

'We don't have to wait, you know.'

'Yes, we do.'

We could hear nothing from inside the house. I would have expected the sound of women's voices, babies crying. There was nothing. I looked at the windows, which were tightly shut and barred. 'It must be stifling in there, with no ventilation on a day like this,' I said to Alan.

He pointed to a condenser on the roof. 'Air conditioned. Didn't you notice yesterday?'

'I thought I was just cold because she was so ... so rigid.'

'They take no chances at all that anyone might get in.'

'Or out,' I said, looking again at the barred windows. 'Alan, I know it's all meant to keep the women safe, but it's an awful lot like a prison. And virtually soundproof.'

He started to make some comment, but the door opened again and the young doorkeeper appeared. 'Mrs Bryant will see you for five minutes.' She opened the door just wide enough to let us in and then closed it carefully, shooting the bolt.

My claustrophobia kicked in immediately. Somehow I hadn't noticed yesterday, but it *was* like a prison in here. There was no lack of space, nor of comfort of a restrained sort. Everything I could see was spotlessly clean, and there was no smell of diapers or sour milk, as might have been expected. Gentle sounds of mothers and babies could be heard from upstairs, and there was a toy box in the front room.

Nevertheless, no one could get out. Only the chosen few could get in. I half expected to be screened for weapons.

The doorkeeper accompanied us to the office, although we could hardly have lost our way; it was just off the front hall.

If we hadn't already guessed that the matron was not pleased to see us, it would have been immediately apparent. She didn't rise from her desk when we came in, and didn't ask us to sit down.

'I cannot imagine how you think I can help you, Mr Nesbitt, and as you can see, I am very busy.'

The surface of her desk had a single folder open upon it. For her, a riot of disorder.

'I told you yesterday everything I knew about Ms Carter. I know no more today.'

'It wasn't about Ms Carter, directly, that I wanted to talk to you.'

'What, then?'

'I wondered if you had any more idea about the identity of the young man calling himself Paul Jones. You were a bit uncertain yesterday, whether you recognized him or not.'

'I thought I made it clear that I was quite certain. I do not know who he is. I have never seen him before. Now, is that all?'

For once Alan didn't have to signal me to keep my mouth shut. It was obvious we weren't going to get anywhere. I smiled sweetly. 'It was good of you to see us. We'll be sure to let you know if we learn anything.'

'Indeed. I should have thought that was the job of the police. Good morning.'

Our doorkeeper was waiting just outside the office. We were not to be allowed to roam about the house on our own; that was plain.

On impulse, as she opened the door for us, I asked, 'My dear, are you happy here?'

She shrugged. 'It's not bad. Better than getting hit all the time.' She pulled up her sleeve and showed us a bruise the size of a saucer, and then she lowered her voice. 'It's not all roses, though. Mrs Bryant won't let us breathe, hardly, for fear our men'll find us. I'm leaving as soon as I can find another place. And, ma'am...' she lowered her voice still further '...she's lying to you about Peter James. We saw him on the telly the other night, and Mrs Stevens, that's the cook, recognized him right away. He used to live here, with his mother and sisters. She's just afraid to tell, like she's afraid of everything.'

'Do you know his real name?' Alan breathed, in the lowest possible tones.

'Libby!' The call came from the office. Mrs Bryant sounded annoyed.

'Gotta go.' The young woman all but pushed us out the door.

'Well, now we know the connection.'

Alan and I had gone back to our cottage, changed into hiking gear, and were wandering over the hills, bound for Sezincote House. We hoped walking would open up our minds as well as our lungs. The landscape would have made any artist set up an easel then and there. The soft

140

colours of late spring sprang to life in the sunshine. Birds trilled in the hedges; lambs gambolled in the pastures. I barely took notice of any of it.

'We know the connection,' Alan replied, 'but does it get us anywhere? The fact that Paul knew Jo Carter years ago, and she was, presumably, of help to his family in a difficult situation, doesn't shed much light on their connection now.'

'Well, let's— oops! Thanks, dear. I had no idea that hole was there. Let's think about what we know about Paul. It's a good name for him, I think. He actually looks a little like Paul McCartney, you know? When he was young, I mean.

'Now, what do we know? We know he and his mother spent some time in the shelter. Libby said something about sisters, so there were other children, too. We don't know how many, or their ages, or anything about them.'

'We can find out,' said Alan, his voice a bit grim. 'If it becomes necessary, we can get a court order to search the shelter's records. I simply do not believe Mrs Bryant destroys them all. And if she does, well, we can insist she tell us what she knows.'

'She's a tough nut to crack.'

'You might be surprised. Sometimes that sort will come apart completely if you can find their weak spot.'

I winced at that. 'Yes, but Alan, I hope we, or rather they, the police, don't have to do that. I don't like the woman, but I admire her. She's doing the best she can in an absolutely horrify-

141

ing job. Imagine dealing, day after day, with stories of human misery on that scale. I think the only way she's able to keep her sanity is to remove herself from the emotion of it all and stick to administration. As you said, keep her desk obsessively in order, her clients obsessively protected, lest the darkness crash in and drown them all.' My voice had risen and I made such an expansive gesture that I nearly crashed into a thorny hedge. 'Sorry about the dramatics. I ... it gets to me.'

'It gets to anyone with a spark of humanity. And of course that's why I don't want to force information out of Mrs Bryant, either. But we have to find Jo Carter. That is, somebody has to find Jo Carter. I'm truly worried about this disappearing act. It doesn't seem at all in character, and too many odd and unpleasant things have been happening to ignore the possibility of something nasty.'

'You don't think she's ... dead, do you? I can't think of any reason why someone would want to kill her.'

'Nobody can think of any reason to kill William Symonds, either,' Alan reminded me.

I negotiated a complicated stile, with Alan's help, and tried to pet a lamb on the other side. Of course it ran away, and its mother told me what she thought of me. 'It all goes back to that, doesn't it?' I said, watching my footing as we strolled across the pasture. 'The death of William Symonds, blameless farmer. And Paul knows who did it.'

'We think Paul knows who did it. That's

conjecture on our part, don't forget.'

'Well, either he does or he doesn't, and there's one way to find out. He shouldn't be hard to find, now that he's famous.'

'If he knows something dangerous, he's going to be very cautious about making his whereabouts known,' Alan objected.

'He can't hide completely. His publicity people would never allow it. His safety right now lies in the fact that what he saw, if he saw anything, was in the persona of Paul Jones. Why should anyone connect that person with Peter James, rock star?'

'Dorothy, you're not thinking. Everyone at the Holly Tree knows. He told Pam about his big surprise, remember? And now everyone at the shelter knows, even though Mrs Bryant is trying to keep it quiet. He's a sitting duck!'

'But ... but then he wasn't worried about anyone knowing ... Alan, we're missing something somewhere.'

'Careful, love, this stuff is loose underfoot. You could take a nasty slide. I agree we don't understand everything. Hardly anything, in fact. But I'd like to find young Paul, myself. When we get back, let's see what we can find on the Internet.'

SIXTEEN

I enjoyed Sezincote. I really did. It isn't quite as over the top as Brighton Pavilion, which it is said to have inspired, but there is an exuberance about it that reminds one of the glamorous days of the Raj, and allows one, for a time, anyway, to forget the darker side of that period of history. It lifted my spirits. I especially enjoyed the two stone baby elephants, nearly life-size, that graced the gardens. And I enjoyed the walk there and back. But Paul Jones was never far from my thoughts. As we strolled the gardens, a bored teenager following his parents jogged to the tune playing in his ears, and I wondered if he was listening to the latest sensation. As we ate a snack lunch, I remembered our lunch with Paul. When Alan caught my arm to keep me from falling at a hill that was slightly steeper than expected, I thought about the quarry.

The first thing I did when we got back to the cottage was to put the kettle on. The second was to boot up the laptop we'd left in the car.

There was a time when I was pretty helpless in front of a computer, but our young friend, Nigel Evans, is a technology wizard, a 'geek' in the very best sense of the word. He taught me the basics, Alan expanded my knowledge, and now

144

I flatter myself I'm as good at finding things on the Internet as many people half my age.

The trouble with searching for someone well-known is that entirely too much information is available. I had little patience for sorting through the millions (literally) of sites mentioning the name of Peter James. Some of them were obviously referring to other people by that far from uncommon name, some indeed to saints and apostles, or churches. Many were repetitive. I was offered the opportunity to buy recordings of his music in various forms, some of which were completely unfamiliar. I could hear excerpts of his work online. (I passed on that, with a shudder.)

'Try that one,' said Alan, who had been leaning over my shoulder. He sometimes has flashes of insight about these things that I will never have. He was a policeman for over forty years, after all, and knows something about seeking information.

I clicked where he pointed, and reached a website that showed, joy of joys, a complete calendar of performances for Peter James, from last week's TV show through the end of June.

'Oh, that was in Birmingham,' I said in surprise. 'I had thought, London. Would that mean he's still in Birmingham, do you think?'

But Alan's mind was following another track. He took the mouse from my hand and clicked on the 'contact' icon.

There was no phone number for Paul/Peter. I hadn't expected that there would be. But there were numbers and email addresses for agents and managers, for media contacts, for 'contract negotiations', for anything under the sun.

'Wow,' I said in a whisper. 'He really is big business. I hadn't quite realized...'

'Yes.' said Alan. His voice was hard.

'What?'

'Don't you see, love? All this makes him that much more vulnerable.'

'And,' I said, thinking aloud, 'makes it that much more surprising that he spent more than a week in Broadway, just before his big night. His handlers must have been tearing their hair out.'

'He had to have had a compelling reason. And I'll wager anything you like to name that Ms Carter could tell us what it was.'

'If we could find her. Alan, we must!'

'Well, someone must, anyway, we or the police. And our best lead, our only lead, actually, is Paul Jones.'

'Yes. Alan, is your email address still "ccnesbitt at belleconstab", or whatever it is?'

He looked a little surprised. 'Yes, it is. They offered me the option of keeping it, and somehow I never got around to getting a new one.'

'So if you sent emails to these people, sounding official as all get-out, and they got the impression you were still a senior police official...'

'Impersonating a police officer is a serious offence, my dear.'

'I know, but you wouldn't be actually lying, just ... allowing them to make an inference.'

'You should have been a Jesuit, Dorothy,' he said with a sigh. 'Am I to call them, as well, allowing the same inference?'

146

'No, I'll do the phone calls.'

'And what story will you spin for them?'

'I don't know yet. Did it never occur to you that I might simply use the truth, that we befriended him and want to see him?'

'Never,' he said with finality, and moved me aside so he could use the computer.

I made more tea and sat sipping it while I thought about my next move. I would obviously have to make up a story that would get me through to someone trusted with making decisions, someone who could actually get me to Paul.

I thought about masquerading as someone else, but I rejected that idea almost immediately. Changing identity these days is almost impossible. If I used my own mobile phone, they could easily trace it to me. If I used the landline at the cottage, they could not only find out who made the call, but where I was at the time. At least mobiles don't suffer from that hazard, or at least I don't think so. Good grief, though, considering that some of them are equipped with GPS systems, maybe ... I shivered. Spying, as a profession, may soon die out, because anyone can do it these days. Privacy no longer exists.

I looked around at our peaceful cottage, out in the lovely countryside, and thought about how absolutely anyone could find us here ... and decided not to think about it. Paranoia is paralysing.

Very well, I would have to be myself, Dorothy Martin. Anyone could of course find out quite a lot about Dorothy Martin: who I was married to, where I lived, probably my bank balance and which brand of underwear I prefer. That would take time, though, and somehow I couldn't see anyone in Paul/Peter's entourage being interested. So probably I could alter the facts just a little. I couldn't disguise my American accent, so I would exaggerate it. I couldn't hide my lack of knowledge of the current music scene, so I could pretend to even less understanding than I had.

I would be ... I would be an American grandmother, desperate to take something home ... no, it was too easy for anyone to find out I lived in England. Something to give to a visiting teenage grandson, something he would really like. And I'd heard that Peter James was the newest music sensation (yes, I could lay that on really thick), and I wanted to give grandson Robert all his records ... CDs ... no, records, I'd use that term. It would reinforce my image as a sweet old lady who didn't know anything about anything.

In which image there was, as my mother used to say, more truth than poetry.

Oh, well, it was a start. I'd play it by ear. I have a fertile imagination; surely I could supply any necessary embroidery as I went along.

I took my mobile into the bedroom and shut the door. I couldn't do this in front of Alan.

It took five calls, to five different numbers, before I was able to talk to an actual human being. My loathing of phone trees grows at every encounter with them. I know no one who doesn't hate them. Why, then, do they continue to spread?

I went into my act. For some reason, when I try

148

to produce an extremely American accent, it ends up sounding as if I grew up in Alabama, y'all. Oh, well. I know many people in America to whom all English accents sound alike, and they include Australian and South African in that group. Maybe all Americans sound alike to most Brits. I hoped so.

'Is this Mr Peter James? Oh, his publicist! Oh, honey, I'm just so excited. I never thought I'd get to talk to someone as important as you. What? Oh, sorry, my name's Dorothy Martin, that's Mrs Frank Martin, and my grandson Robert's comin' to see me in two days, all the way from Mobile, and he's just your biggest fan, oh, I mean Peter's biggest fan ... oh, you'll have to excuse me, just babblin' away ... what? No, I live in England now, but he's never been here before, and his birthday's comin' up, he'll be sixteen ... this trip is his birthday present from his folks, they can't come, him bein' the mayor of Mobile an' all ... no, Robert's *daddy*'s the mayor ... I'm not makin' a lot o' sense, am I, honey? Anyway, I wanted to give him somethin' really special, and the very best thing I could think of is a whole set of Peter James's records ... what? Oh, sorry, what? CDs? Oh, how silly of me! I guess they haven't called them records for a long time, have they, I'm gettin' old and out o' date.' I giggled sickeningly. 'So I thought, if I could buy him the set, and get Peter to sign his autograph on 'em, it'd be so special, you know? So I went out and got 'em yesterday, I hope I got 'em all, they were all they had at the store, anyway, and I'm just prayin' I can come tomorrow and get Peter to sign ... oh, dear me, that *would*'ve been easier, wouldn't it? I never thought of you goin' to all that trouble of mailin' 'em to me. But, y'see, I've got 'em now, and I couldn't send a package to you and get it back in time for his birthday, and ... oh, dear! I was so hopin'...' I allowed my voice to crack a trifle, and sniffled. 'Oh, I do hate to tell his daddy...'

I allowed that to trail off artistically, and sniffed a little more. My fingers were crossed so hard my hands were beginning to cramp.

I had allowed the poor fellow at the other end very few opportunities to get a word in edgewise, but now I let the silence lengthen. His voice finally came across the line. 'Madam, are you still there?'

I had an insane impulse to quote the wonderful line from *The Producers*: 'I ain't the madam, I'm the con-see-urge.' I restrained myself. 'Yes, I'm here.' Sniff.

'Are you anywhere near Birmingham?'

'Why, yes, honey, I'm in ... I'm not far away at all.' I remembered in time that locations could possibly be checked. And 'not far' means something quite different to an American, accustomed to vast distances.

'I can't promise, you understand, but if you could be at my office tomorrow morning at ten, I think we could accommodate you.'

I didn't have to fake my excitement. 'Oh, honey, that's just so wonderful, my grandson will be over the moon, this is just so nice of you, oh, I'm so excited!'

He gave me an address, said again, somewhat
150

wearily, that he couldn't make a firm promise, and rang off.

I dropped the phone on the bed, turned for a tissue to wipe my brow, and saw Alan standing in the door.

He clapped. 'Outstanding performance, love! I take it back, Mrs Bernhardt. You shouldn't have been a Jesuit. You should have been on the stage.'

I fell back on to the pillows. 'Not if one five-minute performance wipes me out. Do we still have any bourbon?'

SEVENTEEN

'I told him we could be in Birmingham by ten tomorrow morning,' I said over a glass of wine, as we did not in fact have any bourbon. 'Can we?'

'Do you have the slightest idea where Birmingham is?' Alan replied, smiling.

'No, only that it's north of here.'

'Up the M5. Right now we could probably do it in an hour. At that time of day, what with rush hour traffic, we'd best allow three. Here, let me have the address.'

He went to the computer and found the best route. The all-knowing oracle inside the box routed him by lesser roads than the motorway, and predicted a travel time of just under an hour.

I took one look at the directions, with what looked like at least fifty roundabouts to navigate, and offered profound thanks that I wasn't going to be the one driving.

'Right,' said Alan. 'We'll leave at seven, then. If we're very lucky indeed with the traffic, and don't get lost or encounter roadworks, we may have time for breakfast when we arrive. And exactly how are you going to handle this interview, my dear?'

'Oh.' I hadn't thought about that. I was still euphoric about my getting this far. 'Well. I guess I'll have to go out and buy the wretched CDs first. Or will I have time to do that?'

'O, what a tangled web we weave ... I suppose you might, if we have all the luck I mentioned, and if we can find a shop open at that hour. WHSmith might have them.'

'I hope so! I'd better make a list of them, so I'll know what I'm looking for.'

'And once you have them?' Alan wasn't letting me forget about this till morning, as I would much have preferred. I was getting extremely cold feet about the whole thing.

'We march up to Mr What's-his-name's office and I tell him my name and ask to see Paul. Peter, I mean! And then after that ... um. He'll recognize us, of course, and we can tell him...'

'Exactly. Tell him what?'

'Oh, dear! Alan, what have I got us into?'

For the difficulties of tomorrow's proceedings were just coming home to me.

We'd found Paul/Peter. We, or rather I, had an appointment to see him. But would there be any privacy at all? Or would he be surrounded by his retinue, and fans, and paparazzi, and goodness knows who-all?

Would he in fact want to talk to us? He knew us only in connection with an unpleasant incident just after he had witnessed a murder, if we were right in that conjecture. He might well not even remember who we were. His mind had certainly been on something else, something that had put him almost into a state of shock. What could I, or we, say to him to persuade him to talk to us, and in private?

'We'll just have to tell him the truth,' I said. 'I don't want to blurt it out in front of everybody who might be there, but I think we have to tell him Jo Carter is missing, and we need help in finding her.'

'I have a better idea,' said Alan, taking pity on me. I was floundering, and he knew it. 'You launch into your ditzy grandmother routine, and while he's trying to remember where he's seen you before, I'll slip him a note, explaining why we need to talk with him at some length.'

'Alan, that's brilliant,' I said with relief. 'He'll know how to manage his people. So now all we need to think about is exactly what information we need from him, and we can talk about that on the way tomorrow. Now, let's have something to eat. Fretting always makes me hungry.'

We set out early the next morning, with only coffee to bring us to some semblance of consciousness. I brought along a thermos of it, and after a few miles felt awake enough to consider our approach to Paul.

'All right,' I asked Alan. 'What are you going to say in that note?'

'I'll keep it simple and brief, so he can read it instantly. Something like "Jo Carter is missing. Urgent we talk." If any of what we have inferred is even remotely near the truth, that ought to catch his attention.'

'And I'll do a reprise of that disgusting act I put on yesterday. Loudly. I want to create enough distraction that no one will notice the note-passing.'

We were tied up in traffic for a while in Birmingham. I stewed while Alan waited patiently behind lorries, avoided bicycles and buses, inched along trying to enter clogged roundabouts. The internal combustion engine is going to be the death of mankind one day, if not by inhalation of its toxic effluent, by apoplexy at its ability to create incredible congestion and inspire road rage.

After what seemed to my overstretched nerves to be a week or so, we found the building we were looking for and, miraculously, a car park not too far away. Our first mission was to find some Peter James recordings, which proved to be easier than I had feared. A small music store featured his picture in the front window, and after parting with an exorbitant amount of money, I was the proud owner of a good deal of music I would hate. That transaction completed, we had nearly an hour to spare, so we went into the nearest café, which happened to be a Starbucks, and got some breakfast.

'I don't really like the idea of American chains
154

taking over England,' I said as I downed my latte and coffee cake, 'but I have to admit this tastes good.'

Alan smiled and sipped his espresso. He knew I was talking about trivialities to avoid thinking about what lay ahead.

It still lacked fifteen minutes to the hour when I could sit no more. 'Alan, let's go. I know we'll be early, but I can't stand it one more minute. Do you have your note?'

He patted his breast pocket. 'Ready for your impersonation of a brash American?'

I swallowed hard. 'Let's get it over with.'

The building was newish, with very little grace or style, but efficient elevators. We were whisked to the seventh floor faster than I would have wished, and found the room number on a plain wooden door with no name.

'After you.' Alan gave me a slight bow and a look that told me clearly he knew exactly what I was feeling.

The office was pleasant, but by no means luxurious. The reception desk, in curved blond oak, might have been an attempt at retro style, but I didn't think it was. Somehow the effect was more garage sale. Not shabby, but definitely not showy.

The desk was also unattended. In fact, there were no humans anywhere in sight, although voices could be heard in the background. They were loud and argumentative, and they were getting closer.

A door opened, and a small riot erupted into the outer office. Only three men were talking, or

155

yelling, but they were plainly upset.

'How many times?! I tell you, I don't know where the bloody hell he's gone! Just left a note, didn't say where, didn't say when he'd be—'

'Didn't say anything about a contract, either, did he? What am I supposed to do with all these damn kids? They can't do a session without—'

'Find him, damn it! He's got to be—'

Alan cleared his throat. Loudly.

One of the men spun around. 'And who the bloody hell are you? We don't run auditions here. Down the hall, 7316. And good luck, darlings.'

Alan ignored the contempt in his voice. 'This is my wife, Dorothy Martin. She has an appointment with Peter James.'

The silence was so sudden I thought for a moment I'd gone deaf. Then the man who had spoken to us, the fat, bald one, turned to me with a look of menace. 'Oh, you have an appointment with Peter, do you? I don't suppose you'd care to tell me where he is?'

I gulped. My prepared speech deserted me. 'Um ... I phoned yesterday about him signing some CDs for me. Ten o'clock, you said. Or somebody said.'

'That was me,' said the spotty young man in the purple shirt and the outrageous tie. 'I remember you. You sound different.'

'Never mind how the hell she sounded,' said Baldy. 'I don't know who you are, madam, and I don't bloody well care. I've got a recording session due to start in an hour, and my star's gone missing!'

156

EIGHTEEN

I turned to Alan. He had adopted a very official look, and pulled out of his pocket, not the note he had planned to give Paul, but his identification.

'Gentlemen, my name is Alan Nesbitt. I have retired from Her Majesty's constabulary, but I still have some police powers. I think we had better sit down and talk about this situation.'

'The police!' said Baldy. His face was dangerously red. In fact his whole head looked like a ripe tomato. He spoke with a heavy American accent, and I thought he ought to have a cigar in one corner of his mouth. 'I told you not to call the police! The publicity—'

He was apparently addressing the spotty youth, who shouted, 'I didn't call anybody. When have I had time to call anybody? I only—'

'Please!' said Alan. He has a knack of sounding authoritative without raising his voice, reminding me of myself, back all those years ago when I taught nine-year-olds. 'The lad is telling the truth. No one called me. I came here simply to accompany my wife. However, since I am here, and since I may know a good deal more about your missing singer than you do, we will get along better if we sit down and speak calmly.

157

Are you expecting any other callers this morning?'

Baldy raised his hands and looked at the ceiling as if imploring the Almighty. 'Expecting any other callers, he says. Only the rest of the band, and the photographers, and the media, and God only knows who else. Why did I ever get in this business, why? Is it worth the agony, I ask you?'

I'd had enough. 'You got into it, sir,' I said, summoning my own sit-down-and-shut-up voice, 'because you thought you would make a great deal of money. I have no idea whether it's worth it or not. What I do know is that a friend of mine is missing, and if your concern is merely the effect this will have on your ulcers and your bank balance, mine is for the well-being of one young man named Paul Jones or Peter James or whatever you want to call him. Now sit down and tell my husband what he wants to know.'

Somewhat to my surprise, they all sat. Somebody's mobile phone began to bleat out *La donna è mobile*. I looked up in surprise, and Baldy said, 'Yeah, well, OK, I like other stuff, too. Culture freak, that's me.' He pulled the phone out of his pocket, looked at the display and put it away.

'I won't ask you to turn off your phones,' said Alan, taking charge without any difficulty at all, 'because an incoming call might be important to our inquiry. I will, however, ask you to set them to vibrate, so as to disturb us less, and we'll lock the office door, if you don't mind. I hope this won't take long. I do realize you're all busy.'

'Not without Peter,' growled the third young man, a nondescript fellow with thick glasses.

'I have introduced myself, Alan Nesbitt, retired Chief Constable of Belleshire, and my wife, Dorothy Martin. Perhaps—'

'Bit off your beat, aren't you?' That was Baldy.

Alan just smiled. 'I am, certainly. And I have very little authority even back on my home turf, now that I am retired. But a policeman is a bit like a clergyman, in that once we take office, we are, so to speak, in it for life. I assure you that, although I have no command in this or any other part of the country, I have the full cooperation of the local authorities. Right?'

There was a hard edge to that last word, a clear warning that they'd best take him seriously. All three of them squirmed in their chairs, but there was no outward disagreement.

'Right. Now may I have your names, please?'

Baldy turned out to be one Morris Rose, artists' representative. His staff consisted of Spotty, otherwise known as Lester Small, who handled publicity, and Glasses, the secretary, bookkeeper, and general dogsbody, whose name was Thomas Fuller.

They did not in fact have much to tell beyond the bare facts, but they took some time to tell it, interspersed with wailings about how this loss was going to affect them.

The firm, Rose & Co., Ltd, was in fact a very small organization. Morris Rose had begun as an impresario, finding new talent and promoting them to performance venues and recording companies. As more and more rising would-be stars

159

came his way, he decided that he could handle more aspects of the business with a little more help. So he hired Small to publicize his people, and soon realized that someone who knew something about business and money was also essential.

So they had struggled along, paying the rent on the office, finding a few modestly talented performers whose flames burned frantically for a brief time, but who turned out to be meteors rather than stars, falling to earth in a shower of sparks after their fifteen minutes of fame.

And then Peter James had come along.

'What is his real name?' asked Alan.

'Thought you was friends of his,' said Rose, suspicion sharpening his voice.

'We are, but we met him as Paul Jones – and he told us that wasn't his real name, but he didn't confide the real one.'

Rose shrugged. 'I don't know any other but Peter James.'

I turned to Fuller. 'You must have filled out forms to pay him. He would have had to show his identification.'

'It was some ordinary name. I don't remember.' Fuller sat on the base of his spine and looked sulky.

'Would you look it up for me, please?' asked Alan. It was phrased as a request, but Fuller knew it was an order. He uncoiled from the chair and slouched off.

'So he came to the office, wanting to audition,' Alan prompted Rose.

'No, he didn't come to us. I found him! Somebody sent me an email with a link to a YouTube video.' He looked at us doubtfully.

'Yes,' said Alan. 'I do know about YouTube.'

'All kinds of stuff out there. Mostly rubbish. But this singer – he was fantastic! Oh, a bit rough, needed some polish, but I knew right away he was going to be *it*! So I dug around a little, found out how to get in touch with Peter James, called him, and the rest, as they say, is history.'

'History is right,' said Fuller, returning. 'There's a wad of money tied up in that lad, and now he's disappeared. Browne,' he said to Alan.

'I beg your pardon?'

'Name's Browne. Matthew Browne.'

I would have chuckled if I hadn't been so worried about Paul. What a lot of fake-sounding names we were dealing with! One forgets that there really are lots of people named Smith and Browne and Jones. I suppose, somewhere out there, there are some John Does and Richard Roes, too.

'May I have the rest of his personal information, please? Age, birthplace, current address.'

'Look, Mr Nettle,' said Rose. 'You said you know something about where Peter might be, but so far you're the one asking all the questions. How about giving a little in return?'

'Soon,' said Alan calmly. 'His personal data?' he asked Fuller again.

'Age twenty, born Winchcombe, Glos., gave a post office box in Cheltenham as his address.'

'Cheltenham,' I said, giving Alan a significant look.

161

He nodded. 'Thank you, gentlemen. Now, may I ask when you last saw ... I'll call him Peter, for now.'

'Yesterday,' said Rose. He stood and began to pace. 'Yesterday afternoon.'

'Just before you called,' put in Small, looking at me.

'And everything sweet as can be. He's got manners, the kid has. Yes, sir, and thank you, sir, and always right on time, every place he's supposed to be. Last thing he said, we'll turn up around nine so there's time to get to the studio, he says. And then we come in this morning and there's this note!'

He pulled it out of his pants pocket. It had obviously been wadded up and then smoothed out. He gave it to Alan and I looked over his shoulder.

'I have to go,' it said, in an almost illegible scrawl. 'I'm sorry. I'll be in touch.' It was signed simply 'Peter'.

'This is his handwriting?' Alan asked the obvious question.

'That's the thing! I don't know!' Rose would have torn his hair out if he'd had any. 'We did everything by phone, text, email.'

'It's his signature,' said Fuller.

'And you didn't find it until this morning? Surely he didn't remain in the office after everyone had left.'

'Slipped under the door,' said Fuller, sliding even farther down in his chair. 'It was on the mat.'

'How could he have got into the building? Is it

162

locked at night?'

'Not till ten.'

'And is there a night watchman?'

'No. Look, Nelton—'

'Nesbitt,' said Alan, his voice neutral. 'Yes, I'll tell you what I know, though it isn't a lot. We, my wife and I, met the young man in Broadway over a week ago. He was staying at our B&B under the name of Paul Jones. We had an ... encounter ... with him on the second day of our holiday, after which he apparently left town. We neither saw nor heard anything of him until the television programme on Saturday night. We had been rather worried about him and were relieved that he was apparently all right.'

'So what?' said Rose. 'Nothing new there. We knew he was taking a little holiday, resting up for the big gig.'

'Yes. But what you don't know is that when we saw him last, he was in a condition of extreme fear. Neither do you know that a man was murdered just outside Broadway that same day. Nor that a woman who had been a mentor to Paul ... er, Peter ... when he was young, and was looking for him in Broadway, has now gone missing herself, failing to keep an important appointment. She has not answered her mobile for several days. Now do you understand why my concern extends beyond an aborted recording session?'

NINETEEN

The silence in the room was heavy. Then Rose cleared his throat. 'I get the point. You're a bleedin' humanitarian, and I'm a crass commercial git. OK. Actually I'm a little nicer than you think. I like the kid. But y'see, I want him back just as much as you do. Maybe not for all the same reasons, but I want him back, bad. So what can I do? What can we do? I put my entire staff at your disposal.' He made an expansive gesture that took in the office, its outdated furnishings, and his two employees.

Alan smiled in spite of himself. 'I appreciate that, sir. Your best approach is simply to co-operate with the police.'

Rose sighed heavily. 'Yeah, I suppose we got to call them. But the publicity...'

'I thought there was no such thing as bad publicity,' I said brightly.

'Having the hottest item in the business mixed up with a murder isn't the greatest,' muttered Small. 'It'll be all over the Net in five minutes.'

'Wait!' I said, an idea bubbling up. 'Wait a minute.'

They looked at me, Alan with the liveliest apprehension.

'No, it's a good idea. Really! A contest! Have

164

a contest to locate Paul, I mean Peter.'

Mystification on all faces except Small's. He began to brighten. '"Where's Wally", or whoever it was?'

'Exactly!' Since nobody else seemed to get it, even Alan, I explained. 'A few years ago there was this silly game, in the comics and I suppose online, though I didn't own a computer back then. You had to locate one face in a huge crowd, and it wasn't easy. I think there were prizes. Now. Peter James is a sensation just now. He has a website, and I suppose all the rest of the electronic nonsense I don't understand, blags and all that.'

'Blogs,' said Small.

'Yes, blogs, thank you. The point is, he's highly visible. Now. Suppose you launch a competition. The first person to spot Peter James – in real life, I mean, not in a picture – wins something. Lunch with him, or something like that. You'd have every teenager in the country looking for him.'

'In the world,' said Rose, beginning to like the idea. 'He's really big in China.'

'Now, hold on,' said Alan. He ran his hand down the back of his head. 'You plan to tell the world that Peter ... Paul ... I wish we could agree on a name for him ... that the young man is missing?'

'No,' said three of us at once. 'No,' I continued. 'Make it seem as if he's part of the fun, that he's hiding. Then people will really look for him, not just hope to spot him by accident. Instead of having a few dozen, or a few hundred, policemen keeping an eye out, you'll have thousands—'

'Millions,' interjected Rose firmly.

'—millions of fans actively searching. He'll be found in no time.'

'And by whom?' asked Alan, very quietly. 'Have you all forgotten that he may have witnessed a murder?'

'Alan, that's not important any more!' I said hotly. 'If someone was after him, he could have been found long ago. It took us about fifteen minutes on the Internet. Whatever he's running from, or to, the murder has nothing to do with it.'

In which I was both right, and tragically wrong.

We argued about it for a few minutes, but with four of us on one side, and Alan on the other, the outcome was never in question. Alan, with a shake of his head, conceded, and went to call the police about Paul's disappearance, while Small hurried to set up a fast addition to the various websites and blogs and whatever, announcing a major competition called 'Where's Peter?'. Fuller unlocked the office door and started dealing with missed phone calls, while Rose coped with the backup group and I sat around feeling fairly useless and somewhat unhappy.

I dislike quarrelling with Alan over anything more serious than beef or chicken for supper. For one thing, he's so often right that I end up making a fool of myself. Especially in anything remotely resembling police matters, of course, he's the expert and I'm merely a hanger-on. Mostly, I just hate finding myself crossways

166

with him.

I got up and found the office where he had found a little privacy for his phone call. He was just putting the phone back in his pocket.

'What? What is it?' He looked extremely worried, his face set, his shoulders rigid. 'Something's wrong. What?'

'Jo Carter made a nine-nine-nine call yesterday, from someone else's mobile. She could speak only in a whisper, but she told them where she was and said she was in great danger.'

My breath was coming in shallow gasps.

'When the response team got to the place, the phone was there, pretty well smashed to bits, but she was gone.'

'Didn't anyone know where she was?'

'There was no one else around. She had called from a disused shed on a farm near Broadway.'

'What on earth was she doing there?'

'That's only one of the things no one knows. But Dorothy ... there were signs of a struggle. Not just the broken phone, but footprints in the mud, as if at least two people had slid in it, one of them barefoot. And...' He paused and looked at me unhappily. 'And smears of blood on the door frame. Fresh blood.'

I blinked away tears. 'And they're looking for her?' It was a silly question. Of course they were. If they'd found any trace of her, Alan would have told me.

'They're doing everything they can, love. They did find her car, almost immediately.'

My question showed in my face.

'In Broadway, abandoned on a side street.

Keys still in it.'

'And now Paul...'

Alan's face showed his distress. 'Of course I told them about Paul, and they'll be looking for him, too.'

'Maybe we'd better call off the competition. This changes everything.'

'No, actually the superintendent thinks it's not a bad idea. We need every scrap of information we can get, and Paul almost certainly has some of the answers.'

'So does that woman at the shelter, what's her name?'

'Mrs Bryant. They went to talk to her again. They're probably there at this very moment.'

I fought down a sob. It turned into a hiccup. 'Alan, that poor woman! What can we do?'

'Not much, I'm afraid. Wait. Try to use our brains. Pray.'

We didn't tell Rose or Co. about Jo. There seemed no reason for them to know. They were doing all they could to find Paul, for their own reasons. We did tell them the police would be calling on them soon to glean every detail about Paul's disappearance.

'We already told you everything,' said Rose. 'Didn't you tell them?'

'They want to hear it from you,' said Alan patiently. 'And you might remember something when you tell it again. People do. That's why the police ask questions over and over again, caus- ing considerable irritation, I might add.'

'Yeah, well.' Rose spread his hands. 'I better get back to work.'

'I don't think,' I said when we were back in the elevator, 'that he has a whole lot of work to do.'

'It does rather look as if Paul is his only important client, doesn't it? No wonder he's furious.'

'At least it means he'll make every possible effort to find him.'

We drove back to the cottage in near-silence. It was still early. 'Shall I make some tea?' I asked. 'Or shall we walk? It's a beautiful day ... and walking helps me think.'

'Why don't you bring your notebook?'

I dropped it in a pocket, found my sunglasses and my walking stick, and set out.

It truly was a beautiful day. The rain earlier in the week had washed the earth until it looked newly made. 'This is England,' I said softly, echoing my thoughts of a few days before.

'Oh, no,' said Alan, smiling at me. 'There's no smell of salt, no sound of waves or sea birds.'

I smiled back. Alan had grown up in Cornwall, in the tiny village of Newlyn, his father a fisherman. 'Ah. Like cornfields and red-wing blackbirds.'

Alan had visited Indiana with me. He understood, and took my hand. 'Nevertheless, this is very pleasant. Far too pleasant for our subject matter.'

'Yes.' I dragged my mind back to the disagreeable task at hand and pulled out the notebook. 'Shall we go back to our list of queries?'

Alan nodded.

I studied the page. 'Well, we've answered some of the questions about Paul. We know his real name, though I can't think of him as anything but Paul. We know something of his background, which we didn't even think to ask before. We don't know what he was doing in Broadway, though.'

'We'll find out all the answers about him when we find him – or somebody finds him. What else?'

'The really important one, I think. Why was Jo looking for Paul? Why was she so concerned about a missed appointment? We can figure out why she stayed in Cheltenham to look for him – because that's where he stayed when she knew him before.'

'And he did go there. Let's not forget that.'

'You know, I had almost forgotten. And he ran away when I saw him.'

'And yet, a few days later, he was appearing on television for the whole world to see. It was a live broadcast, wasn't it?'

'Yes, I checked.'

'So he really was in Birmingham that night, and not in hiding. He was there the next several days, too, and making no secret of it.'

'That implies that if he left Broadway out of fear, it must not have been fear for himself, or he would have stayed in hiding. Fear for someone else?'

'We had thought that earlier. Maybe ... Alan, maybe he went to Cheltenham because he was afraid for Jo. Maybe he went to warn her! Remember, she said, when we met her in the church, he had made an appointment with her and not kept it.'

'I wasn't sure she was telling the truth.'

'I wasn't either, but suppose she was. Suppose he made that appointment, and then something made him change his mind.'

'What? And why would he need to warn her, as you put it, about anything? What threat might there have been to her?'

'I don't know.' I stopped in the middle of the footpath; Alan nearly fell over me. 'But whatever it was, it's caught up with her, hasn't it?'

He put an arm around my shoulders and we stood for a few moments, looking out at the beautiful hills, the silly, innocent sheep, and thinking about the evil that could hide there.

'Even in Eden, there was the serpent.' Alan spoke my thoughts.

TWENTY

We walked, not paying much attention to our surroundings. 'Alan,' I said after a while, 'do they have your phone number?'

'"They"?'

'The Gloucestershire police. Rose and Co. Anybody who might hear from Paul.'

'Yes, love. I'll know when anyone learns anything.'

'And meanwhile there's nothing we can do.'

'We can walk. And breathe this lovely clean air, and look at the beauties of the earth. And try to remember that the earth doesn't turn at our twirling.'

'Thank you, Eliza Doolittle.' We walked on, each absorbed in our own thoughts.

'Alan, she's a town person,' I said suddenly. 'What was she doing in a shed?'

He didn't have to ask who I meant. 'How do you know she's a town person?'

'She lives in Cheltenham, and has for a long time.'

'How do you work that out?'

'She's been working at the shelter for years.'

'Doesn't mean she lives there. She could live in any village nearby. As to what she was doing in a shed ... we don't know that, do we?'

'You said it was a disused shed. Does that mean rundown, falling to pieces, or just not in current use? And on whose property? And whose phone was she using?'

'I don't have answers to any of those questions, but you may be sure the police are looking into all of them.'

'I know they are, but do you think you could find out? Without putting their backs up, I mean. I know you're not officially on the case, but they don't seem to resent your lending a hand.'

'Probably, but to what purpose, Dorothy? We could go and inspect the shed and the farm it belongs to. We could talk to the owner of the phone; I'm sure they've established that by now. We could ask people all the same questions the police are asking, and annoy them no end, but why?'

'You're saying we're helpless.'

The compassion in his face was answer

172

enough.

'There must be some way we can help.' I was talking to myself as much as to Alan, trying to convince myself. 'Alan, do the police know about Sarah Robinson?'

'What about her? He frowned doubtfully. 'I know you're worried about her, but...'

'No, I mean, do they know she's a friend of Jo's? Have they talked to her, do you think?'

'Hmm. I have no idea. Certainly, I didn't mention her to the police in Cheltenham.'

'Then let's go talk to her ourselves! It would be something to do, anyway, to keep from feeling so useless.'

'She wasn't exactly forthcoming the last time we spoke,' Alan pointed out.

'Jo wasn't missing then. Or at least, she wasn't in trouble. Now she's in danger. I think Sarah will want to help. She called Jo her best friend, remember?'

'No, I'd forgotten. I do remember quite distinctly her telling us to peddle our papers.'

'Your American is coming along nicely, dear, but your accent needs work. And you still look English. Something about the way you walk...'

We had a quick snack lunch at the cottage and then got in the car for the short trip to Broadway. It took about ten minutes. Walking it, even along the roads, would have taken most of the day. I began to appreciate Alan's point about the advantages, on occasion, of mechanized travel.

The arts festival was beginning to wind down a little, but the village was still crowded. We found a place to park, with some difficulty, and

173

walked to the gallery where Sarah Robinson worked. It wasn't heavily patronized, on a Thursday afternoon, but a few customers wandered about, looking at paintings and drawings and sculpture, mostly sightseeing, I surmised. We scanned the ground floor quickly, then Alan went upstairs. He was down in less than five minutes. He shook his head.

'Lunch?' I whispered.

He shrugged and walked over to the owner, who was being gracious to an elderly couple who looked as though they had money.

'I beg your pardon,' he said in that stifled tone one adopts in galleries and churches, I have no idea why. 'I'm so sorry to disturb you, but we were looking for Ms Robinson. We're friends; you may recall seeing us one day last week. I wonder if you know when she might return.'

'Do forgive me,' she said to the couple. 'I'll let you talk it over. I'll not be a moment.'

She led Alan to her desk in the corner of the room. I tagged along. 'I don't think I remember your name, Mr...?'

'Nesbitt. Alan Nesbitt. And I'm not sure we were ever introduced, but I assume you own the gallery.'

'Clarendon. Elizabeth Clarendon. Yes, this is my gallery. Have you known Sarah for a long time?'

'Actually, we've only just met. In fact...' He lowered his voice to an almost inaudible level. 'In fact, we are quite worried about another friend of hers, a Ms Carter.'

'Jo? Is something the matter with Jo?'

'That's what we'd like to discuss with Ms Robinson. If you could tell us when she might return...'

'But you see, I don't know!' Her voice held a mixture of exasperation and fear. 'She's been acting peculiar all week—'

'Peculiar how?' Alan interrupted.

'Nervy. Jumped at every noise, and ... well, clung to me, rather. That's not like her at all. She's a bit quiet, but not clingy. Determined, independent. But I expect you know all that.'

'Go on.' If Alan was as impatient as I, he hid it well.

'She came in this morning quite early, before I got here. She was looking ... well, like something the cat dragged in, if you want to know the truth. Pale and shaky. She said she hadn't slept well and thought she'd get a start on the work. We've done rather well out of the festival, so there's masses of paperwork to be got through. But then mid-morning she took a phone call—'

'On her mobile?' asked Alan, interrupting again.

'No. I prefer that mobiles not be used in the gallery. No, it was on the phone here. I answered, and the voice on the other end was so scratchy I could hardly make out what he said. Eventually I caught the word "Sarah", so I called her to the phone. She listened for only a few seconds, then she dropped the phone, picked up her handbag, and said, "I have to go." And she was out the door without another word, and I swear, Mr Nesbitt, she was as white as that paper.'

175

Her voice had risen as she spoke, and the elderly couple, looking alarmed, slipped out the door, as did two other customers.

'I'm sorry,' Alan murmured. 'I'm costing you custom. If it weren't important...'

'Never mind. I'm more worried about Sarah than about lost business.'

'Two more questions, and then we'll leave you in peace. Does your telephone keep a record of recent calls?'

'Yes, a few, at any rate. But there've not been many today, so perhaps...' She was pushing buttons as she spoke. 'Yes, this must be the one. Nine twenty-two this morning. No name, I'm afraid, just the number of a mobile.' She read it off, and Alan wrote it down.

'Second, do you have any idea where Ms Robinson might have gone?'

'She went up the High Street. I know, because I ran to the door to ask her what was wrong, and she was running as if the hounds of hell were after her.'

It was a turn of phrase I would not have expected from the woman, who was bland and conventional, or so I had thought.

'I suppose she might have gone home. She lives up that way. But I did try ringing her later, around noon, and there was no answer.'

'Can you tell me exactly where she lives?' Alan's voice was steady, and probably no one but I would have noticed the underlying urgency.

'I don't remember the number, but it's in the Upper High Street, not far from the end, on the south side. Masses of yellow roses in front.'

176

'Thank you. You've been most helpful.' Alan shook her hand.

'And you'll let her know I'm worried about her!' she said as we opened the door.

'Alan, that's the house...' I said as soon as we were well outside.

'It may be,' he said cautiously. 'Yellow roses aren't exactly a rare commodity in this village.

'No. But I don't remember any others that far up, on that side of the street.'

'We'll soon know.'

We left the car where it was and walked up the street at a pace that left me breathless. 'Alan, I know you're eager to find out what we can, but remember my knees!' I cried plaintively, panting along in his wake.

'Sorry, love. I can't help feeling anxious about this whole situation.' He slowed a trifle, but I was at least as worried as he, and I hurried as best I could.

We rounded the bend and saw plainly the house with the cascades of yellow roses. We stopped at the same moment and looked at each other. 'Alan, I don't like this,' I said in a small voice.

The house was, as I had been sure it would be, the one we had seen Paul Jones leaving on our first night in Broadway.

As we approached, Alan straightened his shoulders. His face changed in some indefinable way. I understood that it was Chief Constable Nesbitt making this call, and that he wanted me as silent and inconspicuous as possible.

Even the rap on the door sounded solid and official.

We waited.

There was no answer, but I saw the curtain twitch. It was only the slightest movement, but Alan caught it too, and held his finger to his lips.

The silence was alive – the tense silence of fear, not the dead silence of an empty house.

'Ms Robinson, it would be better if you would open the door. It is of the utmost importance that we talk, and privacy is essential.' Alan's voice was quiet, but carrying. These houses were solidly built, but with someone obviously in the front room, he could certainly be heard.

'We have information that you need, Ms Robinson, and we believe you have information that we need. We mean no harm to you or yours. This concerns your friend Ms Carter. Please let us in.'

The silence took on a different quality, a hesitancy. Then with no warning creaks or clicks, the door opened a crack.

Paul Jones, aka Peter James/Matthew Browne, stood in the doorway.

178

TWENTY-ONE

'Hello, Paul,' I said in as normal a voice as I could muster. 'I thought we might find you here. I believe I'm entitled to a lunch with you.'

'What are you talking about?' His voice was low and hoarse. 'For God's sake don't stand there on the street. Anyone could see you!'

He opened the door just wide enough to let us in, then closed and locked it. I took Alan's arm. I wanted to cling to him, but I managed to keep my touch light.

Sarah Robinson was in the front room, standing by the window. She dropped her hand from the curtain and came towards us, moving slowly and carefully, as if she were afraid a sudden movement would cause her to disintegrate. 'What information?' she asked Alan, her eyes never leaving his face.

'May we sit down?' he asked quietly. 'Some of what I have to say will come as a shock to you.'

'Sit, stand, do as you like!' Sarah's control was slipping. 'But tell me!'

Paul took her hand and pushed her gently on to a love seat. He stood behind her. 'What is it?' he demanded.

Alan sat in front of her. His voice was very gentle. 'We have reason to believe that Jo Carter

179

is being held prisoner.'

Paul caught Sarah as she slumped in a dead faint.

Alan is trained in basic medical skills. While he ministered to Sarah, I shooed Paul out to the kitchen, where we made tea. 'Is there brandy somewhere, or whisky?' I asked. I was quite sure he would know.

He found a bottle of brandy. I added it to the tea tray and returned to the lounge.

Sarah was sitting upright again. Her skin was so pale it was nearly transparent, and her eyes were sunken, with purple circles underneath. She opened her mouth to speak, but I shook my head. 'Not until you've got some of this in you.' I poured the tea and added three lumps of sugar.

'I don't take sugar,' she said in a near-whisper. 'Just milk.'

'You're having sugar now. It's good for shock. And no milk. The brandy might curdle it.'

I had found a rather tired lemon on the kitchen counter and sliced it. I dropped a slice into the cup and added a healthy dollop of brandy. 'There. Now drink that as soon as it's cool enough.' I stood by her side until I was sure her hand was steady enough to hold the cup without spilling hot tea all over herself, and then retired to a dim corner, giving Alan a quick glance. He nodded. My role now was to watch and listen. Paul sat down beside her, close enough to steady her if she felt faint again.

'Mr Jones,' Alan began, and then hesitated. 'I hardly know what to call you, young man. You have many names.'

'Paul will do, sir. Peter James is my professional name.' He had lost his belligerence, but there was deep fear and distress in his eyes and in his manner. Even so, he couldn't keep a small note of pride out of his voice.

'And you are ... Ms Robinson?' Alan allowed his scepticism to show.

'I, too, have many names,' said Sarah, with great sadness. 'I was born Susan Browne. But you can call me Sarah.'

'And Paul here is your son.'

In my corner, I suppressed a triumphant cry. I had been sure, from the moment Paul opened the door, of the truth, but I had feared Alan would ask, and be lied to. I should have had more confidence in my experienced policeman.

'I'm not sure how you found that out, but yes, he is. My oldest child.'

'You have other children?'

'Two daughters. I've sent them to stay with a friend for a little.'

Alan didn't ask why. Her situation here at home was plainly difficult at the moment. He simply nodded. 'There's a good deal more I need to know and understand, but the first, urgent matter is: have you heard anything from Jo Carter?'

'Nothing!' It was an anguished cry from Paul. 'I've been phoning her for days. Her mobile doesn't answer. The shelter doesn't know where she is, or won't say. She's ... she's vanished from the face of the earth, and now you say she's a prisoner?'

'We very much fear that is the case. When I

say "we", I mean the Gloucestershire police, with whom I am cooperating. A fairly complicated series of events, in which you are very much involved, Paul, led us to believe she might be in danger.' There was a quiet moan from Sarah, which Alan ignored. 'A great many people have been looking for her. Last evening the police received a nine-nine-nine call from her, or from a person claiming to be Jo Carter. She said she had escaped from a captor and was hiding. She gave the police careful directions to her location. When they got there, no one was there.'

'What do you mean, a person claiming to be Jo?' Some of Paul's belligerence was back.

'She was using someone else's mobile phone, apparently stolen. The phone was found, smashed to pieces.'

'But ... why would she steal a phone? Jo isn't ... she wouldn't...'

'We believe she was not able to take her own with her when she ran away. We don't know how she managed to find someone else's. What we do know is that the woman who made the call was in great distress.' He let that remark hang in the air. I watched Sarah, who was crying quietly, her tea cup still in her hand, forgotten. She had drunk some of it. Enough, I hoped, to help a little. I moved forward, took the cup from her hand, and put it on the table.

'Where was she?' Paul hunched forward, elbows on his knees. 'Maybe they haven't searched well enough.'

'The location she gave the police, on the

phone, was a disused shed not too far from Broadway.'

'Are they sure they found the right place?' Paul shot to his feet. 'She could be out there, hurt—'

'They found the right place. I forgot to say, Dorothy, but they found her wristwatch.'

'But a watch could be anybody's.' Paul wasn't ready to give up hope.

'They took it to the shelter where she worked. It was positively identified.'

'Do sit down, Paul,' said Sarah wearily. 'You can't think when you're in a rage.'

He glared at her, but he sat.

'And speaking of the shelter,' said Alan, watching both of them closely, 'I need to know a good deal more about your family history. All I know is that Jo was your counsellor there. If counsellor is the right word.'

'The word is angel,' said Sarah. She was still crying, but she paid no attention to the tears, which rolled down her face unchecked. 'We wouldn't be alive now, any of us, if not for Jo.' She sniffed and reached in her pocket. I spotted a box of tissues and passed them to her.

Paul put his hand over hers. 'It's OK, Mum. I'll tell him.' His voice still had a bit of a hard edge, but his anger was directed inward, not at his mother. At himself, I wondered? Or something in his mind?

'I'll have to go back quite a way,' he said, 'so you'll understand. I was born when Mum was pretty young, and my dad was never in the picture. I guess we had a pretty hard time of it. I was

183

too young to remember much, but I do remember Mum crying sometimes, and I remember there wasn't always a lot to eat.'

I looked at Sarah, pale and thin, and at Paul, taller than his mother and with a lean hardness that spoke of good health. *And what little there was, she gave to you*, I thought. I've never had children, but I could understand the fierce love that would protect a child at whatever cost.

Sarah gripped his hand, but didn't interrupt.

'So when I was about seven, Mum met this man. He started seeing a lot of her, taking her out, bringing her presents. He brought me presents, too. I took them, but I never liked him, not from the very first.

'Mum told me they were going to get married. I think I was a right stinker about that. Temper tantrums, the lot. Mum tried to tell me it wouldn't make any difference for us, that she'd always love me, but we'd live in a nicer place and have better food and that. I didn't care. I didn't want that man around.'

'And how right you were, darling,' murmured Sarah.

'But for the wrong reasons. I was jealous and selfish. I see that now. But of course they married.' He swallowed hard. 'Is there any more tea?'

'I'll make some fresh. This is cold.' I got up and went to the kitchen, but I left the door open. I wanted to hear this.

'He started in, almost from the beginning. It would be after I was sent to bed, and I'd hear him talking to her. She never answered back. He

184

didn't shout, not at first. He just went on and on about how she did everything wrong, she was a terrible cook, she didn't keep the house clean enough, she wasn't trying to look her best.'

He stopped again. I brought him a glass of water. 'Until the kettle boils,' I said, and he took it and drank thirstily.

'Then he started drinking. Well, he always drank, ever since I can remember, but it got worse. He'd yell and scream and throw things. Then one night...'

I brought the tea in and saw Sarah wince. 'Paul...'

'All right, Mum. I won't go into all the gory details. But they have to know part of it. She was pregnant by that time, and he hit her. Hard. She fell, and...'

Sarah took a deep breath. 'I almost lost that baby. I would have left, then, but there was no place to go. You don't want to know all of it. Believe me, you don't. But I put up with it for five more years. An eternity. Then...' She couldn't go on.

'Mum caught him ... messing around with Jemima. She was only five. He would have killed Mum then, I think, but I ... I stopped him.'

'You were how old?' Alan asked, very quietly.

'Thirteen. He was big, but soft, and very drunk. And I had a knife.' He and Sarah both looked as if they might be sick.

Alan gestured a 'go on'.

'My son barely scratched him!' Sarah said fiercely. 'Ben fell, trying to get away from Paul, and hit his head on the Aga. Oh, yes, we had an

185

Aga. We had a beautiful house. Everyone had beautiful clothes. The neighbours all thought we had a beautiful life.' Sarah shuddered and took several deep breaths. 'I didn't know if he was alive or dead, but I was afraid he was alive. I got his car keys and some money out of his pocket, threw a few clothes into a suitcase, packed up the kids, and left.'

'Did you go to the police?'

'No. I didn't dare. Paul had stabbed him, and I had stolen the car and quite a lot of money. And he could be so charming and plausible. I knew he'd twist everything around, make it all my fault, and Paul's. I just drove till I was so tired I thought I couldn't drive any farther, but I had to hide the car. That was the first thing he would do, tell the police the car was stolen and send them looking for it. I knew of a little wood near Winchcombe, where I was born, so I drove there. It was night, and the roads kept turning out wrong, and I thought I'd never find it, but eventually I did. We slept in the car that night. At least the kids did. I woke at every sound, terrified he'd find us.'

She sipped her cooling tea, and Paul took up the story. 'You don't need to know all about the next few days. They were bad. But Mum finally found a church in Cheltenham where they told her about the shelter. You seem to know about that.'

'A little,' said Alan.

'Well, we went there. I don't know if Mum expected much. I didn't, just maybe beds for a night or two before we had to go on the run

186

again. But Jo ... sir, you've got to find her! You've got to. She saved our lives, and if she's in trouble now, it's because of us!' He had risen and was pacing the room.

'Because she's trying to protect you?' Alan asked, sure of the answer.

'No! Well, not exactly. Because he's after her!'

TWENTY-TWO

'I don't understand.' Alan and I said it simultaneously. It was to me that Sarah turned, her face wiped clean of all emotion.

'Besides my family, Jo Carter is the only human being on this earth who knows that Sarah Robinson of Broadway is Susan Browne of Winchcombe. We thought we were safe here, the girls and I. But Paul saw my ex-husband in Broadway, just a few days ago. He's still trying to find us, and he knows that Jo was my counsellor. He'll know she knows where we are.'

Whole floods of light were pouring into the dim recesses of my mind. Of course! That explained so many things! The terrible fear we had seen in both Paul and Sarah. Jo's worry. And...

'Where did you see him, Paul?' Alan's voice was very quiet, very controlled.

Paul looked at his mother, licked his lips, and swallowed. 'On the street. He didn't see me. He wouldn't know what I look like now, anyway. I

187

was a kid when he saw us last, and I've had a little plastic surgery. We all did. But I've been trying and *trying* to get Mum to move away from here, with the girls. If he's around, it isn't safe any more. She won't listen, she says—'

'But that isn't the only place you saw him, is it?' Alan's voice was still quiet, but it was as pointed as steel.

'He ... I...'

'You might as well tell him, lamb. I think he knows, anyway.'

Paul looked from Alan to Sarah, like an animal trying to escape a trap.

'Shall I tell you?' asked Alan. 'You saw him push someone into the quarry.'

Paul's face was sufficient answer.

'I won't ask you why you didn't go to the police at once,' said Alan. 'But you must do so now, you know.'

'You don't understand. It wasn't just that I was afraid,' said Paul, very subdued now. 'I *was* afraid. I still am. You've heard the story. You know why. But it wasn't just that. The thing is, I know nothing about him, not even his name or where he lives, unless he's still at the big beautiful house, but somehow I doubt it. It was probably never even his, really.'

'His name?' I finally felt free to pose a question. 'But surely...'

'No.' Sarah had had just about all she could take. 'I knew him as Ben Elliot, but I found out, or rather Jo found out, when she was working with us, that he had married me under an assumed name. He was already married. So,

188

although I call him my ex-husband, he's really nothing of the kind. I was never legally married to him. And I don't know his real name. Jo thought it better that I not know.'

'And Jo is missing,' I said bleakly.

'Records at the shelter...?' Alan suggested a little hopelessly.

'They're destroyed soon after clients leave.'

'You're quite sure, Sarah?' Mrs Bryant had told us that, but I'd hoped she'd been exaggerating.

'Quite sure. Before they started doing that, someone lied, got access to the records, found out where his girlfriend was ... and killed her.' She made a little face at my involuntary gasp. 'Mine is not an unusual story, Mrs ... I'm sorry, I've forgotten your name.'

'Martin, but Dorothy will be just fine. I do understand.'

'Appearance, then,' said Alan. 'What does this man look like?'

Paul looked a little helpless. 'I'm not good at things like that. He's big, soft. He looks like a drunk, red face and all that. He looks ... he looks sort of like Falstaff. We did Shakespeare in school,' he added in response to my astonished look.

'Now, this is extremely important, Paul.' Alan leaned forward and looked at Paul intently. 'Are you absolutely positive that the man you saw at the quarry was the man you knew as your step-father?'

He hesitated. 'No. I mean, I'm sure, in my own mind, but I suppose I couldn't swear to it. I saw

189

him first in the street, and I was sure then. That was Ben, all right, or whatever his name is. I swear to you, I nearly died of fright until I realized he hadn't even noticed me. And then later ... well, I never saw his face, and I wasn't all that close. But it was him,' he finished, stubbornly.

'What exactly did you see? Or no, first, what were you doing there?'

'I saw Jo. See, this was the same morning that I saw ... him. And he saw Jo, too. I watched it, and there was nothing I could do. He saw her, but they were both in crowds of people, and by the time he got to where she was, she'd gone away. But I heard her tell somebody she was taking a little time off work, and was going up to the Tower later. And ... I was pretty sure he heard her, too. So I had to follow.' He leaned forward, too, his hands nearly touching Alan's. 'Do you understand, sir? This woman is like a second mother to me. She saved my life, saved all our lives, because he would have killed us all. I couldn't stand by and wait for her to be killed!'

'I understand. Go on.'

'I followed. I had a motorcycle. Well, you know about that.' He had the grace to blush. 'I really am sorry about that, ma'am.'

Sarah looked mystified, and Paul rushed on.

'I have a car, of course, but it's red and ... well, pretty conspicuous. And I didn't want anyone to notice me while I was in Broadway, so I borrowed the bike from a friend. And ... oh lord, I still haven't had it repaired. Anyway, I rode up the hill as far as there was a track, and then shoved it into some bushes and went the rest of the way on foot.

'When I got to the Tower, I couldn't see either of them. So I thought maybe I'd got there too early, and I waited around. There was quite a crowd of people, and I had the beard and all, to make me look really different, but I was still pretty nervous about him showing up and maybe recognizing me.

'So after I'd waited a while, I thought maybe they'd both already been there and left, or maybe Jo had changed her mind about coming. And, oh God, I thought maybe he'd found her down in the village. So I started back. And I guess I wasn't watching where I was going, because I was lost in minutes.'

'I can relate,' I said, but very quietly.

'Well, so pretty soon I found myself in a sort of wood. I don't know much about the country. There were brambles, and flies, and it was miserable. I was hot, and scared. And then I saw him.'

'Ben?'

'Somebody who looked like him, anyway. He was quite a long way away, on the edge of the wood. I only saw his back, and his hands. He was ... doing things with his hands.' Paul made a gesture of clenching and unclenching his fists. It was extraordinarily menacing.

'He looked just like he used to when he lived with us and was getting ready to blow,' he went on. 'So I was scared worse than ever, and I thought I'd better follow him. I didn't really want to, because I didn't like the idea of what he
191

might do if he saw me, and we were all alone out there. But I really had no choice.'

'No,' said Alan. A single word, but Paul looked grateful.

'Well, I kept well back. I thought for a while I'd lost him, as well as the path, and then I was scared silly that he would come up behind me ... well, what with the midges and one thing and another, I was pretty well out of my mind when I heard him call to someone.'

'Call to someone! To whom?'

'I don't know. The flies were buzzing around, and there are odd echoes up there, from the quarries, I suppose. I wasn't close enough to see, but he sounded furious. I thought I heard him say "Stop", and then he swore at whoever it was.'

'Did the person answer at all?'

'Not that I heard. But I was getting worried, because I was afraid he'd found Jo. So I moved a little closer, and that's when I saw it.'

Alan waited. When the pause became extended, he said gently, 'You can't stop now, you know.'

'I know. I just ... well. I saw someone walking near the edge of the quarry, looking down. I saw ... him ... shout again, but the person never looked up. And then he started to run, and I'm not sure if he tried to grab the person, or pushed him, but the person fell, and he started to swear, worse than I've ever heard him before, and then he left.'

'What did you do?'

Paul looked at his feet. 'I went back in the bushes, and was sick.' He looked up to see if

192

anyone was going to laugh at him. He was, I thought, still very young, poor boy.

'And then I ran hell-for-leather to find my bike, and roared down into town, and ran into you, Mrs ... Dorothy.'

'And all you could think of was finding Jo, or your mother, and we coerced you into having lunch with us,' I said. 'No wonder you were a nervous wreck.'

'I didn't want to be rude,' he said, betraying once more his extreme youth, 'but I had to talk to Jo, and to Mum, and I was afraid he would see me. And then Mum wasn't home, of course, and I couldn't talk to her in the gallery, and I couldn't find Jo, and I couldn't think what to do. I was about half-crazy, I think. So I hitched a ride to Cheltenham, hoping I could find Jo.'

'Did you phone her to make an appointment?'

'Yes, but I only got her voicemail. And then I saw you near the racecourse, and I was afraid you were chasing me, or something, so I went back to Broadway and got my things and took off for Birmingham. There was the concert, and then this morning we were supposed to do a taping, but I tried calling Jo again and suddenly I couldn't stand it any more. So I rang up Mum and told her about Ben, and came here.'

'And we know the rest.' Alan frowned and started to go on.

'But Paul, you don't know the rest. We went to your ... is *"agents"* the right term?'

'More or less.'

'Well, everyone there was in a tizzy because no one knew where to find you, so we – well, I
193

actually, dreamt up a scheme that would have the whole world looking for you. Or for Peter James, not quite the same thing. It was to be publicized everywhere, and the first person to find you was to get a prize of lunch with you.'

'Oh, so that's what you meant ... but that could be...'

'Yes, it could be quite dreadful if this horrible man figures out who you are. I had no idea of course, but...' I trailed off. I felt as though I had lit a very long fuse to a very large cache of dynamite.

'You'll have to go into hiding, I'm afraid,' said Alan, 'all of you.'

'My daughters are quite safe, Mr Nesbitt. I would rather leave them where they are and not frighten them. They think I've simply given them an illicit holiday from school, and they're thrilled to be with Nancy.'

'I'll need their address, please. As for the two of you ... have you any ideas?'

Sarah's sigh came from deep within her. 'I hate to say it, Paul, but I think we're going to have to go back to the shelter.'

'I'm not a child, Mum. They won't take me. And Jo...' he struggled for a moment to regain his control '...Jo isn't there to speak up for us. I have a better idea.'

So it was that Alan and I found ourselves, a couple of hours later, driving up to London with two passengers, elderly grey-haired ladies in charity-shop dresses. And if one of them had a slight five-o'clock shadow by the time we arrived at the Ritz, nobody appeared to pay any

194

attention. The doorman had probably dealt with more unusual guests than this pair, and was as suave and unflappable as I had expected.

We saw them up to their suite, which was the last word in luxurious elegance.

'Now you won't go out at all, right?' I said nervously. 'You can have all your meals served in your rooms, and if you need anything, just call the concierge and he'll arrange to get it. I do feel terrible about putting you in this position.'

Sarah was pale, but holding up. 'We're just lucky that my remarkable son can afford this sort of thing. When I think back...'

'Well, Mum, just hope it doesn't go on for too long. I'm not quite as rich as the Queen.'

'One last time,' said Alan. 'I hate to go on about it, but as I've asked at least twenty times already, can either of you think of any possible reason why your nemesis should have wanted to kill a perfectly harmless Gloucestershire farmer?'

'He's mad, I think,' said Sarah. 'I always thought he was near the edge. Now he seems to have gone over.'

Alan shook his head. 'Even the mad live by logic, their own insane logic, but they do things for a reason. Well, if you think of anything, you know how to reach us. Day or night, remember.'

I gave Sarah a hug and Paul an impulsive kiss. 'You're perfectly safe here,' I said, which must be one of the oddest tributes ever made to the impeccable luxury that is the Ritz. 'And it's sure to be over soon. Try to get some rest.'

Alan stopped at the concierge's desk to give

careful instructions about telephone calls. 'No one except me, and I do mean no one. I'll identify myself with a number.' He wrote it down. 'I'm trusting you with the lives of those two people.'

'Yes, sir. Certainly, sir. We do quite often have very important guests, sir.'

Since the hotel had, in its many years of operation, probably housed enough celebrities to populate Texas, that was one of those wonderful British understatements that I cherish so.

We set out for home.

TWENTY-THREE

We were greeted by our next-door neighbour Jane and her bulldogs, and two sleepy cats. The dogs were voluble with welcome, sniffing ecstatically to learn all they could about where we'd been. Sam and Emmy woke briefly from their nap. Sam stretched, poking Emmy in the stomach with two stiff Siamese legs. Emmy reacted with some half-hearted feline profanity, and they both went back to sleep.

'The silent treatment,' observed Jane. 'Been abandoned. Won't warm up for a while.'

'Abandoned, my foot! I'm sure you spoiled them rotten.'

'Hate to see animals hungry,' said Jane gruffly, and changed the subject. 'Didn't expect you

196

home for another week, or did I get the dates wrong?'

'No,' said Alan wearily, 'you're right. And we're not really home.'

Jane cocked one shaggy eyebrow.

'We were in London this afternoon, and this was so much closer than driving back to the Cotswolds,' I explained. 'But we're off again after a night's sleep. That's if you don't mind?'

She just looked at us. Jane is a woman of few words. She is also the best friend and neighbour anyone could hope to have, and she adores pet-sitting our cats.

She didn't ask why we had been in London, or why we'd chosen to drive many miles in the wrong direction, if we were planning to resume our holiday. She simply cocked her head towards her own home next door. 'Didn't get any food in for you yet. I've ham and salad and fresh bread. Could you do with a meal?'

It was bliss to sit in Jane's kitchen, stone-floored and cosy, with bulldogs nuzzling our feet and good, plain food in front of us. Jane poured some wine, and we talked about things other than fear and murder and madness. We waxed enthusiastic about the beauty of the Cotswolds, the charming villages, Sezincote House, and John Singer Sargent. Jane kept her peace, knowing we were talking too much about trivialities, willing to wait until we wanted to talk about the important things.

We were staggering with weariness when we finally got to bed, after the longest day I could ever remember. The cats decided, provisionally,

197

to forgive us for our absence, and settled themselves comfortably on the bed, leaving barely room for us. It was heaven.

'I'm glad,' I said with a mighty yawn, 'that we're getting this little holiday from our holiday.'

My answer from Alan was a snore.

I had to struggle with my conscience next morning. It was a lovely May day, the beginning of the long Bank Holiday weekend. The roads would be clogged with holidaymakers heading to the chilly seaside, where the children could dig in the sand, or the pebbles, and the adults could either wear winter coats and be comfortable, or proper beach clothing and turn blue. Here in Sherebury it looked like being a warm day, not too hot, with perhaps a shower later on. The garden was beautiful, thanks to the efforts of Bob Finch, our devoted if sometimes drunken gardener. Alan had got up early and fed the cats, and they were back on the bed, purring. I wanted nothing more than to stay there with them, dozing and sipping tea and being lazy.

And in London, a mother and her son waited in luxury and terror, while in or around Broadway, an extremely dangerous man walked free, and a woman lay captive ... captive, or ... I wouldn't let myself consider the alternative.

I was out of the shower by the time Alan brought my tea.

'Side roads, I think, love,' was Alan's only comment as we got into the car. There was no other decision to be made. 'Less traffic, possibly.'

It used to amaze me how long it took to get anywhere in England. The whole country is only something like 800 miles from one end to the other. How could it take most of the day to drive a couple of hundred miles? That was before I understood the complexity of the roads, and the traffic.

America is laid out in a grid, more or less. We are a young country, whose aboriginal peoples travelled only on foot, and seldom more than a day's walk from their tiny villages. When the white man came, they laid out towns according to the compass, and when they started building roads, they built long ones, from one town to the next. Later highways were built for the purpose of carrying people and freight long distances as quickly as possible. I had a friend, years ago, who lived in northern Indiana, and when she visited me and my English friends asked where she lived, she said, 'Not far from Chicago,' knowing they might have heard of that huge city. When pressed, she would admit that 'not far' meant about a hundred miles. She never quite understood why the English greeted that remark with hilarity. Subdued, of course, but definite.

In England, the roads are organic. They grew out of the needs of the people. Foot traffic first, of course, then beasts of burden with wheeled carts. Paths became tracks, tracks became roads, eventually roads were paved and, in very recent history, motorways were established from one big city to another. But given the density of the English population, the motorways are often hopelessly clogged, and side roads ... well, the old doggerel 'The rolling English drunkard made the rolling English road' too often seems apt. My favourites are the euphemistically named 'narrow roads with passing places'. That little phrase means that the road consists of one narrow lane, and if you meet another vehicle, perhaps on a blind curve, one of you must react in time to avoid a head-on collision, and one must back up until there is a small layby to pull in to, so that the other may pass.

Then there are the roundabouts. Don't get me started on roundabouts.

Alan does the driving. I'm great with a map; I navigate.

It took us most of the day to get to our holiday cottage. I looked at it with a jaundiced eye as Alan stopped the car in front of the house. The rain which had promised, in Sherebury, to be a gentle sprinkle, had been in this part of the country a downpour for the last hour. The drive was sodden and rutted; the house looked bleak and forlorn. I thought of our solid, beautiful Georgian house in Sherebury and suppressed a sigh as I got out and made a dash for the front door.

'Are we out of our minds?' I asked my loving husband as we sat and sipped bourbon. He had built a fire, and the cottage was beginning to get warm, but it smelled damp, and there was nothing much to eat except cheese and limp biscuits and canned soup. I would bestir myself soon and put together a scratch meal. We certainly had no desire to go out into the drenching rain.

'Probably,' said Alan. 'We could be home in

front of our own fire at this very moment. We could let the very efficient police deal with all the problems here.'

'But we can't, can we? I can't, anyway. If that dreadful man found Sarah, Paul, and the girls, we'd never forgive ourselves for not trying to ... Alan, what's that noise?'

The back door was rattling. I'd thought at first it was the wind, but the wind died down for a moment, and the rattling continued. 'Is someone trying to get into the house?' Despite my best efforts at control, my voice rose almost to a squeak.

Alan had the sense to grab the poker before he went through the tiny kitchen to the back door. 'Who's there?' he shouted, his voice an intimidating roar.

The rattling became frenzied, and was accompanied by a barrage of barks and whines. I started to laugh. 'A dog?'

Alan opened the door cautiously, and a bedraggled black and white creature crept in, belly low to the ground, tail between its legs. It looked up at Alan and whined gently, then shook itself vigorously, spraying water all over Alan, the kitchen floor, and everything else within range.

'Well, old chap, where did you come from? Love, get me some towels, would you? The poor thing is freezing.'

He led the dog into the front room and knelt in front of the fire, holding out his hand. The dog, still uncertain of its welcome, licked his hand and tried a tentative wag of his tail. I brought towels, and the two of us managed to remove

201

quite a lot of water, along with a great deal of mud, from the shivering animal.

'He – is it a he?' Alan investigated tactfully and nodded. 'He's not a very prepossessing specimen, is he?'

'Not at the moment.' The dog's fur was matted and still very muddy. He still shivered in hard spasms, but he had uttered no more barks or whines. 'Let's feed him, and bathe him, and then see what we have here.'

Alan's voice had taken on a foolish, motherly quality. Alarm bells began ringing in my head. 'We need to find his owners,' I said firmly.

'Of course. But we can make him clean and comfortable first. I refuse to share a small house with a dog this dirty.'

There was little to eat, even for us, and almost nothing that was suitable for a dog. But I found a dab of pâté in the fridge, and a can of beef and barley soup. He accepted both offerings with an alacrity that suggested he hadn't eaten for some time, and then lapped up a soup bowl full of water.

'All right, sir, it's bath time.'

I cravenly retired back to the fire while distressing sounds issued from the bathroom.

When my beloved emerged, much of the mud appeared to have transferred itself to his person, but the dog, though horrified after his ordeal, and looking very small with all his fur clinging to his body, was much better-looking.

'I'll just go and change,' said Alan.

'What does the bathroom look like?' I called after his retreating figure, but he pretended not to hear me.

The dog, meanwhile, sank down in front of the fire, burped gently, and went to sleep.

Alan also looked much more respectable when he came out of the bedroom. I poured him an extra tot of bourbon and gestured to the crackers and cheese I had set out. 'That's supper, I'm afraid. Buster here got the rest.'

'The old boy was starved, Dorothy.' That fond, foolish tone again. 'I think he's been living rough for a while. You can feel his ribs, sharp under the fur.'

I opened my mouth to say something, saw his face as he looked at the dog, and changed my mind. 'What breed do you suppose he is?' I asked mildly.

'Mixed, certainly, but I should think mostly spaniel of some sort. When we get the brambles out of his fur it will be nicely feathered, and he certainly has a spaniel's muzzle and ears. He'll be quite handsome when he's dry.'

Again I took breath, and again stopped myself. I was too tired to argue. In the morning Alan would have come to his senses and we could discuss what we were to do with this animal.

In the middle of the night, I was awakened from a troubled sleep by the sensation of an earthquake. The bed rocked. I sat up, trying to banish the shreds of disagreeable dreams, and saw a pair of liquid eyes a foot from my face.

The dog cocked his head to one side and smiled at me. Then he turned around several times and burrowed contentedly into the nest he had made for himself, squarely in the middle of the bed.

I sighed loudly, turned over in the small space left to me, and went back to sleep.

The rain continued all night, and I slept late. Rain is such a pleasant background for sleeping. I woke, finally, to find myself alone in bed and, indeed, in the cottage.

I staggered to the kitchen and found the coffee already made, and cold, and a note on the counter. 'Buster and I went to town for provisions. Back soon.'

Taking the dog with him in the car. This was a bad sign. We were going to have to have a serious talk when he got back.

I microwaved a cup of the coffee and lit a fire, and then sat and made plans. What could we do that the police couldn't?

Well for one thing ... good grief, had Alan called Rose & Co. to call off the 'Where's Peter?' campaign? If not, I'd better do that right away. I booted up the laptop, found the agent's website, and saw with dismay that the search took centre stage. I called instantly.

Busy. Of course. Everyone in the country would be calling. What had I done? I buried my head in my hands and tried to remember how to make the phone keep placing the call until someone answered, and finally gave up. Instead I sent an urgent email, not at all sanguine about the results. This was all my doing, and it was appalling, but if I couldn't do anything about it, I couldn't. All right. Set that aside for the moment. Next thing.

Plainly the urgent matter was finding Jo. But

what could we do about that?

Very little, I concluded, that the police weren't already doing. We could ask Paul and his mother about her usual favourite places, but what good would that do? She wouldn't be in any of them. If she was able to run away again, she'd try to get to the police. If not...

I wished I could push the picture out of my head, the picture of that sturdy, sensible woman held prisoner somewhere, prisoner to a man with a history of violence. The only dim ray of hope was that he wanted her alive, because only she knew where to find Sarah.

But she didn't! Oh, dear heaven, she didn't! Alan and I had removed Sarah and Paul, hidden them in London in the most luxurious security cell imaginable. What if Jo, in desperation, told whatever-his-name-was where to find them, and he went, and they weren't there! From what I'd heard of him, I was sure he would explode into a fury of hatred and anger, and...

Calm down, Dorothy, I told myself firmly. She's kept the secret all these years. She won't tell now.

She wasn't being tortured before, the other voice retorted.

I started pacing. I wished I had a warm cat to hug. I wished Alan would come back. I wished I didn't feel so bloody useless.

Think, Dorothy. Think. What do you know, what skills do you have, that might help?

Well. I knew something about the general situation, certainly. I hadn't taught all those years without learning things, things I would

205

very much rather not have known, about abused children and their mothers. Sometimes, though rarely, it was the fathers who were abused. I knew about abuse turning into a family trait, children growing up thinking nightly fights were a family norm.

I didn't see how that could help, but I tucked it away.

I'd done volunteer social work of various kinds for many years, through my church in America. It had mostly been of the soup kitchen variety, but I'd brushed elbows with a good many professionals along the way. Did that perhaps give me some insight into the way they think? Could that help me find Jo?

I shrugged and kept pacing.

When I'd first moved to England, I'd been able to ask questions and generally pry into matters that were none of my business, because I was an outsider, who didn't count. It was the shipboard romance pattern. Anyone could say anything to me, because I was a foreigner who might never see them again.

That didn't work any more. My accent and vocabulary had altered enough that, while the English still knew I was American, my American friends said I sounded perfectly English. I was no longer a foreigner, quite. My friends in Sherebury thought of me as almost belonging. I never would, completely, of course. My ancestors were from Indiana, not Belleshire. But I was enough one of them that they were cautious about what they said in front of me. I knew too many official sorts of people to whom I might pass it on.

In these parts, though, I was instantly recognized as an American, even before I opened my mouth. Furthermore, I was a tourist, that species of humanity both welcomed into a community for the commercial value, and despised for the nuisance factor.

Hmm. That element of negligibility might prove useful, after all.

What else?

I racked my brains, my eyes surveying the room restlessly, as though the very walls would give me an inspiration.

My searching eyes lit on the book I'd been trying to read. My mind had been too fidgety to stay with it for long, but it didn't matter, since I knew it virtually by heart. Dorothy L. Sayers' *Gaudy Night* is, for me, the finest mystery novel ever written, with development of character and setting worthy of the finest 'straight' fiction, with intriguing subplots, fascinating jaunts into Sayers' philosophy of life and her idea of a university ... meat enough to warrant the many re-readings I had devoted to it. The book was nearly falling apart, but I was loath to throw it away, as it was a Gollancz edition with the brilliant red and yellow cover so characteristic of its period.

The point, my wandering mind informed me sternly, was that I was an avid and experienced reader of detective fiction. I knew every plot device that had ever been used. I knew, in theory, how to interrogate witnesses, how to interpret clues. I knew that, in contravention of the tradition of English common law of 'innocent until 'proven guilty', everyone should be considered a liar until proven to be truthful. I knew how to be an amateur detective ... or at least I ought to.

I made myself a cup of tea and sat down again, thinking hard until Alan came home. By the time he walked in the door, I had a plan.

He had brought plenty of food, for us and, I saw with misgivings, for the dog. It romped inside after him and came bouncing over to me to administer a thorough sniffing. I patted it gingerly on the head and went to the kitchen to help Alan unpack.

'I'll get a collar and lead this afternoon,' he said, putting packages away. 'He's full of energy and needs exercise, and the rain should stop soon.'

'Alan.'

He turned to look at me, surprised at my tone.

'He's not our dog.'

'Well, I know that!'

'Do you?' I pointed to the tins and boxes of food and treats, the new bowls. 'He belongs to someone, my dear. We can't just ... appropriate him. And we have two cats.'

Alan's smile faded, and I felt awful. 'Most dogs get along well with cats,' he said, 'given the right introductions. He's a friendly fellow.'

'Oh, love. I didn't mean to be heartless. He is friendly, but it's just ... I've never had a dog, and I don't know how to treat one. And he's come from somewhere. Somebody's probably frantic, wondering where he's gone.'

'I had dogs, always, when I was a boy. You know I love cats, but ... oh, well, you're right.

We'll have to try to find his owner.'

'We could just let him out. He'll probably go home.'

Alan said nothing, but opened the back door. He looked like a small boy who had just had his ice cream cone snatched by a bully.

The dog gave us both a friendly smile and trotted outside. Before Alan could shut the door again, the dog came back, shook the rain off his coat, and sat down, tail thumping.

'Oh, well.' I conceded the battle ... but not the war. 'You'd better feed the poor thing, and I'll feed us. Then we can make some plans.'

'Yes, we need to decide where and how to advertise. The local newspaper, I suppose, and perhaps posters...'

'I meant, about finding Jo.'

Alan turned slightly red in the face and became very busy opening a can of dog food.

TWENTY-FOUR

Alan and I ate our breakfast in a slightly strained silence and then sat down on the couch to try to map out a plan of action. The dog, full of food, settled himself comfortably between us, and soon began to snore softly.

I sternly refused to give in to his obvious charm. He wasn't our dog. And Sam and Emmy would have forty fits if we brought him home. However, this wasn't the time to quarrel about it. We had more pressing issues.

'Alan, I've had some ideas. Obviously the first thing we have to do is tell the police everything we learned yesterday. There are lots of leads they can follow up that we can't, or not nearly as effectively.'

'I'm surprised to hear you admit that the police can do their job better than you can.'

Oh, dear. He was still sulking about the dog. Amazing how like a little boy a man of seventy can be at times. I hurried on. 'I've never claimed to be better than the police at *their* job. What I can do, sometimes better than they, is ask questions. I'm not only an old woman, I'm a foreigner. I've lost that edge in Sherebury, where everybody knows me and knows I'm married to you. They've become more cautious about

210

telling me things. But here I'm just an American tourist. Almost nobody knows me. I think I can go around and talk to people, around here and in Broadway, and who knows? I might just pick up something interesting.'

Alan made a non-committal noise. 'Questions about what?'

'I don't know yet. Social work, maybe. The problem of abuse. It'll come to me. The thing is, I have to do it alone.'

This time the noise was definitely displeased. 'I think that's a very bad idea. You're looking for a man who's already killed, for apparently no reason at all. I'm coming with you.'

I'd been prepared for this. 'Alan, it won't work that way. You know how people say I look like an American, somehow? Well, you look like a policeman. A superior one, intelligent and courteous, but unquestionably a copper. Nobody's going to say a thing if you're along.'

He said nothing, just sat there looking stubborn. We'd been over and over this for years: his need to protect me versus my need for independence. I sighed inwardly and played my last card. 'And look, I've just had a thought. If you go ahead and buy that collar and lead for Buster, here, I can take him along with me. He'd be protection, and the perfect excuse for calling on strangers. I can say I'm looking for his owner, and that will lead to more conversation. You know what a good ice-breaker a dog is.'

'You,' said Alan deliberately, 'are trying to manipulate me.'

This time my sigh was audible. 'You know me

211

too well, that's the trouble.'

'I know your capacity for getting into trouble. And quite honestly I can't see what you hope to accomplish. Besides taking my dog away from me.' But he smiled. 'You know, if we do end up keeping him, we must come up with a better name. "Buster" just won't do.'

I looked at the dog, still soundly asleep. His paws were working as he chased something in his sleep, and he whined a little now and then. 'I agree. Not a good name. He knows it isn't his ... doesn't respond to it. But of course we're going to find his proper owner. He's a nice dog. Someone will be missing him.'

'You really want to carry on with this, don't you?'

'Alan, I do. I don't know what I hope to accomplish, either, but I can't just sit here and pretend everything in the garden is lovely. Oh! That reminds me. I tried to call Rose and Co. this morning to tell them to call off the hunt, but I couldn't get through. And I couldn't remember how to make the phone keep on trying.'

We sorted that out, and then Alan got out his car keys. 'Want to come with me for that collar and lead?'

We took the dog with us, of course, and dutifully asked everyone we saw in Upper Pinnock if they knew anyone who had lost a dog. The English do love their dogs, and everyone was very sympathetic, but no one could help. At Alan's suggestion (reluctant, but resigned), we stopped into a vet's office to enquire. They obligingly took a picture of the dog, who revelled in the attention, and promised to post it on their website and make a few copies to show around. 'Lovely dog,' said the receptionist, patting him fondly. 'His owner will soon turn up, I'm sure.'

'Thank you,' said Alan morosely, and we went back to the cottage.

'Very well, my dear,' he said on the way. 'Broadway first, or the farms near the cottage?'

'The rain's stopped, and Buster and I both need some exercise. What is there within walking distance?'

'I left the OS map in the cottage. We'll take a look.'

It turned out there were only three farms near enough to walk, or near enough for me, anyway. Alan insisted I take the mobile with me. 'But what if you need it?' I asked with a frown.

'I shall be here in safety, with a landline and a car in case of emergency. You will be out hunting a murderer, armed with a walking stick.'

'And a dog. Don't forget the dog.'

'A dog that greets everyone with joy and wants to lick their hands. He'd be about as much use against an attacker as ... as Emmy.'

Emmy, Esmeralda really, is our elder cat. She is a large grey beast whose idea of hostility is twitching her tail while watching the birds outside the kitchen window.

'Oh, well, all right. I'll take the phone. But I don't expect to meet anyone more dangerous than another dog.'

'Dorothy, you don't know anything about this animal. He could turn mean if another dog came

213

along. They could fight ... I do wish you'd re-think this.'

'I'm not sure if you're more concerned about me or the dog. Stop fretting. I'll be fine. And I'm taking the phone, I promise.'

I made some sandwiches, enough for me and the dog if we were out that long, packed them and a couple of other necessities in my back-pack, and set out, OS map in hand and Buster on the lead.

It became obvious after about five minutes that (a) Buster wasn't accustomed to restraint, and (b) I couldn't manage him, the map, and my stick. I stopped and looked at him. He sat, pant-ing and smiling at me.

'You are a considerable nuisance, you know.' My tone was indulgent enough that his smile never altered. 'If I take you off the leash, will you stay with me, or run away? Alan would never forgive me if you ran away. He's decided you're his dog, no matter what he says.'

I looked down the footpath. A stile loomed ahead, and beyond it a pasture full of sheep. Oh, dear.

The dog looked at me, still smiling.

'Very well, I have to either risk it or turn around and go back. Off the lead until we negotiate the stile, and then I'll have to buckle you up again, because if you chased the sheep, the farmer would probably shoot both of us, and with good reason.'

Fearfully, I unhooked the lead. The dog shook himself, explored a couple of bushes, anointed one in the traditional fashion, and then trotted happily down the footpath, looking back every now and then to make sure I was following. Maybe this would work, after all.

He made short work of the stile, flattening himself to slip under it. It took me quite a while longer. The steps were awfully far apart, and hard for my knees, especially with no one to help. I was terrified that the dog might charge into the flock of sheep, but he was apparently well-trained and waited patiently for me to join him. He even put up with being re-leashed.

'You know,' I said, studying him thoughtfully, 'if I'm not careful I'll begin to think you're our dog, too. And obviously you belong to someone. I must *not* get attached to you.'

He grinned at me, wagged his tail, and trotted obediently by my side across the pasture. The sheep ran away, of course. They always do, silly animals. But the dog paid no attention to them beyond a casual glance now and then. Definitely well-trained.

The stile on the other side wasn't quite as steep, and when I'd got over it I found myself in a barnyard, a couple of bantam hens and one absurdly pompous little rooster hopping about. The dog paid no attention to them, either.

A woman in blue jeans and a plaid shirt was working in one of the outbuildings. I got near enough to see that she was grooming a pretty little black mare.

'Hello!' I called. 'May I come in?'

She glanced up, pushing back her floppy straw hat. 'Is your dog well-behaved?'

'He's not my dog. That's why I'm here, looking for his owner. But he's been very good so far.'

'Come on in, then. But keep him on the lead. Coco here spooks easily.'

The pony stood quietly enough, however, when we came nearer. The two animals eyed each other with mild interest, then the dog sat down and began to worry at a spot somewhere in the middle of his back.

'I take it he isn't yours, then,' I said, stating the obvious. 'My husband and I have taken a holiday cottage nearby for a few days, and yesterday this fellow turned up in the middle of the rainstorm.'

'He looks a nice dog, but no, he's not mine, and I don't know of anyone around here who's lost a dog.'

'Of course it's only been a day. I suppose the word might not have got around yet.'

'Have you advertised?'

'Not yet. I wasn't sure how or where.' I allowed my accent to become slightly more Transatlantic. 'Back home, we'd tack posters up on utility poles, but I don't know if you do that here.'

'Ah, you're American. Or Canadian?'

'American, but I've lived in England long enough I ought to have lost the accent.' This was getting me nowhere. How was I going to bring the conversation around from lost dogs to lost women? 'Beautiful animal,' I said lamely, nodding at the pony.

'Welsh mountain pony,' she said proudly. 'I'm training her to the saddle. She's very clever, but

216

very naughty.'

'You have children, then?'

'One child.' Her face closed, and she turned back to the pony.

Any sensitive person would have read the 'no-trespassing' sign and changed the subject, or ended the conversation. But I was beginning to get the glimmer of an idea, and I couldn't afford to be sensitive. This might be the lead I was looking for. 'Oh?' I said brightly. 'Boy or girl?'

'Girl. She's ten,' the woman added reluctantly.

'Oh, my, at that age they're horse-mad, aren't they? I never had any children of my own, but I taught them for many years. We lived in a smallish town in southern Indiana, and every little girl who didn't have a pony envied the ones who did.'

The woman nodded. Her lower lip trembled. I hated myself for persisting, but there was tension here, and where there is tension and trouble, there might be some information.

'There was an organization I thought did good work, called Reins of Life,' I went on, feeling my way. 'They trained ponies to work with children who had various disabilities, especially autism. They did wonderful work. I saw several children begin to come out of their lonely worlds and learn to love.'

The woman said nothing. She twisted the pony's black mane in her fingers.

'Is there something like that in this country?' I went on, doggedly.

'Look, who are you, and what are you doing here?' She was angry at last.

217

The dog stood and whined. I tightened my hold on the leash. 'My name is Dorothy Martin, and I'm sorry if I've disturbed you.' I held my hand out. She ignored it. 'I have a special interest in children in trouble, you see. The disabled, the abandoned, the abused ... I can't see them without wanting to do something.' Well, that was true enough, especially just now. 'But I can see you'd rather not talk about it, so I'll be on my way.'

'How did you know?' Her voice was barely a whisper. 'Who told you?'

'That you have a child with ... problems? I didn't know. I guessed, from your manner. But as you were about to tell me, it's none of my business, so...'

'No. Don't go. I ... I suppose it would really be rather a relief to talk about it. Would you like a cup of tea?'

The sun had come out and was beating down fiercely on the wet earth, raising clouds of humidity. My clothes were sticking to me. There was nothing I wanted less than a cup of hot tea. 'I'd love one, thank you.' I followed her across the farmyard, the bantams scurrying out of the way. 'May I bring Buster in with me?'

'Buster? Is that his name?'

'Well, he doesn't have a name, really, not that I know, anyway. It's just that I have to call him something, for now, until we can find out who he belongs to.'

'Well, bring him in, anyway.'

'You daughter won't be afraid of him?' I wasn't sure I should ask.

'She's not here just now. Sit down, Mrs Martin. Oh, my name's Helen. Helen Hoster.' She pulled off her hat and wiped her brow. 'Look, would you rather have some lemonade?'

'Much rather, thank you.'

While she went to the kitchen, I looked around with interest. The house was furnished casually, with squashy, comfortable chairs and rag rugs, but it was exquisitely, almost painfully tidy. Nothing was out of place by so much as an inch. No books or magazines lay on the tables, no flowers were in evidence. There was no evidence that a child lived here, no evidence, indeed, that anyone lived here. It might have been a stage set. English Farmhouse, Scene One, before the prop man put in the little touches that made it seem real.

Somebody, I thought, has some serious control issues. The dog seemed a little uneasy in the room. He whined once or twice and looked questioningly at me before settling down beside my chair.

My hostess brought in two glasses of lemonade on a tray with a pitcher, napkins, and coasters. My glass even had ice in it. I looked at it and smiled at her. 'Catering to an American's peculiar tastes? Thank you.'

She set the tray down in the exact centre of the low table, placed coasters so precisely I wondered if she'd made measurements earlier, and handed me my glass and a napkin. I carefully wrapped the napkin around it so it wouldn't drip, and drank gratefully.

'Mrs Martin.' Mrs Hoster put her glass on its

coaster, untouched. 'You said you have a special interest in ... troubled children. Did you teach special children, then?'

'No. At least, not exclusively. Back then, in a small Indiana town, all the children were lumped together, no matter what their problems, so in forty years I did deal with my share of unhappy stories.' I kept an eye on her as I told my story. 'There were the ones who were just a little slow, and the ones who couldn't learn at all, poor things. The others picked on them, though I did my best to stop it. Then there were the simpler problems, poverty, mostly. Ours was a caring community. We could usually see the parents through the worst times, and help the kids with food and clothes. Of course the kids who had more picked on the poorer ones. I think it's universal: the ones who are different are outcasts.'

I had seen no important reaction so far. I sipped my lemonade. Mrs Hoster said nothing, but she was watching me as closely as I was watching her.

'The really tough cases were the abused children.' She looked away from me, down at her hands. Bingo. 'We didn't always even know,' I went on, 'unless the abuse was obviously physical, and even then there was little we could do. Laws were somewhat primitive then, and unless a family member was willing to file a formal complaint, we couldn't interfere. It used to break my heart.' I put my glass down. 'I tried to give them all the love I could, but if the abuse was bad enough, they often seemed beyond my reach, beyond anyone's reach. Perhaps one or two of them were autistic, rather than abused. Even now, it can be hard to tell.'

By now Mrs Hoster had tears coursing down her cheeks.

'My dear woman ... I didn't mean...' I was truly appalled. I'd gone way too far. Had my detective enthusiasm led to this, to outright cruelty? Should I leave now, abandoning the damage I'd done, or stay and make things even worse?

'That's the thing, you see,' said the poor woman. 'We don't know if Gillie is autistic, or if it's just her background. She's adopted; we couldn't have any of our own. We knew she came from an abusive home, but we thought ... with lots of love...' She couldn't go on.

I looked around for a box of tissues, but seeing none, pulled a wad out of my pocket. 'Go ahead,' I said. 'They're crumpled, but they're clean. And if you'll excuse me for a moment, I think my dog needs some water.'

At least I could give her a bit of privacy. I went to the kitchen and rummaged a bit, finding a bowl that was probably meant for cereal. I filled it from the tap, looked at the gleaming floor, and put the water outside the back door. 'Don't you bother that nice pony, now,' I said, and went back into the house.

Mrs Hoster had regained control of herself and was sipping at her lemonade. I still felt like a monster. To what purpose had I brought this poor woman to tears?

'I'm sorry,' she said. 'I don't usually...' She

made an ambiguous gesture.

'I'm the one who should apologize. I'm thoroughly ashamed of myself. I had no right to come in here and pry.'

'It doesn't matter. I told you I was relieved to talk about it. We don't see many people, living out here away from town. My husband works in Cheltenham, so he isn't home a lot, and I can't really get out much, what with Gillie and the animals.'

'You said Gillie was away just now?'

'Her therapist thought an outing might be good for her, so she's gone to see the pictures in Broadway. Gillie loves art. She's always drawing.'

'Horses, I'll bet.' I looked around the room, rather pointedly.

'She likes to keep her pictures to herself,' said Mrs Hoster in answer to my unspoken question. 'They're in her room. She stays in there most of the time. She's so – so silent, so withdrawn. And so neat. She wants everything to be where it belongs. Oh, I saw you looking around. No, it doesn't look like a real home, but Gillie gets terribly distressed if anything's the least bit out of place.'

'How does she feel about the animals, then? Even the best of them aren't exactly precise in their habits.'

'Well, the bantams drive her to distraction, but my husband loves them, and he's put his foot down. They stay. We don't have dogs or cats, just because Gillie'd worry so if they weren't where she thought they ought to be. And Coco, of course...'

'Is special. Ponies always are.'

'Mrs Martin. You said you have a special interest in troubled children. What would you recommend we do for Gillie? I mean, we're doing all we can think of, but...' She lost control of her voice again, and looked down.

'I'm no expert, Mrs Hoster, but I do happen to know someone slightly, who has worked a great deal with families in abusive situations. She's ... away just now, but she might be able to make some suggestions when she returns. But your own therapist—'

'What's her name?' asked Mrs Hoster eagerly. 'When will she be back?'

I made a decision. 'Her name is Jo Carter.'

'Oh, Jo! I know Jo. Not well, and I've not seen her for years. She helped a bit with some of the legalities of the adoption. I thought then she seemed both competent and sympathetic.'

'A rare combination,' I commented.

'You are so right! Most of them are either briskly efficient or treacly. Where can I get in touch with Jo? She might be just the person to point us in the right direction.'

I could see nothing in her face but concern for her child. *I hope this is the right thing, Lord*, I thought, and took the plunge. 'I'm afraid Jo Carter is missing. She may be in some danger. That's another reason I'm out this morning: to look for her.'

TWENTY-FIVE

'What do you mean, missing?'

'I don't know all the details.' Well, I honestly didn't know them all. 'But she isn't responding to her phone calls, which is most unlike her. She is neither at her home nor at her job with the women's shelter in Cheltenham, nor anywhere else anyone can determine. Her friends are very worried about her.'

'Hasn't anyone called the police? How long has she been missing?'

'Yes, the police are looking for her. But they can't be everywhere at once, so I decided to have a go myself.'

'What makes you think she'd be out here in the country? She could be anywhere!'

'I don't think she would be in the country, particularly.' I had no intention of mentioning the abortive phone call. 'It's just that this is where I happen to be, with a dog who needs an owner, and I thought I'd see if I could find any trace of Jo while I was at it. I don't suppose you've seen her, have you? I believe she liked to walk in the country, so she might—'

I heard my mistake as soon as I uttered it, but it was too late to take it back.

Liked to walk in the country? Past tense?

What are you saying?'

I opened my mouth to claim a slip of the tongue, and then shut it again. 'I hope it isn't true. But I admit I'm afraid for her. I can't go into details, but—'

'Why can't you? I'd think the details would make it easier to find her.'

'Some of them are confidential, and not mine to disclose. I'm sorry. But there is reason to believe she might be in considerable danger, to put the best face on it.'

'Only she? Or anyone?'

And there was the root of it, and the question I couldn't answer. 'I don't know, and that, Mrs Hoster, is the absolute and honest truth. I think probably the ... the danger to Jo Carter is directed only at her, but I can't say for certain. If I were in your position, with a child to look after, I'd make sure she stayed under very close supervision. And please, if you do see or hear anything of Jo, let me know. I don't have a card, but my mobile number is...' I pulled the phone out of my pack and punched a button or two, since I can never remember the number, and read it off to Mrs Hoster. 'Do be extremely careful, please. There's too much we don't know, and there could be danger to you and yours if you approach the wrong person.'

'I understand. But I do know several people who might be able to help. Gillie's had quite a few therapists in her short life, poor dear, and most of them would know Jo Carter by sight. I'll put out the word, shall I?'

I thought about that. 'I think that would be a

good idea ... so long as—'

'So long as I'm careful whom I tell. I understand.' She leaned forward. 'And what you must understand is that I would never, ever say or do anything that might harm Gillie.'

Somehow her flat tone of voice, sounding almost devoid of emotion, conveyed the ultimate in conviction. 'I think I do understand.'

She relaxed a little. 'Well, then, I'll phone you if I hear anything, and please phone me if you find her.' She handed me a card. 'There are both the numbers. *Please* do call. I don't think I'll be able to sleep until she's found.'

'And I brought this upon you. Mrs Hoster...'

'Oh, for heaven's sake, call me Helen. Now that I've told you my life story! You didn't cause all this, you only told me about it. I suppose eventually I'll be glad you did. But just now...'

'Just now you'd rather I left you in peace.' I realized I was holding a leash. Oh, good grief, where was the dog? If he'd run off...

But he hadn't. He was snoozing peacefully in the farmyard next to the empty water bowl. I clipped his lead back on, detoured into the kitchen to return the bowl, and set off at as brisk a pace as I could manage. I was quite sure that the sooner I was out of sight, the happier Helen Hoster would be. And I didn't blame her in the least.

When we were well away from the house I let the dog off the lead, found a convenient rock, and sat down for some lunch. The sandwiches were pretty well squashed, but I was starving, and apparently Buster was, too, for he ate his

226

share with obvious enthusiasm. 'I am going to have to think of a name for you,' I said firmly. He cocked his head at me. 'Even if we have you only for a few days, I can't go on calling you Buster. It just won't do.'

He shook himself in vigorous agreement, and I had my first good laugh of the day.

I shared with him the bottle of water I'd brought along. He didn't particularly enjoy drinking out of a bottle, but I managed to get a little water into him before I stood up. 'Now what?' I asked. 'Home, admitting utter defeat, or the next farm?' I unfolded the map, wishing, not for the first time, that they were smaller and easier to manage. At least it wasn't raining. Trying to read a large and floppy map in the wind and rain is no fun at all.

'The next farm looks to be a couple of miles away,' I informed the dog, 'and there's supposed to be a good footpath. Then from there it should only be a mile or so to get home. Shall we try it?'

Buster smiled and bounced a little, eager to be off. I folded the map to the relevant bit, consulted the compass in my stick, and set off.

For once the path was well-marked and easy to follow. The dog trotted along with me quite happily, running off to explore matters of importance to him, but always returning before I could be anxious about him. In only a little over half an hour we were nearing the stile that led into the farmyard.

There had been a purposeful, occupied feel about Helen's farm. This one felt different. I slowed as we approached the stile, and Buster stayed closer to me, whining a little. The sun went behind a cloud, and I felt a chill that wasn't entirely external.

'Maybe we won't stop here, after all,' I whispered. 'I've got a bad feeling about this.' I felt foolish, quoting movie lines to the dog, but I'd have felt sillier talking to myself. It was, in fact, nice to have him along. He was far too friendly to make a good guard dog, but just his presence was reassuring. I began to hope we wouldn't find his owner.

I climbed warily over the stile while Buster crawled under, and then put him back on his lead. 'You stick with me, boy,' I said as we walked slowly on.

The front door of the farmhouse was shut tight, and no one answered my tentative knock. I was just as happy about that. I was being silly, I told myself, but I genuinely didn't like the feel of the place, and neither did the dog. He whined. He was probably just reflecting my own impressions, but for whatever reason, I was eager to get away from there.

'You couldn't be from a place like this, little friend,' I said to the dog. 'You're much too nice to belong to whoever lives here.' He tugged at the lead, pulling me down the path. 'You're as eager to get away as I am, aren't you?'

And then he stopped dead and began to growl, low in his throat. He took a stance that looked threatening even to me, unaccustomed to dogs, and refused to move.

'What? What is it? What's the matter? You're scaring me, dog.'

And then he began to creep towards one of the outbuildings, belly low to the ground, still growling. I had no choice but to follow. I wasn't about to drop his leash when he was acting so strangely.

It was a shed that hadn't seen much use for a while. It was empty. No cat lurked inside, no fox, nothing I could see to disturb the dog, but he came to a stop in the doorway and stood there trembling.

I saw the tiny shards of plastic first. There were only a few of them, in the angle of the wall and the floor, and I wouldn't have seen them at all if a ray of sunlight hadn't struck just there. They were a silvery colour. Just like the casing of the mobile phone in my pack.

Then I saw the dark stains on the door frame.

My legs turned to jelly. I reached for my stick, but it couldn't hold me; I slid to the ground.

This was the place. Had Alan known it was so close? Was that why he had been so opposed to my little expedition?

No. He would have told me. Protective as he was, he would never have left me to find this unwarned. I was a muddy mess, I realized after sitting there for a while. The dog was standing over me unhappily, whining. 'Yes, well, me too, old boy,' I said. 'The trouble is getting up. It's not as easy as it looks. I'm going to have to roll over on my knees, and that's going to hurt.'

I had little choice. I couldn't call Alan, because I had foolishly not noted the number of the landline at the cottage. I made a resolve then and there to get a mobile of my own. However, that

229

didn't help in this situation. I could hardly call 999 and ask the emergency forces to come and give me a hand standing up. What I needed was something sturdy to lean on, but the only thing available was the dog, and while willing, he wasn't anything like big enough to bear my weight. I sat a little longer, working up my nerve, and then, with a series of grunts, worked myself around to my knees and then to one knee.

I paused to get my breath, and that was when I saw it. The sun was getting lower, and shining more directly into the shed. The doorway faced south-west, so the frame was illuminated as if by a spotlight. It was rough wood, and I saw, caught on the jamb, a single long blond hair.

Jo's hair was short and grey. Moreover, this hair was coarse and dry-looking, not shiny.

It was, I was quite sure, not human hair at all, but a hair from the mane or tail of a horse. Not Gillie's pony Coco; she was black.

I had with me my trusty Swiss Army knife, without which I never stir. Ignoring the pain in my knees, I got to my feet, pulled out the tiny scissors, cut off a bit of the strand of hair, and stuffed it carefully into my pack. Then the dog and I were off home as fast as our respective two or four legs could carry us.

Alan wasn't quite pacing the floor when we walked in. He did, however, give the impression that he had just sat down. The newspaper in front of him was open to the sports pages, which he never reads. 'Ah, there you are,' he said with the utmost casualness.

'Here we are, safe and sound,' I said, equally

230

casually. 'And I have something for you.'

'And I have something for you.' He pointed to a small plastic bag on the end table. I dropped the dog's lead and picked it up, expecting chocolates, the traditional 'I'm sorry I was unreasonable' gift.

Instead... 'Oh, you are the most wonderful man!' I bent over and kissed him, smearing mud on his clean shirt.

'Goodness, what is this about? It's only a phone.'

'Oh, it's just that I was so wishing we both had one. And I'm sorry I got you all dirty. I need to go and change.'

'You fell.' It was almost an accusation.

'Not exactly. And I'm perfectly all right, so don't fret. Just give me a few minutes.'

I took the time for a lovely scented bath. I needed to wash the impressions of that day away. When I had soaked until I was pink, I put on corduroys and a sweater against the cooling late afternoon and joined him in the front room.

He was sitting in front of a small fire, the dog by his side. Both were comfortably asleep and snoring. It was such a sweet picture, man and dog relaxing at the end of the day, that I hated to disturb them.

I tiptoed to the kitchen, poured two glasses of wine, and waited for at least one of them to return to consciousness.

It didn't take Alan long. He sleeps like a cat, after long years as a policeman required to be awake and alert at a moment's notice. He gave me an appreciative smile. 'You look clean and scrubbed, like a nice baby.'

'And here I was trying for sultry and seductive. Alas for jilted hopes. Cheers.' I raised my glass.

'All right, love, tell me about your adventures. How did you get into all that mud?'

'Uh-uh. You first.' I was happy and comfortable, and I didn't want to recount my story quite yet.

'I've nothing much to tell. I drove into town, Upper Pinnock, that is, to get the phone and see if anyone had reported a missing dog yet. No one had done, of course, so I went on to Broadway with more pictures to distribute, and stopped in at the police station. No joy there, either. No progress at all. Oh, and I did manage to reach Rose and Co. to call off the official hunt for Paul. They were not best pleased. Their Internet connection and phone lines have been jammed for hours with calls and emails. And of course I wouldn't tell them where he was, and that rather upset them, too. Then I went to Cheltenham to mention the dog, though that's rather far afield for the little chap, and then home to wait for you.'

And to fret, I thought but didn't say. I took another sip of wine. 'You certainly covered a lot more territory than I did. I only made it to two farms. On the other hand, I learned something at both.'

'Oh? No claim for Buster, here?' He nudged the dog, who snorted, licked Alan's shoe, and went back to sleep.

'You know I'd have told you. No, I talked to

one woman, who knew nothing about a missing dog.'

'I thought you said two farms.'

'Yes, but no one was home at the other one. In fact, it looked deserted. But at the first one, I met a very interesting woman. She told me a long story, but the short version is, she has an adopted child with major psychological problems, perhaps stemming from early childhood abuse. And she knows Jo Carter.'

Alan raised his eyebrows.

'Only slightly, but ... well, Alan, I told her a little about the situation. Only a little, so she could be another set of eyes and ears.'

'Do you think that was wise?'

'I think she's trustworthy. I worry, of course, that I've put her in some danger, though I did warn her to be cautious. And the fact is, she might have been in more danger if she came upon Jo and/or her captor unawares. And Alan, she's going to spread the word about Jo among the therapists she knows. There are a lot of them, because her daughter has needed so much help. And she says they'll all know Jo, and will be on the lookout for her.'

'Mmm.' Alan is very fond of those equivocal noises. I used to try to interpret them, but over the years I've realized they simply mean 'I hear what you say. I may not agree, but go on.' So I went on. 'It surely can't hurt anything, and it might help. With that many people looking...'

'You may be right. More eyes are a good thing. There are never enough police to do the job right, and never enough reliable members of the public to help. The characters in *The Thirty-Nine Steps*, the alert and vigilant citizenry who spot Richard Hannay all over the length and breadth of Scotland, do truly belong in fiction.'

'It's an awfully good book, though. Anyway, that was the one farm. But what I learned at the other one was really important. Toss me my pack, will you?'

I rummaged inside, found the bit of hair, and reached over to hand it to Alan. 'What do you think that is?'

He frowned over it, turned on the light beside him to see it better. 'Too long to be dog or cat hair, too coarse to be human. I'd say it's from a horse's mane. Or tail, but somehow it looks more like mane hair to me. Where did you find it?'

'That's the point. I found it in the shed where Jo Carter was recaptured.'

'*What? Where?* How did you—'

'It's all right. It's all *right,* Alan! Let me pour another glass of wine, and I'll tell you all about it.'

So I did, not even leaving out the creepy feelings I'd experienced. 'The dog felt it, too, I'll swear he did. In fact, that's actually why I went into the shed to begin with. The dog was uneasy, and I wanted to see why. You know I've always believed in atmosphere, Alan, and the atmosphere in that place was thick with menace.'

I waited for him to smile away my fancies. He didn't. He studied the single strand of hair. 'So your theory is that Jo was taken away on a horse?'

'There weren't any tyre tracks, or tracks of anything wheeled. I'm sure the police noticed that. What was their theory of how she was taken away?'

'I didn't ask. Were there hoof prints outside the shed?'

'After yesterday's rain? There was a lot of mud everywhere. I brought quite a lot of it back with me, as you noticed. So stupid of me to fall that way, but I was...'

'A trifle out of countenance?'

'Just a trifle.'

We sat silent, considering the implications. At last Alan stood and stretched. 'You'd better try to lead me there in the car. I need to see exactly where the hair was. Did you mark it?'

'What kind of detective do you take me for? I left half of it there, of course. And it's firmly attached to splintery wood. It isn't going anywhere for a while. So what you are going to do is phone the Broadway police and tell them about it, and then I'll put on some slightly fancier slacks and you will take me out for a bang-up dinner. I think I deserve it.'

TWENTY-SIX

We took the dog with us. There was never any real question about that. Ostensibly we wanted as many people as possible to see the dog, in case his owner turned up.

Most fine restaurants don't allow dogs, even in England where dogs are welcomed almost anywhere. So we searched out a pub in Upper Pinnock that had a terrace and a promising menu. Buster settled down under our table with no fuss at all, though he remained alert to the possibility of falling titbits.

'We're not going to feed him under the table,' said Alan sternly.

'Of course not.' Accidentally dropping the occasional bite of steak doesn't count as feeding.

We didn't discuss Jo's situation over dinner. There were too many people around, and we both needed some time to think. But on the way home, a replete dog fast asleep in the back seat, Alan said, 'I've been thinking about the implications of what you found.'

'Me, too. What have you come up with?'

'Well, let's assume, for a start, that Jo was being held prisoner somewhere in the country.'

'Yes, because if she were in a city or town, or even a village, and she managed to get free, she

236

would have gone to a neighbour, or straight to the police.'

'Right. Also because it's harder to hide someone in a place where there are lots of other people around. Even bound and gagged, a person can make some noise.'

'And except in very large cities, neighbours notice unusual activity. One of the things I've always liked best about England is the way neighbours know each other, and look after each other.'

'It isn't that way in America?'

'Not except in the very smallest towns. Back in Hillsburg, I knew almost everyone casually, but it would never have occurred to anyone to ask me, in the grocery store, how my Aunt Susie was coming along after her operation. Here that sort of thing is a commonplace.'

Alan slowed for a nasty corner, our headlights sweeping a hedgerow and illuminating for an instant the eyes of some wild creature on its nocturnal business. 'You surprise me,' he said. 'Americans are such friendly people.'

'Yes, in a way, but ... well, anyway. We're supposing Jo was kept somewhere out in the country. And that means...'

'That means, among other things, that she must have escaped either at night or at some time when her captor had left the premises for some reason.'

'How do you ... oh. Because she would have had to take off across country, and would have been highly visible in the daytime.'

'Exactly. Now. You're Jo Carter. You've been

237

abducted and mistreated. We'll not think about how. You see your chance to get away. You get out of the house, or wherever you're being held, and ... do what?'

I shut my eyes and thought hard. Somewhere on the other side of that hedge, a horse whinnied. The dog sat up and gave a sharp bark, and then subsided.

'I would try to think how to get the farthest away in the shortest possible time,' I said, thinking aloud. 'Let's say it's night, and he, the villain of the piece, is still around. I don't have the car keys, and even if I did, starting it would make too much noise. The country is very quiet at night. So I suppose I'd start out walking. Or no. You said she was barefoot.'

'The smaller footprints the police found outside the shed were barefoot. It's reasonable to suppose they were hers.'

'So she didn't start out walking. Some of the footpaths are very rocky, and some of them cross stubble fields. Clever of the guy to take away her shoes.'

'Oh, we're dealing with a wily one. But go on. You're doing fine.'

Suddenly I smacked my head. 'Oh! Of course! What an idiot I've been. The horse!'

'I think so, don't you?'

'That's how she *got* there!. Maybe that's how they took her away, too, but she arrived on horseback. Either it belonged to her captor, or she stole it somewhere along the way. She could have walked a little way barefoot, I suppose.'

'Depends on the terrain around wherever she

238

was kept, but it's possible. I'm inclined to think, though, that the horse belongs to the villain of the piece, because if she could walk as far as a nearby pasture, she could have walked on to the farmhouse and sought help. I think we're looking for a fairly isolated farm where at least one horse is kept, though I'd prefer two.'

'So he could ride the other one after her. And one of them is palomino, or at least has a blond mane and/or tail. Where are we, by the way?' I peered out into the unrevealing darkness. 'I may be completely turned around, but shouldn't we be back at the cottage by now?'

'We're going to drop the horsehair, and our hypothesis, off at the Broadway police station.'

'Broadway? Not Cheltenham?'

'Broadway's closer, and it's the same force. I'll ask that they get in touch with Superintendent Davids.'

Alan was tact itself when he presented our bit of evidence, and our conclusions, to the police. Even so, the sergeant on duty was not exactly overjoyed. 'Very pretty piece of reasoning, Mr Nesbitt,' he said, with a geniality that didn't quite conceal his annoyance. 'Quite the Sherlock Holmes, your lady wife, is she?'

I bared my teeth in what may have passed for a smile.

'I'll certainly see the inspector gets this in the morning, first thing,' the sergeant went on. 'He has your number if he needs more information?'

Alan murmured something and got me out of there before I exploded.

'They're not going to do a thing about it!'

239

'Oh, they will. They don't just discard leads, even if they are the product of amateurs.'

'Amateur! You're a chief inspector! You're a famous policeman!'

'Easy, love. Not any more, I'm not. I'm a doddering, interfering old busybody, with a wife who's even worse, and American, to boot.' He grinned to tamp down my fury.

'Well, I think they're being extremely stupid. Here we've come up with this brilliant idea, which is more than they have, and they patronize us.'

'I told you from the start that we had to be careful about stepping on official toes.'

'They need to be stepped on,' I grumbled. We were back at the car by that time, where Buster was still asleep. He roused at my tone of voice, though, and whined a little.

'No, it's all right, dog. I'm not upset with you. You're a fine boy. You led me to the most important find in a week. You're a real ... Alan, that's his name! Watson! We'll call him Watson.'

'He is not,' said Alan as he backed out of the parking space, 'our dog.'

Alan and I have not always agreed on how to approach the unravelling of a problem, or even whether we ought to try. In the morning, though, we were as one. We didn't even need to discuss it. We all ate breakfast, Watson went out briefly, and then we all piled in the car. It was Sunday, but for once there were more pressing duties than church. I had the OS map at the ready, along with our road atlas and a pencil.

240

It was another glorious day, what we used to call, back in Indiana, Chamber of Commerce weather. We would have enjoyed it more if it had not been for the urgency of our quest.

'All right,' I said briskly, unfolding the map. 'Here's the centre of our circle.' I tapped my pencil on the location of the shed I'd found, the shed where Jo Carter had hidden, however briefly. 'What kind of a radius do we want to use?'

'We don't actually know, do we?' said Alan, negotiating an especially tricky curve. 'We can't speculate about the distance the horse might have travelled, because we know neither when Jo might have left her place of captivity, nor when she arrived at the shed.'

'We know when she made that call from her mobile, though. I mean the mobile she had with her. I suppose the police told you the time.'

Alan consulted his capacious memory for a moment, and said, 'Twenty forty-two.'

'Eight forty-two p.m.,' I translated. 'Now, I think we're safe in assuming she made that phone call the very first moment she could. So she arrived at the shed around eight thirty.'

'No, I'm afraid we can't make that assumption. She had to find a phone, don't forget. That may have taken her some time.'

I chewed on that for a bit and then started to think out loud. 'OK, let's go back to our little scenario of yesterday. I'm Jo. The bad guy ... can we call him Ben for the moment?'

Alan shrugged.

'OK, Ben, then, has left me alone for a while. I think that's more likely than our other hypothe-

241

sis that she left at night. Because on a horse, if it took her almost twenty-four hours to get to that shed, she would have had to be very far away indeed. Agreed?'

Alan nodded.

'I do wish you wouldn't talk so much. You're derailing my train of thought.'

He grinned, and I stuck my tongue out at him.

'OK. Ben's gone. I'm a sturdy sort of person, and I decide to take my chance. He's taken my shoes, crafty villain that he is. I'm prepared to walk as far as I can barefoot, if that's my only choice, but I look out a window and see some horses. I've ridden since I was big enough to clamber up on a pony.'

'How do you know that?'

'It speaks! Miracle of miracles. I don't know it. I'm forming a hypothesis. Inferences are allowed. I'm sure she wouldn't have taken time to saddle the blasted animal, and it's almost impossible for a person who's never ridden to get on a strange, unsaddled horse. It's hard enough for an experienced rider, but she was desperate.'

Alan nodded judiciously. 'Very well. You're an experienced and intrepid rider. You whistle to the horse; it obediently comes to you. You get yourself up on its back, presumably by climbing on the fence. Now what?'

I'd been working that out as he spoke.

'Now I ride like the Headless Horseman. I have to take a chance on direction, since I don't know where Ben went, but as the car isn't there, he's gone somewhere by road. Therefore I take off across country, avoiding roads. And ... oh! I

242

head away from Broadway, because Sarah is there, and even in my own desperate situation, I refuse to take the slightest risk of leading Ben to her. And I think ... here's another inference ... I *think* I stay away from planted fields, for two reasons. Good manners, and a wholesome respect for my own skin. A horse leaves a trail through a crop that a blind man could follow.

'So I use bridle paths, sometimes footpaths. My manners aren't so good that I worry overmuch about leaving hazards for pedestrians. When it's a matter of my life or death, they can step around a pile of horse droppings.

'I need police help, but I don't dare approach a village, or even a farmhouse, because he might be there. I have no money; he's taken my handbag. Now that I'm over my first panicky flight and able to think sensibly, I don't know what to do, where to go. It's just blind luck that gives me what I think will be my salvation. Someone has dropped the mobile phone by the side of the bridle path. Maybe it fell out of a pocket while they were trotting along. At any rate, I stop and pick it up.'

'Why don't you use it right then?'

'Hmm. Oh, because I don't know where I am. Also, it's hard enough to stay on this animal, which you will remember has no saddle or bridle, without also trying to make a phone call. I need to find a place where I can take shelter, work out where I might be, and then make the call,' I finished triumphantly.

'So you find the shed, get your bearings as best you can, make the call, and wait for the police,

243

but Ben finds you first.'

'Yes, and oh, Alan, we've got to find her, too! That man is a murderer!'

'Easy, love. We'll do better if we keep on thinking of it as a game. When too much emotion starts to work, logic flies out the window. Speaking of which, I think there's one flaw in your reconstruction.'

'Oh, and I was so proud of it!' I tried to get back in the spirit. 'Where did I go wrong?'

'You think she wouldn't have fled in the direction of Broadway. I would agree with you, except ... how did she know where Broadway was? When Ben snatched her, wouldn't he have made sure she didn't know which way she was going? All the best kidnappers blindfold their victims.'

'Oh. Good point. Unless maybe she could see the Tower, and work out directions from the sun. But that's pretty iffy, I agree. And it might have been raining, too. It has a lot, these past few days. I do think she would have avoided the roads, though, don't you?'

'That's a reasonable assumption. Of course,' he added maddeningly, 'you know we're building up this entire elaborate scenario on the slender basis of one strand of what we think is horsehair.'

'Well, we have to start somewhere,' I retorted. 'Now. We don't know when she started out, but there's another way to approach the problem. You know something about horses and riding, don't you?'

'Precious little. My father was a fisherman,

not a farmer, and I've never owned a horse. But yes, I probably know more than you do, town mouse.'

'Well, then. How far do you think someone could ride an unfamiliar mount, bareback?'

He thought about that for a while, as he drove on down twisty country roads. I tried to look for horses, but too often we were hemmed in by tall hedgerows on either side, and I could catch only the occasional glimpse of a chimney or rooftop.

'Dorothy,' he said at last, 'I'm afraid the only answer I have is "It depends." How fresh is the horse, how rough the terrain, how heavy and how practised the rider. Given ideal conditions, I should think a good horse could keep up a moderate pace for hours, and many miles.'

'Oh, dear. That's no help, then.' I was beginning to get discouraged, and my voice showed it. 'I won't let myself think it's hopeless, but these hedgerows ... this could take days, and I'm sure we don't have days. Hours, perhaps.'

Alan patted my knee. 'Well, then, we just have to rely on the dog.'

'To find her, you mean? But he's not a hound, and anyway we don't have anything of hers to give him.'

'No, as an excuse, I meant. You used him as an excuse to go poking about yesterday. We can do the same. Call on every farm we find, and ask if they've lost a dog.'

Watson, in the back seat, barked what sounded like enthusiastic approval of that scheme, making us laugh. And then we both stopped laughing and looked at each other. The ruse was all very

245

well, but what if we actually found the dog's owner?

Well, I could do a Scarlett O'Hara and think about that tomorrow.

'We passed a farm a few miles back,' I said with determined brightness, 'while we were trying to be brilliant and scientific about the search. At least I think we did. I saw a chimney.'

'Good. As soon as I can find a place to turn around, we'll go back.'

It would be tedious to relate how many farms we visited that morning, how many farmers we talked to, how many had no blond horses of any description, how many had lost no dog. Most were pleasant; a few were surly. None was in the least helpful.

We stopped at midday in a tiny village and found a delightful pub where we had an excellent ploughman's lunch. Instead of the usual resident dog, the pub had a fat cat who made the rounds of the room letting it be known that if we happened to drop some food, she'd be happy to tidy it up for us. She didn't exactly beg. Cats don't beg. But her purpose was apparent.

Watson behaved admirably. When the cat first appeared, he uttered a low growl, but then with an almost visible shrug he conceded that this was the cat's territory, not his, and proceeded to ignore her.

As we finished our lunch, I had an idea. 'Alan, I've just thought of something. Do you remember that man who owns the horse farm? The one we saw in the pub, and I thought he was the mayor?'

'I'll never forget, my dear.'

'Well, wouldn't he know who in the area owned a palomino, or anyway a horse with a blond mane and tail?'

Alan smacked the table. 'Do you know, he might. He just might. Shall we drive in to Broadway and ask him?'

'We'll have to be sort of careful, though. I really, really don't want Ben to know we're looking for him. I have the distinct impression that might not be good for our health.'

'Make up a story, love. You're good at that.'

So I racked my brains and cudgelled my imagination, and by the time we got to Broadway I was prepared.

'I suppose we're prospective buyers,' said Alan in a low voice as he found a parking place near the horse farm.

'Not at all. Follow my lead. I have the basic outline worked out, but we'll have to play it by ear.'

'Ah. Improvisatory theatre. I see.'

I had decided that it was risky to try to be anything but what we were. Broadway is a village, and we'd stayed there a week. By now, virtually everybody in town would have heard at least a little about us. So Alan directed me to the door at the side of the big barn where, he said, the office was likely to be.

Sure enough, a modern no-nonsense office had been set up in what might have been a tack room at one time. A couple of computer screens glowed, filing cabinets reached nearly to the ceiling, and behind a sturdy if rather battered desk sat an

247

attractive young woman who reminded me of someone I couldn't place.

She looked up with a smile. 'Good afternoon. Lovely dog.'

I smiled back. Watson, who of course had accompanied us, sat and offered the woman a paw to shake. I was as proud of him as if we'd taught him the trick ourselves. 'We think he is, but unfortunately he's not ours. He just walked in one day at our holiday cottage, and we've been looking after him until we can find the owner. You don't know anyone who's lost a nice spaniel, do you?'

'No, but I'll ask around. If he were mine, I'd certainly want him back. Such manners! But how may I help you?'

'Well, I should tell you straight off that we're not looking to buy a horse, just needing some advice, so I'll understand if you're too busy to talk to us.'

'Not at all. Dad isn't all that much of a slave-driver. Do sit down, if you can find a place.'

She stood, swept a pile of papers from one of the chairs, and offered Alan the one she'd been using, which he declined with a smile.

'Now. What can I do for you?'

I had finally recognized her. 'You're very like your father,' I said. 'He's an impressive-looking man. I thought at first he was the lord mayor.'

'Oh, I remember you now! At the Swan. We noticed you because we didn't know you, if you know what I mean.'

I was very glad I hadn't invented an identity. 'I know exactly what you mean, and I'm really

248

impressed that you remember a couple of strangers seen briefly. My name's Dorothy Martin, by the way, and this is my husband Alan Nesbitt.'

She held out a clean but work-worn hand. 'Annette Burton.'

'But I'm taking up your time,' I went on. 'I'm sorry. Let me explain my errand. I have a cousin back home ... oh, you'll have guessed that I'm from America.'

She simply smiled.

'I can't hide it,' I said with a sigh. 'Not that I want to. Anyway, I've lived here for a long time, but my family is still back in the States, and one of them, a distant cousin, told me in her latest letter that she's moved to Wyoming and is planning to buy a horse, a golden palomino. Now that worried me a little, because my first husband always used to say that palominos were beautiful but really stupid, not unlike the common perception of some human blonds.

'I don't know a thing about horseflesh, myself, and my cousin is headstrong. I wanted to be sure of my ground before I wrote to warn her off the breed. So what can you tell me? Is it true that they're dumb blonds?'

Annette had begun to look a bit distressed. 'I wish I could tell you it isn't so. I love the breed myself. Well, most say it's not really a separate breed, just a colouring; almost any horse can have the colour pattern. The original ones, though, were from Spain, Queen Isabella's favourite horses, and the best ones even today have that breeding. We've had some splendid palominos here over the years. But I won't

249

pretend that there's never a problem. The trouble crops up with careless breeding. If horses are bred purely for looks, leaving out other considerations, eventually you get inbred animals that can barely find their way to the feed trough. It's not fair to the horses, but some breeders are really unscrupulous. They don't care if a horse can be trained; they'll sell somebody a beautiful colt and then claim it's the owner's fault when the horse doesn't prove satisfactory.'

'Oh, dear! I guess I'll have to tell Maisie to be really careful. I don't suppose ... are there any palominos in your stables now?' I held my breath.

'Not at the moment,' she said, and I nearly gave the game away with a sigh of relief.

'Oh, I was hoping you might give me some tips about what to tell my cousin to look for in a good specimen.'

'Well, I could show you some pictures, but the important details are more in the horse's behaviour than in looks. But I'll tell you what you might do, if you want. There's a lovely palomino living not far from here, a mare that's beautiful and smart as can be. We didn't sell her, but I wish we had. She's a horse to be proud of. I know the owner would be happy to show her to you, let you put her through her paces.'

'I don't ride, but I'd love to look at the horse.'

'Here. I'll write down the owner's name, and directions to the farm. And I think I have the phone number around here somewhere, if you'd want to call first.'

I glanced at Alan. Was it going to be this easy?

250

He smiled. 'We've struck a bit of luck, it seems,' he said, and if I knew what he meant and Annette didn't, that didn't matter.

She gave Alan a slip of paper with the information, and I managed to restrain myself and not look over his shoulder until we got back to the car. He handed me the paper, his face a perfect blank.

The owner's name was Jo Carter.

TWENTY-SEVEN

'But ... but...'

'You're sounding like Paul's motorbike,' commented Alan unhelpfully.

'It's just that ... our theory ... her *own* horse?'

Watson, riding courteously in the back seat, whined a little. My tone of voice was upsetting him.

'You're jumping to conclusions, love.'

'I am not! I'm not within sight or smell of any conclusion, much less jumping range. All my ideas have just been blown away.'

'That's what I mean. Jo Carter owns a palomino mare. You have leapt to the conclusion that it is the only palomino in Gloucestershire and therefore must have been the horse at the shed. If indeed there ever was a horse at the shed, and not just a bit of yellow sewing thread.'

251

'Hah! That hair was from a horse. I'll swear to it.'

'"I don't know a thing about horseflesh, myself,"' he quoted. I swear, that man does know how to be maddening.

'I do, however,' I said through clenched teeth, 'know the difference between hair and sewing thread. I have been sewing on buttons for well over sixty years, including, I would remind you, a good many of yours. I can't swear that was horsehair. If you can find me, somewhere near-by, a woman, or indeed a man, with bleached blond hair down to the waist, I will concede your point.'

'Why bleached?' asked Alan with real interest.

'You felt how coarse it was. The only time I've ever seen human hair like that, it had been so badly treated over the years that it was like straw. And of course the poor woman had split ends and couldn't grow her hair longer than four or five inches before it broke off.'

'I bow to your expert knowledge. And I'm sorry for teasing you. But—'

'I know. You're right. I did jump to at least one conclusion. But Alan, I don't believe in coincidence. It really bothers me that Jo owns a palomino, and also stole one to ride away on.'

'You're still upset and not thinking clearly. If Jo owns a palomino, and she sees two horses, or more, in a field, which one is she apt to choose to ride? Which one will more readily come to her?'

'Oh. The one she's familiar with, I suppose. Do various kinds of horses have various personality traits, like dogs?'

'My dear, I know almost as little about it as you do, but it would make sense, wouldn't it?'

'I guess. Oh, Alan, I thought we were so close, and now it's all to do over again.'

'Not quite. We have Jo's address, and directions to her farm. We didn't know before where she lived.'

'The police do, though.'

'Doubtless. But we'd more or less agreed that the police need some help. So what's to prevent our going out to have a look? Your famous intuition might find meaning in something the police have overlooked.'

'Surely someone's on duty at the place. Will they let us in?'

Alan just looked at me and grinned. I admit, I do tend to keep forgetting how important he is.

I had no idea what we might learn at Jo Carter's farm. Something more about her, perhaps, but I wasn't sure information about her was relevant at this point. If she had gone somewhere voluntarily, yes. Knowledge of her habits and preferences might lead to an understanding of where she might go. But she had been taken away forcibly.

'It is extremely frustrating,' I said to Alan, 'to know, almost to a certainty, who kidnapped Jo, and yet know nothing about him, not even his name.'

'Mmm,' said Alan, concentrating on the winding Cotswold roads.

I shut up, knowing he hates to be distracted while driving, but a few minutes later when the

253

road ahead was ironed out and became straight and level for a few hundred yards, he said, 'Yes, I agree. It is frustrating. But we know one important thing about this man. Ben is a sociopath. That means he follows a certain pattern of behaviour and is, in his own twisted, evil way, as predictable a criminal as any out there. We know his essential credo: all his misfortunes, all his plans that have miscarried, are someone else's fault. We know he has a driving, an insatiable need to get what he wants, as strong as the craving of an addict for the drug. His drugs are power and control. We know he has no conscience, but can be extremely clever and convincing to get his way. We know enough about him to recognize him, when we find him.'

'When we find him,' I echoed.

We were silent the rest of the way to Jo's farm.

The farm looked very much like Jo. I got the notion that I would have known it was hers without being told. It was a foolish idea, of course, but the whole place did seem to suit her personality perfectly.

It was small, compact, and very tidy. It wasn't a farm at all in the strict sense, I suppose. No crops were apparent and there was no barn, only small outbuildings and an immaculate two-stall stable. A well-kept rail fence enclosed a paddock, and a good-sized pasture behind the house was thickly green with sweet grass.

The house itself, like the other buildings, was built of the golden Cotswold stone and roofed in slate. It was a cottage, really, and the front garden was a cottage garden, glowing with flowers

254

in that profusion envied by gardeners the world over. In back a kitchen garden sported neat rows of vegetables and herbs, and fruit trees trained against the walls.

There was no sign of a golden palomino. There was, however, a neat black car parked in the drive, and as we drove up a trim young woman got out of the car. She was in uniform.

'May I help you?' Her attitude was pleasant, but with an unmistakable air of authority.

'My name is Alan Nesbitt.' He pulled out his identification. 'Retired, as you see, and with no official status whatever, but your chief has asked me to look around a bit and see if I can help. I doubt it very much. He's a most capable man, and I know he has a fine staff. But I wondered if my wife and I could just take a look at the house?'

The constable hesitated for a moment, and I could almost see the wheels turning. Technically, Alan was simply a member of the public, and unwelcome. But the constable had heard of him, of course, and had, I was sure, been told that he was to be granted every courtesy.

She smiled and handed his identification back. 'Of course, sir. You'll be careful to touch as little as possible?'

Alan nodded gravely, and the constable's fair face was flooded with colour. 'Sorry, sir,' she muttered. 'Of course you know...'

We followed her into the house. She might be embarrassed, but she wasn't going to allow anyone, even a retired chief constable, to roam the house unsupervised.

Alan stood in the minute entryway and looked around. The house appeared to be in perfect order. 'This is not being treated as a crime scene,' he said, with a slight lift to his voice. It wasn't quite a question. The answer was obvious. No fingerprint powder anywhere, no crime scene tape, no sign of police presence.

The constable flushed again. 'Well, sir, we don't actually know that a crime has been committed. That is, we have no evidence, other than the phone call and the disturbance at the shed. We did take a quick look here, of course, but we're pretty sure she wasn't abducted from here.'

'Yes, far more likely from her abandoned car, I agree. All the same, I'd like to see over the house, if you will.'

'You sound as though you're planning to buy it,' I whispered as the constable led the way upstairs.

'Too austere for my taste,' he whispered back.

I agreed with that assessment. After that riotous garden, the house was an almost shocking contrast. It was so painfully neat and clean, I thought Mrs Bryant would have felt right at home. The walls were painted a pale grey, and I saw no pictures hanging on them. The stair treads were unadorned oak, and when we reached the top landing, the wide oak boards were bare.

There were two bedrooms upstairs, along with a tiny bathroom, almost certainly a late addition to the house, which I guessed was of eighteenth-century vintage. Both bedrooms might almost

256

have served as monks' cells, save for the width of the beds. Each was a double, covered with a plain white coverlet. It was obvious from the flat, smooth look of the beds that there were no duvets under the coverlets, though the house was chilly even on this late spring day. No rugs lay on the floors; no curtains hung at the windows. There was a large mirrored wardrobe in each room, two uncushioned Windsor chairs, and a washbasin, another obvious twentieth-century innovation. In the front bedroom, a bedside table held a small lamp and two paperback books, the only sign of habitation.

I shivered, not entirely from the cold.

Wordlessly we went back down the stairs.

Downstairs the house was the same. Clean and tidy to a fault, but everything hard-edged. The 'lounge' belied its name, with only two chairs, one of them wooden. The other, the only chair in the place that appeared to be at all comfortable, was covered in brown leather and looked more as if it belonged in a man's den. The kitchen was modestly equipped – the kitchen of someone who cooks but doesn't make a religion of food. Table and countertops were bare.

'May I?' Alan asked the constable, gesturing at the refrigerator.

She moved forward and opened it for him, using a tissue and touching only the very edge of the handle.

Inside were an opened carton of milk that even I could tell, from where I stood, was sour. Some cheese looked fairly fresh, and there was most of a loaf of wholemeal bread and an unopened jar of Branston pickle. The bottom shelf held a lettuce that had seen better days and a couple of apples.

We dutifully visited the tiny room at the back, which Jo apparently used as an office. There was no room for a real desk, but the bookshelf had a pull-down panel that revealed a few pigeonholes with bills (unpaid in one stack, paid in another), stamps, envelopes. There was no computer in evidence, no printer or other appurtenances. Those must be at her professional office. The two-drawer file cabinet was as exquisitely neat as we had begun to expect, and held no surprises.

We had been in the house less than half an hour when Alan thanked the constable. 'There's just one more thing,' he said. 'The stables look well maintained, but I don't see any horses. Can you tell me anything about that?'

'Oh, yes. There were two horses in the pasture when we arrived, beautiful animals, a golden palomino and a bay, both mares. They seemed to be in excellent condition, but when Ms Carter didn't return after another few days, and we had all that rain, a neighbour asked if he couldn't take them in and look after them.'

'That was kind of him,' said Alan. 'I'm fond of horses myself. Might I have his name?'

Again her thin, fair skin betrayed her. 'Um ... I'm afraid I don't know his name. My DI took that information, and I wasn't there. But he lives on the next farm.' She pointed over the hills. 'You can just see the horses in his pasture.'

Well, maybe her young eyes could. All I could

258

see was a blur of movement that might equally have been dogs, cats, goats, or motorcycles. But I nodded amiably.

We had, of course, left Watson in the car. Now we let him out for a brief comfort stop, and told the constable about looking for his owner. She admired him, but knew nothing about him. We both thanked her again and climbed into the car.

'Alan!' I said the moment we were away. 'You don't suppose...'

'It is,' said Alan sententiously, 'unwise to calculate the quantity of juvenile poultry until the period of incubation has been completed.'

'And where did you get that one?' I asked after a period of stunned silence.

'Our friend Ed Walinski, last November. He specialized in dreadful puns, but altered aphorisms also formed part of his repertoire. I rather liked that one.'

'Yes. Well.' I put my mind back in gear, and said, 'Alan, tell me what you thought of that house.'

'Schizophrenic. Warm, welcoming, beautiful outside, clinically cold inside. Of course we don't really know Jo Carter, but I find it hard to imagine her living there.'

'Would you like to know what I thought?'

Alan grinned. 'I imagine you're going to tell me.'

'Allergies.'

Alan gave me one of his 'Have you lost your mind?' looks. 'Allergies? *Allergies?* What *do* you mean?'

'I knew someone once who had a house just

259

like that. Lovely garden, sterile house. It wasn't quite as bad as this one, because she had a lot of money and had bought beautiful bright paintings to liven things up. But there was nothing soft in her house, because although she could tolerate pollen and the like, she was deathly allergic to mould and dust mites. And I do mean deathly. An attack could close off her air supply and kill her.'

'So you're saying ... what, exactly?'

'I'm saying Jo Carter is allergic to dust and probably to mould spores, that's all.'

'And how is that going to help us find her?'

'I have no idea, but I do know that it increases her degree of risk by a very high factor. I can't imagine that any kidnapper would worry much about the cleanliness of his prison, let alone our sociopath Ben.'

Alan said nothing, but his hands tightened on the wheel, and he drove faster than the road would really allow.

TWENTY-EIGHT

The farmer next door wasn't home, but his wife was. She was a cheerful soul, short and plump, shaped rather like the Mrs Noah dolls that used to inhabit Arks in English nurseries. She happily showed us both horses, grazing in the pasture with their own two. 'And we'll be missing Jo's when she comes home. They're lovely mares, just lovely, both of them, though Jo's always fancied the palomino. Beautiful, isn't she?'

She was. And we were no closer to finding her owner than when we first started out.

We were on our way back to the holiday cottage, discouraged, when the same thought hit both of us.

'Pharmacy!' I said at the same moment Alan said 'Chemist's!' He turned the car around at the first opportunity and headed for Broadway.

This time, fortunately, the inspector, one David Owen, was on duty and listened with attention to what Alan and I had to say. He sighed when he had heard it all. 'It's speculative, but of course you know that. And we've no better lead. You'll understand I haven't the resources to put someone in every pharmacy in the county, but I can telephone them all and ask that they call the police if anyone they don't know comes in with

261

a prescription for epinephrine. If you're right, Ms Carter would surely have the prescription with her.'

'My friend was never without it.'

'You might go one step better,' said Alan diffidently 'if you don't mind my making a suggestion. If anyone knows what doctor Ms Carter usually sees...'

'Of course! That will pinpoint it, and save us a lot of useless telephone traffic. And we can call the doctor, as well, and verify your diagnosis, Mrs Martin.'

He remembered my name, and he was polite, and he apparently believed us. Three points in his favour, to offset the many points his sergeant had lost with his boorish behaviour.

'You'll let us know...' I said as we left.

'I will. You've both been of the greatest help, and we owe you that much.'

We were, all three of us, both tired and hungry. We stopped at a pub with a nice garden and ordered beer for two and bangers and mash for three. 'Alan, I don't think mashed potatoes are very good for dogs,' I objected.

'If he doesn't want them, I'll eat his serving. I'm hungry enough to eat one of those palominos, bleached blond mane and all.'

We finally dragged ourselves home and let Watson out for a good long run while Alan built a fire and I poured us some bourbon. I was hesitant about letting the dog off the leash at night, but Alan insisted. 'He'll either come back or he won't, and if he doesn't we can assume he's gone back home.'

'Yes ... but...'

'I know.' Alan patted my hand and took his glass. Neither of us uttered the words 'He's not our dog.' Increasingly with every day, every hour, he *was* our dog, and I knew we'd both be miserable if we found his owner.

'What's next?' I asked after we had sipped enough Jack Daniel's to blunt the edges of our unfruitful day. 'Do we just wait until someone shows up with that prescription? If someone shows up? I don't think we can count on Ben having a lot of compassion, any more than a clean house.'

'Actually, he probably does have a clean house. That sort of sociopath usually does. He's as obsessive/compulsive as they come. But he certainly isn't hiding Jo at his own home, and I agree that he's not likely to care overmuch about her comfort or cleanliness. There's one reason, though, why he might care about her health.'

'Yes, I'd thought of that. If she had an asthma attack, it might scare him into getting her medicine. Because he needs her to be alive. Dead, she can't lead him to Sarah and Paul and the girls.'

It was a depressing thought. I picked up my glass and then put it down. The way I was feeling, it was too tempting. Drowning my sorrows would only add to them in the end. I saw that Alan hadn't drunk much, either. I queried him with my eyebrows and went to the kitchen to make tea, 'the cup that cheers but does not inebriate'. It causes other difficulties, taken in the evening by people with bladders our age, but we could deal with that more easily than with a hangover.

'So. We wait?' I said when we were settled with tea.

'Unless you think we should keep on looking for the palomino that was at the shed.'

I shook my head. Today had convinced me that was a wild goose chase.

'Then we wait, until we can think of something more productive.'

I turned on the television. We don't watch much TV, but I didn't feel like talking. There was nothing to talk about except our problem, and we'd been over and over that until there was nothing more to say. Rehashing it was like biting down on a sore tooth to find out that, yes, it still hurt. Television would fill the silence.

I hit a news programme. I don't like watching the news. It's all bad, and there's nothing I can do about it, and on the whole I'd rather be an ostrich. I reached for the remote to change channels, but Alan stayed my hand.

'...rumours circulating earlier in the pop music scene. Peter James, the latest singing sensation, was earlier reported missing. Now his agents are saying there's nothing in it, that it was simply a publicity stunt, but they're being very close-mouthed about the whole thing. Unusual for an agent not to talk about his superstar, isn't it, Derek? They're apparently not wanting publicity for their publicity stunt.'

A man in another location appeared on the screen. 'It's very unusual, Glenna, and there's more. Our sources have learned that odd things are going on in and around the Cotswold village

264

of Broadway, where Peter was last reported seen. The police still have no leads at all in the murder of an elderly man just outside Broadway last week, and now someone else seems to be missing. No one's talking about that, either. Coincidence? Or is there something rotten in the village of Broadway, the "jewel of the Cotswolds"?'

'Damn and blast!' Alan smacked his hand on the arm of his chair, and clicked off the TV. 'We wanted all that kept quiet, and now some perishing reporter's got hold of it somehow!'

'But how, Alan? And how did they get the idea that Paul was in Broadway? He was in disguise!'

'Who knows? Some fan spotted him, I suppose. We don't know that he took any great care not to be seen when he first got back from Birmingham. And of course the murder is a matter of public record. How they know about Jo, I cannot imagine. But I think the first thing we need to do is call Sarah and Paul and reassure them, tell them progress is being made and they need to sit tight.'

A lie, I thought but did not say. I suppose the agonizingly slow process of elimination we'd been going through was progress of a sort. And I agreed that they'd probably be in a bit of a panic if they'd seen the news.

Alan pulled out his mobile to make the call.

'Yes, this is Alan Nesbitt, and I'd like to speak to the concierge, please.' After a brief pause he repeated his name and the code number he had given the hotel, and asked to speak to Sarah Robinson. Pause. 'What? Repeat that, please.

265

When? Did they say ... I see. Thank you.'

I didn't really need him to tell me, but I asked anyway. 'They've checked out?'

'A few minutes ago. Said nothing to anyone, used the automatic checkout system. No one apparently saw them leave. They're gone.'

Of course Alan called the police immediately. Unfortunately, the same condescending sergeant we had encountered before was on duty, and he was not inclined to take the matter too seriously. 'After all, sir, they've not committed a crime. Not under arrest, are they, or wanted for anything? They've a right to go where they wish.'

Alan's temper was getting shorter and shorter, and he finally clicked the phone off and paced the room, while I worried about his blood pressure. When he could trust himself to speak calmly, he placed the call again and asked the front desk for the inspector's home telephone number. Of course he met with resistance. 'I realize that,' he said, his voice growing dangerous. 'This is Chief Constable Alan Nesbitt, and I must speak to your inspector immediately.'

It worked. Alan redialled, and waited. And waited. I could hear when the voicemail system picked up and the tinny voice issued its instructions. Alan left the briefest of messages, and when he sat down again, breathing as if he'd been running, I had a glass of bourbon waiting for him. There is a time to be sensible, and a time to abandon sensibility and soothe one's irritations.

The inspector did not call back, and we spent

266

the rest of the evening in fruitless speculation. The one bright spot in the entire day was the return of Watson, shortly before we went to bed.

TWENTY-NINE

Things looked a bit brighter in the morning, as they often do. Alan seldom stays angry for very long, and by the time he'd had some coffee and my super-deluxe scrambled eggs, he was ready to concede that the supercilious sergeant did perhaps have an operating brain cell or two.

I wasn't so sure. 'What more does he want, for heaven's sake? These people have been threatened, Jo's missing and maybe ... well, missing and in danger, we know that for certain, we know that the guy who's after her has a record of violence and has already killed one man, apparently for kicks. Where in that can he not find a reason to get upset that Paul and his mother have vanished?'

'I think I'll wait to answer that until you don't have a pot of hot coffee in your hand,' he said, looking at me over the top of his glasses in a way I always find hard to resist.

'You're going to go all calm and reasonable, aren't you? I don't *feel* like being reasonable!'

'I don't either, really. I'm still annoyed with

the chap. He's far too full of himself, but to give him his due, he was only following procedure. I lost my temper and bullied the poor girl at the front desk into giving me the inspector's phone number, a thing I had no right to do – and a fat lot of good it did me. The sergeant's only problem is—'

'That he's terminally stupid!'

'Not stupid, not really. Only stolid and lacking in imagination. He'll never rise far in the force, because he can't see into a criminal's mind and work out what he's likely to do. I expect he's a real whizz at writing up reports and checking number plates.'

'That,' I said, my good humour restored, 'is the nastiest thing I've ever heard you say about anybody. Except Ben, of course.'

'Ben is a special case. And I wish to heaven I knew what we were going to do about him. With or without the help of the Gloucestershire constabulary.'

His mobile rang. He glanced at the number and shrugged at me. Not one he recognized. 'Nesbitt here.' A silence followed. 'I see.' More silence.

I was nearly dancing with impatience.

'Pity, but it couldn't be helped.'

I gave him an anguished, silent query with upraised hands. He shook his head.

'Yes, of course. And thank you.' He clicked off.

'*What?*' I asked, unable to wait another second. 'What's a pity?'

'The fellow came in to fill the epinephrine prescription, but the pharmacist was very busy

268

and didn't remember to phone the police until about an hour later. By then, of course...' He spread his hands.

'He was long gone.' I sat back, deeply discouraged. It was a bad blow. 'Well, at least he did fill it. That's more than I expected of him, the monster. I don't suppose he gave an address.'

'False. He went to a big Boots in Cheltenham and gave a Winchcombe address. Said they'd spent the day in Cheltenham and his wife was in a bad way, forgot to bring her medicine with her and didn't want to risk driving all the way home. The clerk who served him said he was very convincing.'

'Aren't they supposed to check addresses when it's someone they don't know?'

'Not if they recognize the doctor's name and registration number. Which of course they did; it's a legitimate prescription.'

I was near tears. 'It was our only hope, Alan! Jo's only hope. Why can't this guy make just one teeny mistake? Just one. He's not perfect. Nobody's perfect. Why can't our side get a break, just once?'

Alan said nothing. There was nothing he could say.

I poured more coffee, just for something to do. It was cold. I zapped it, but it never tastes as good reheated; neither of us wanted it.

'He apologized, by the way.'

'Sorry, I wasn't paying attention.' I was wallowing in the doldrums.

'Inspector Owen apologized. I gather he gave

269

the sergeant a wigging and told him he was to be informed immediately when I, or you, for that matter, gave the station some information.'

'That's nice.'

'Here, buck up, old thing. That means they're looking for Paul and Sarah, and they've put out a call all over the southern half of England.'

'Wonderful. They haven't been able to find Jo, and we pretty much know she's not more than a few miles away. I'm sure they'll be just as efficient finding Paul and Sarah.'

'What is it, love? You're not usually so ready to give up.'

'Oh, Alan, it's all my fault!' I gulped some cold coffee to hide the quiver in my voice. 'If I hadn't thought up that fool publicity stunt, no one would have ever known Paul was missing, or Peter or whatever you want to c–call him...' I was crying in earnest now.

Alan, over many years of marriage to his first wife and then to me, had learned to cope with a woman's tears. I suppose he'd seen his share of hysterical women in the course of his work, as well. At any rate, he fetched the box of tissues, put it in front of me, and let me get it out of my system.

When I had reached the sniffling stage and started to mop up and blow my nose, he brought me a glass of water, a damp washcloth, and a bottle of ibuprofen. I washed my face and took the medicine and said, 'How did you know I was getting a headache? I don't have crying jags all that often.' I was embarrassed and realized I sounded belligerent.

270

'You may not believe it, but I've wept from time to time myself. I know what happens.'

Of course he had. If I'd cried buckets when my first husband died, certainly a warm, caring man like Alan had cried at the death of his wife. She'd been quite young, too. I felt like an insensitive clod.

'Now, don't start again. I put the kettle on, and we're going to have some tea and talk sensibly. Are there any biscuits?'

'In the cupboard over the microwave. They might be a bit stale.'

He rightly ignored that remark and brought, in short order, a tray with all the necessities except the teapot, which followed as soon as the water boiled. I rather enjoyed the novel sensation of being waited on, and began to feel better.

'Now, then.' Alan tented his fingers in his lecturing mode, and I relaxed. 'First of all, get rid of any silly notion that any of this was your doing. How long do you think it would have been before word would have leaked out that the fabulous Peter James had disappeared?' He didn't let me answer, but pushed ahead. 'Second, because of your idea, Rose and Co. were able to pass the thing off casually. You watch, they'll have begun damage control the moment the story went out, and if they can pull it off, and I have every confidence in them, the whole thing will die down like a damp squib.'

'But it made Paul and Sarah run away. You can't brush that off.'

'Something made them run away. It was a dam' fool thing to do, but you can't take responsibility for other people's foolish actions. And my third point – and you're going to think me a hard man – my third point is that playing the blame game is not productive. We could trace blame back to Ben's parents, assuming he had them, and their folly in conceiving him in the first place. Or back to Adam, if it comes to that. None of it helps with our present agenda, which is deciding what we're going to do next.'

I had been sipping tea while I meekly listened to Alan's pep talk. It had cleared my brain a little. Not much. 'I don't have any brilliant ideas, Alan. The only thing I can think of is to try once more to find that horse. I know we've done that, and not had any luck, but what other leads are there to follow up? And at least that's one place where we wouldn't be getting in the way of the real police. I mean, they don't have enough personnel to look all over Gloucestershire for a horse. Even if they wanted to, which I don't think they do, very much.'

'I agree. We were tired yesterday when we decided to give up. We can start out again. And I'd also like to talk to that pharmacist in Cheltenham, and the clerk. They might just remember something they didn't tell the "real" police, as you put it, that would give us some ideas.'

'But if we do that, we won't have a lot of time to go around to the farms,' I objected. 'Cheltenham is busy, and congested. It could take half a day just to find the right drugstore, let alone talk to anybody.'

'Hmm. You have a point. Well, you could drop me at the outskirts of Cheltenham, maybe at the racecourse, and then—'

'Whoa. Stop right there. You know how much I enjoy driving in the wilds of rural England. I'd be lost before you crossed the street, and then there'd be one more missing person for everyone to be looking for.'

'Well ... what do you suggest? I know I'm a skilled, trained policeman, but I never quite mastered being in two places at once.'

'We hire a car and driver. That same nice driver who took us to church the other day, if we can get him. He can drive me around while you do your thing in the big city. And Alan, it would really work out better that way. He knows his way around all the farms, and the shortest way to get anywhere, and he might even know who keeps palominos. And you can look around outside Cheltenham, when you're finished at Boots.'

Alan looked at the teapot. 'What did I put in there? I thought it was just tea, but there must have been a nice little extra something for inspiration. That's a very good idea, love. Brilliant, in fact. But you'll take Watson with you.'

'Of course. Where is he, by the way?'

'Right behind you, all fed and dancing with eagerness. I'll see if I can find the number of the driver, and if not, I can phone Pam at the Holly Tree. You get dressed. And don't forget to take your mobile, and leave it on in case I have to call you.'

Well, that caused a little flurry, because I didn't know my phone number and couldn't remember quite how to work the thing. Then I had to find

273

the dog-biscuit treats we'd bought for Watson, in case he got hungry, or showed a tendency to run and had to be lured back. But in less than an hour the car was at our door, and after a quick kiss Alan went off and Watson and I were packed in the hire car. 'Where we goin' then, luv?' asked the driver.

'I don't actually know. I'm wanting to drive around to all the farms in the area that keep horses, especially palominos.' I wondered if I should offer some explanation, but apparently the fact that I was American was explanation enough. No telling what those foreigners will want to get up to.

'You've got a nice day for it. Mind you, it'll rain later on.'

I could see no sign of rain, but he lived here, after all, and could presumably read the weather better than I. I thought about taking an umbrella, but decided against it. I'd be dry in the car.

'Palominos, eh?' he went on. 'Not so many of them about. Now that Ms Carter, she has one, a beauty, too, but I hear she's gone away.'

'Yes, actually I saw hers yesterday. A neighbour is looking after it while Ms Carter is ... until she comes home.'

'If you're looking to buy yourself a horse, I don't know as anyone's selling a palomino.'

Ah. So an explanation *was* in order. 'Actually, I just want to look at a few of them. I have a cousin...' And I launched glibly into the story I'd used yesterday. I certainly hoped it was a cousin, in case the driver compared notes with anyone. Oh, well, I was old enough I could always claim

I'd simply used the wrong word. Goodness knows it happened often enough for real.

'Hmm. Never noticed, myself, that it's a stupid horse. As horses go, that is. I've never met a horse yet that's as smart as a cat, or even a dog.'

Watson made a comment from the back seat. I supposed he was just responding to the word *dog*, but it certainly sounded like a protest about the judgement of relative feline and canine intelligence. We both laughed.

'I've certainly had some smart cats in my lifetime, but Watson here is my first dog, and he isn't even really mine. He just turned up one day, and we're still looking for his owner.'

'Nice animal.'

'Yes, and to tell the truth I sort of hope we won't find the owner. He's such a nice dog, and Alan and I have grown very attached to him. But that's a very selfish attitude, so if you hear who might have lost him ... oof!'

We had turned into a rutted lane, and my head nearly hit the roof.

'Sorry. All that rain the other day, you see, and this drive needs a tot of gravel.'

It would take more than a tot, I thought. The drive wasn't very wide, but it was long enough to use several loads of stone, and from the look of the farmhouse, there wasn't a lot of money to spare for such niceties. The place wasn't shabby, exactly. There were crisp white curtains at the windows and pots of geraniums here and there, but the woodwork needed fresh paint and the thatched roof had seen better days.

I knew the moment I saw the curtains and

flowers that this wasn't the farm I was looking for, but I could hardly tell my driver that. Watson and I got out and rang the bell. It really was a bell, a very old one by the look of it, that hung by the door with a chain to pull it by. It set up a clamour that set Watson barking, and of course that set off the dogs in the house, a pack of Baskerville hounds by the sound of it. I was glad we hadn't tried a surreptitious approach.

The pleasant woman who came to the door hadn't heard of any missing dogs. Her own always stayed close to home, for a wander. (There were only two of them, after all, and they were smaller than Watson.)

A palomino? No, she'd had a stallion two or three years ago, but had sold him. 'Can't really afford to keep horses these days, can I?' She looked around ruefully. 'You see the state of things. Ever since ... now that I'm alone, it takes all my time just to keep things going. Sorry I can't help.'

I didn't ask until we got back to the car.

'Lost her husband in Afghanistan. Helicopter crashed.'

I was very glad I hadn't raised the subject with the woman. She had to have recognized my accent, and many English blame the Americans for getting them into that war. I'm inclined to agree with them, actually.

We went on. Farm after farm. Horse after horse. When the owners were at home, I asked. When they weren't, I nosed around. There were only a couple of palominos, one of them geriatric and the other not even a year old, if my untutored eye could be trusted. Both of them lived at well-kept farms. Nothing looked at all promising. No one knew of a lost dog.

We had pretty much covered the area north of Broadway by lunchtime, skirting villages and hamlets with delectable names like Church Honeybourne and Cow Honeybourne (side by side), Mickleton and Aston Subedge, when occasional whines from Watson reminded me that he was hungry, and so was I. It seemed to me we were in the depths of the country, and I despaired of finding anything to eat, but our driver read my mind.

'Nice little pub around the next corner,' he said. 'Good beer, nice garden.'

'Dogs?' I asked, and Watson's ears pricked up.

'O' course.'

So we stopped. Watson and I shared a huge hamburger and a pint. I got most of the chips and all the beer; the proprietor kindly gave Watson a bowl of water and let me lead him discreetly around back. We were on our way, much refreshed, in less than an hour.

THIRTY

The southern part of the county was less familiar to me. We agreed that we would avoid the countryside immediately around Cheltenham, where Alan would have had ample time to explore. It was really too far away for my purposes, anyway, but again, I didn't want to confide that bit of information to my driver. But there were lots of farms between Broadway and Bourton-on-the-Water and Stow-on-the-Wold. (I never get tired of English place names.)

I don't even remember how many farms we visited. I got to the point of wishing I had taped my little speech so I could just hit 'play'. Lots of horses. No farm that looked at all like what I wanted.

I was growing very tired indeed, and Watson was plainly getting tired of riding in a car, when we passed a field not far, according to my OS map, from our cottage. And lo, there were two horses, one some dark colour this side of black, and one a gorgeous golden palomino.

'Look! Stop! Who do those belong to, do you know?' For there was no farmhouse in sight.

There was no place to pull off the road, but there was no traffic in sight, either, so the driver simply stopped in the middle of the road. 'No,'

278

he said decisively. 'Never seen those horses before. Must be boarding somewhere about.'

'But we have to find out! I'm sure that horse is the one I ... I mean...'

He turned and looked me full in the face. 'What're you after, then? Load o' taradiddle you told me before, isn't it?'

'I ... yes. I'm sorry. I can't tell you the real story, not yet, anyway. I'm looking for a particular horse, with a particular owner. I don't know his name or where he lives, except it can't be too far from Broadway. And I think this could be the one, but I really, really need to find out who owns this horse and where it's usually stabled.'

'Would've saved some time if you'd told me that to start with.'

I was silent. I'd apologized once.

'Pam tells me your man is a Scotland Yard tec.'

I sighed. So much for trying to keep anything confidential in a place like the Cotswolds. 'Not quite. He was chief constable for Belleshire for a good many years, but he's now retired.'

'But you're not.'

I opened my mouth and then shut it again. What on earth could I say to that? Had I stopped beating my wife?

The car was shaking oddly. I looked over and saw that my driver was convulsed with silent laughter.

After a moment I gave in and laughed myself. 'All right. Throw discretion to the winds. Yes, I've helped my husband with his work, both when he was an official policeman and in his retirement. And if you want the whole truth, I've done quite a little poking around on my own, too. Now are you happy?'

'Miss Marple, that's who you are!'

'Mrs Marple, if you please. But honestly, it's no laughing matter. I still can't tell you exactly what I'm looking for, because it could be dangerous for everybody. But I can tell you that at least one person's life may be at stake here.'

That sobered him in a hurry. He sat quiet for orders.

'Good. Now what can you tell me, or what can you guess, about the owner of these horses?'

'If it's a guess you want, I'd say they're runaways. See that gap in the hedge down there?'

He pointed to a far corner of the field. I couldn't see the gap he mentioned, but I took his word for it and nodded.

'I'll wager those horses got in through that gap. That's a field, not a pasture. Arable land?'

He sounded uncertain that this peculiar American knew the term. I nodded. 'Yes, but not planted. I'd have thought it was a bit late to start a crop, though of course growing seasons are different where I come from.'

'It won't be planted this year. That's because, far as I know, nobody's bought this farm. Owner moved to Spain two or three years ago, and hasn't been able to find a buyer.'

'Then it is part of a farm? Where are the buildings?'

'House is over the hill; can't see it from here. Stable's there, too. Barn's down the road.'

'Fred,' I said, irrelevantly, 'how long have you

lived around here?'

'All my life, and I'm not telling you how long that is.'

'I can give a pretty good guess, though. You know this county like the back of your hand.'

'Hereabouts. Not so much down Cheltenham way.'

He made it sound a thousand miles away.

He cleared his throat. 'See, this farm is all bits and pieces, like. That's one reason it's been so hard to sell, I reckon. Besides bein' rundown, like. This field used to belong over yonder, but that bloke sold up.' He gestured with his head. 'Some say there was some scheme to build holiday cottages on the land, but the builder went bust. Don't know myself. Anyway, the other chap bought it, few years back, said he needed some arable. Grew rapeseed for a while, but the ground wasn't suited for it, and it wasn't easy to harvest, the barn being so far away and all. So now it's all sitting empty, and the house needs repairin', and the fields're goin' to ruin. Shame, that is.'

I hadn't been listening closely to his narrative. The important part was, the field belonged to a distant farm which was sitting empty! What more ideal place to hold a captive? There were no other houses nearby, no one to see unexpected lights or activity. 'Listen, Fred,' I said, interrupting him. 'I need to take a good look at that house, and I'd rather not be seen. Is there a way to do that?'

'Nobody there to see you,' he said slowly. 'Far as I know.'

281

'You're probably right, but just in case some-one is there, I don't want them to see me. It might be someone who ... who has no business being there.'

'Same as you,' he said. I looked at him in some alarm, but his shoulders were shaking again in that disconcerting silent laughter.

'Same as me,' I agreed. 'Are there any trees or anything near the house?'

He scratched his head. 'Don't recall. Remember the general layout, not the details. Haven't been down this way in years. Will the dog go with me?'

It was such a non sequitur, I couldn't think what he meant.

'If I was to be going along,' he said slowly, patiently, 'walking my dog as you might say, would he go with me?'

'Oh. Well ... I have no idea, actually. He's very friendly, but in the last few days I think he's decided Alan and I are his masters. Here's his lead. Try it for a little way and see.'

Watson bounded out of the car. He was definitely tired of sitting and riding, and would have preferred a nice run over the hills, but he accepted his lead quietly enough. I handed the end to Fred, who squatted down and gave him a hand to sniff.

'Who's a good boy, then? Who's a lovely boy?' He used that same foolish, doting tone that Alan adopted towards the dog. Were all Englishmen potty when it came to dogs, I wondered.

Watson's tail was wagging furiously, and he licked the proffered hand so eagerly that I felt a small pang of jealousy, instantly suppressed.

'Who wants to go for a nice walkies, eh, old chap?' Watson indicated that he was the one, oh yes, indeed. His whole body was quivering with joy.

'Everybody around here knows me, you see. Even if I'm seen, it won't matter. Old Fred's got a new dog. I can spy out the land for you. What am I looking for?'

'Any sign of occupation. Smoke from the chimney, maybe, though there'd scarcely be a fire on such a warm day. Lights or an open window or ... well, just anything to show anyone was inside, or had been. But I shouldn't let you do this.'

'Safer for me than for you. I'd not let you go alone.'

That male chivalry again. 'Yes ... well, all right, but be careful. This is ... there could be ... just be careful!'

'Right. Yes, old boy, we're off, then.' And he set off, not down the road, but across the field where the horses were placidly grazing. Watson stopped and gave me a backward look.

'It's all right, sweetheart. Go with the nice man.' And how silly to think that the dog understood a word I said, but he turned around as if satisfied and trotted along beside Fred as perfectly as if they'd been at some elite dog show.

Whoever Watson's master had been, he had trained his dog very well indeed. It was odd that he hadn't put up advertisements for him all over England. I certainly would have. I'd never have guessed I could become so fond of a dog in such a short time, I who had kept cats for well over fifty years. I shouldn't let myself think of how the cats were going to react to Watson. It might never come to that.

What would Fred find at the house? I shouldn't have let him go. I knew what he might be getting into. He thought I was just being melodramatic. If Ben really was there, with Jo, he'd do anything to keep from being seen. Oh, dear heaven, he might even ... no, I wouldn't think about that. He didn't want Jo dead. She was no use to him dead. I had to cling to that idea.

But Fred was of no use to Ben whatever. He would have no compunction about disposing of Fred. And, oh, Watson! What if Watson barked and made a fuss and Ben...

My cell phone rang. I didn't know what the sound was at first. I hadn't taken the time to figure out how to reset the ringtone, and I thought someone was approaching with a radio tuned to some dreadful rock station.

I managed to click 'send' just before the thing went to voicemail, thinking as I did so that the coding was very odd. 'Send' ought to be for transmitting a call, not receiving one. However ... 'Hello?' I croaked.

Of course it was Alan. Who else had the number? 'I have a little news, love. Where are you?'

That put me in an immediate dilemma. If I told him what was happening, he would be extremely upset. I should have called him the minute I saw the horses, he would say. I shouldn't have sent Fred into danger. I should get away from there right now. And so on.

And he was right. I should have done all that. The trouble was, I'd had the blasted phone about five minutes and hadn't got used to the idea that I *could* call Alan in a dicey situation.

On the other hand, if I didn't tell him, I'd lose the chance of valuable help, and only defer his wrath until he found out later.

'Dorothy? Dorothy, are you there?'

'Yes. Alan, I've done something awfully stupid, and I think you'd better come right away. I'm *all right*!' I could tell from the quality of his silence that he was about to go into a tailspin. 'But let me tell you where I am, because I do think you'd best be here as soon as you can get here.' I looked at my map. 'It's off the B3462. There's ... well, there's nothing really distinctive in the way of landmarks, but Fred says there's an abandoned farm just over the hill, a place that's been for sale for a couple of years. A local might be able to locate it for you. But no, look. Are you close to any place where you could buy a copy of this OS map? Because the quickest way is if I give you coordinates.'

'Right. I'll go buy the map and call you as soon as I'm on my way. Don't explain now, it'll just waste time.'

Amazing how much better I felt, just hearing his voice. Never mind if he scolded me later. I deserved it. The main thing was that he was coming, and everything would be all right.

'Are you lost? Is there something I can do to help?'

I nearly had a heart attack then and there. I hadn't heard the man approach. A large friendly

285

man was leaning in the window on the driver's side, smiling at me in a concerned sort of way.

'Goodness, you startled me! Yes, I'm fine. I'm just waiting here for my driver to return.'

'Out of petrol? I'm afraid he'll have an awfully long walk. There's no village for miles, not even a farmhouse where he might borrow some. You chose a bad spot to be marooned.'

'Oh, no, we've plenty of gas ... er, petrol. He just...' What on earth *was* he doing? My usual gift of a ready lie seemed to have deserted me.

The man was giving me a peculiar look. I had to say something. I said a quick prayer for inspiration, but my mind was concentrated elsewhere. In fact, I was badly in need of a loo. Nerves, probably.

Aha! I tried hard to blush. 'Oh, dear, this is embarrassing! He ... I think he went in search of ... that is, we had some very hot curry for lunch, and ... well, there's no farmhouse in sight, but he hoped there might be at least an outhouse somewhere. I'm sorry, I don't know if that's the right word in England. In America we call them outhouses—'

'I'm familiar with the term. I don't know that there are any nearby, though I'm a stranger to this part of the world. There are plenty of bushes, however.'

'Yes, well ... that isn't quite his problem.'

'Needs must when the devil drives, however, eh? Well, it's a lonely spot. I'll just wait with you until he returns, shall I?'

'Thank you, but there's no need. I'm sure he'll be back soon.' I wasn't sure why, but something about this man was making me nervous. He also looked vaguely familiar.

He was apparently determined to discourage me about Fred's fictitious search for a WC. 'Not if he's determined to find a proper toilet. The nearest farmhouse is boarded up and deserted.'

'Oh, dear!' Oh, dear, indeed. If this man knew that, what about his claim to be a stranger? And where had he come from? I glanced up and down the road. There was no car anywhere in sight. 'Are you on a walking tour, then?' He carried no stick or pack.

'Not precisely a tour, but I have been walking. Actually, I'm a trifle tired, and I wouldn't mind a bit of a sit-down.'

Uninvited, he opened the driver's door and got in the car. I was liking this less and less. Oh, how I wished Watson hadn't gone off with Fred!

I cleared my throat. 'I hope you won't think I'm rude, sir, but I'd rather wait alone. I get a little nervous around men I don't know.' Actually, I did know him, I realized, finally placing him. He was the man who wanted the horse and then changed his mind. I'd thought him rather pleasant at the Swan. I didn't think so any more.

'Of course. That's exactly why I'm waiting with you. A bit of protection, eh? Not that there's anyone else around.'

My phone rang. I jumped and reached in my pocket.

'I wouldn't answer that if I were you.' There was a sharp click as the intruder locked all the doors from the driver's console. 'Can't risk you telling someone too much, can we?'

THIRTY-ONE

My mouth was suddenly dry, every sense quivering like the whiskers on a cat, and my instincts kicked in. 'I'd better answer. It's my cousin. I gave her this number to call when she needed a ride, and she'll wonder why I don't answer.'

'Let her wonder. You're not giving anyone a ride any time soon, anyway, are you?'

'My driver...'

'You surely don't think your driver's coming back! You've a very inventive mind; I must give you that. Hot curry, indeed.' His laugh conveyed no amusement whatever.

My phone stopped, and then started ringing again.

'Turn the damn thing off!' my captor barked.

I complied, with a shaking hand. When I dropped it on the floor of the car and tried to pick it up, he nudged it away with his foot.

'What...' I licked my lips and tried again. 'What do you mean, my driver's not coming back?'

'Come now, you can do better than that. "What do you think you're doing? Let me go at once! You can't do this to me, I'm an American citizen!" Any of those spring to mind?'

'I just want to know what you've done with

288

my driver.'

'And suppose I don't want to tell you?'

Think, Dorothy! Alan knows where you are, sort of. He'll know something's wrong when you don't answer your phone. All you have to do is stall. I licked my lips again. 'Oh, for heaven's sake! You sound exactly like a character in a bad melodrama. I don't know what you're trying to do, but if it's money you want, you're out of luck. I don't have more than pocket change on me. And I can't imagine you're after my virtue. There are lots of younger, prettier women around if that's what you had in mind. So what *do* you want of me? I'm sure I'm quite ready to co-operate if you'd only tell me—'

'Shut up!' He backhanded me, or would have if I hadn't seen it coming and turned aside just in time. As it was, he knocked my glasses off, and his heavy ring caught my ear, which began to bleed copiously. I started to feel on the floor of the car for my glasses and my handbag, which held my tissues, but he hit me again, this time with his fist, on my upper arm. It hurt so much I cried out, and looking up, saw the satisfaction on his face.

If I had cherished any lingering hopes that this wasn't the man I was seeking, that look on his face settled the matter once and for all. This man, who derived such pleasure from the mean-ingless battery of a helpless woman, was un-doubtedly Ben. Wife-beater and murderer. And I was alone in a car with him, miles from any-where.

I could do nothing but try not to provoke

another attack, and wait, and pray. But I was not, I was *not* going to be a doormat. I could still hold on to my dignity.

I sat and bled in silence.

'Sulking, are we?'

'You told me to be quiet.' I made my tone as neutral as I could.

Not neutral enough. He slapped me, with the palm of his hand this time. No ring. That was marginally better, but my lip was crushed against my teeth. More bleeding.

I held my breath to keep from crying out.

'Had enough?'

'Yes.'

'Going to do what I tell you?'

'Yes.' I would not plead, I would not bargain. I would say and do as little as possible, and trust in God and Alan.

'Then tell me what the hell you're doing here.'

'Looking for a horse.'

He didn't expect that. 'A horse? What do you mean, a horse?'

'Four-legged animal, used for riding and for farm labour...'

'Dammit, woman, you said that! Don't try to be smart. Why were you looking for a horse?'

It was, I thought, perhaps time for the unvarnished truth. 'I wanted to see if its mane matched a hair I found.'

Another slap. 'Stop playing games with me, bitch! Why did you want that fucking horse?'

'If you don't stop hitting me, I'm going to pass out, and then I can't tell you anything.' It came out as a mumble, through bloody and swollen lips, but it seemed to penetrate through his rage. He turned away from me and slammed his fist on the dashboard instead.

'You wanted to know why I was looking for the horse. I thought it would lead me to you.'

That was the last card I held. I was in too much pain to think clearly, and I've never been a poker player. Maybe I should have held it back, but it was too late now.

He leaned over me, digging both hands painfully into my shoulders. Somewhere in what was left of my brain I knew that if his thumbs moved a bit higher, to my carotid arteries, it would be all over. *'Do you know who I am?'*

'I don't know your name. I do know who you are. I hope your wife is feeling better. Going to Spain, weren't you?'

He gave me a wolfish smile. 'So you finally recognized me. Sam Smith isn't my name, and I never had a wife, you know. Just playing a little game.' Then his mood changed and he released me with a suddenness that made my head swim. Unlocking the doors, he swore fluently and said, 'Out, bitch! Get out!'

I opened the door, but couldn't seem to get out. Ben swore some more. 'God, are all women stupid as lice? Seat belt, bitch!'

I fumbled for it, released it, and tumbled out of the car on to the unforgiving ground. If I'd had any vague idea of getting away, it was dashed. I could hardly crawl, much less run. Never again, I thought sourly as I struggled on excruciatingly painful knees to get to my feet, would I believe the stories about the plucky heroines who survive untold abuse and still manage to use some form of judo on the bad guy and then flee for their lives. Another illusion destroyed.

It was beginning to drizzle. That, of course, added to my misery. But the cool water on my battered face, and the sharp pain of my knees, took the cobwebs away. Where in the world was Alan? And what had Ben done with Fred? And ... no, I couldn't bear to think about poor little Watson.

'Going to take all day, bitch? I'm getting wet!'

I bit back the obvious retort and managed to stand upright, clinging to the car. There was nothing wrong with me, I tried to tell myself, beyond some scratches and bruises and those knees, which would stop setting off nerve explosions any time now.

'Not quite ready to run the marathon, are we? That's too bad, because we're going for a walk. Hurry up!' He strode off.

I didn't have my stick. I didn't have an umbrella. I didn't have anything at all except a grim determination to put one foot in front of the other as long as I had to. And oh, sudden bright thought! The rain was turning the dust of the road into mud, beautiful mud that would take beautiful footprints. They wouldn't last long if the rain started coming down harder, but with any luck at all Alan would be here soon.

And then we turned off the road, towards the field. There was a stile.

'I can't,' I said flatly.

Ben was far ahead. He turned around and glared at me. 'Did you hear me? Hurry up!'

'I can't. I can't climb that stile. I have artificial knees and they won't do it.'

He came thundering back and pulled back a fist. I looked him straight in the eye. 'You can hit me as much as you want. I still can't climb over that fence.'

If profanity really did turn the air blue, the cloud would have been enough to pinpoint our location for Alan. Unfortunately, all it did was lacerate my sensibilities. I've been known to swear myself, on those rare occasions when I was too upset to care, but I made a solemn vow right then to watch my mouth from now on.

In the end he gave up. I was too heavy to be boosted over, and it was against his nature to help a woman do anything, anyway.

'It means the long way round, then. Serves you right for being stubborn. Hurry up!'

He returned to the road winding down into the valley, a road where we could leave those lovely footprints.

It was a nightmare walk. I don't suppose it was even a mile, but it was downhill, which anyone with bad knees knows is much harder than up. I had nothing to give me any support, and I was so afraid of losing my balance that I walked a lot more slowly than Ben wanted. I would even have taken his arm if he'd offered, but of course he didn't, just raced ahead of me and turned back every now and then to fling abuse my way. He was very sure I wouldn't try to escape, and he was absolutely right.

Stumbling along in his wake, I wondered if there was anything else I could leave for Alan, by way of a trail of breadcrumbs. It would be lovely if I had a nice breakable string of beads, but I almost never wore beads any more, except for the pearls Alan had given me as a wedding present, and I would be da— I would be very reluctant to break that string, even if I had them on, which of course I didn't. Buttons? Just one, holding up my jeans, and it was riveted on. I always carried plenty of tissues, but they were in the car, in my bag. So was everything else that might be useful. Blast! (I congratulated myself mentally on my choice of language.)

I trudged on, digging my chilled hands into my pockets. And I was rewarded.

I had forgotten Watson's biscuits. Light in colour and shaped like little bones, they would be very visible against the mud of the verge. And as far as I could tell, they were so hard that little short of Noah's flood would cause them to disintegrate. I looked up to make sure Ben didn't see me, and dropped one, and a few yards on, another.

I had nearly run out when we came to a bend in the road and there, unexpectedly, was the farmhouse. Or *a* farmhouse. It certainly looked deserted, and the shutters were drawn across most of the windows. Ben was waiting for me, and dragged me roughly to the door. 'Come into my parlour, my dear!'

I tried not to think of the obvious parallel.

One shutter was hanging off a glassless window, providing a little murky light to the front room. The first thing I saw was Fred, trussed to a chair with his head drooping forward. I managed to bite back a cry. He isn't dead, I kept thinking. He wouldn't have had to be tied up if he was dead. But his face was a nasty mess, and he didn't stir.

I wanted to go over to him, but Ben had tight hold of my arm. 'Now isn't that touching! She wants to make sure her toy boy is well enough to service her again. I wouldn't be too sure of that, my dear. He might not do too well in that department for a while. Now, what shall I do with you? I wasn't planning on so many guests today, so my cleaner hasn't been. You'll have to forgive the mess.'

He shoved me towards a door at the back of the room. In the near-darkness, and without my glasses, I could barely see. I banged my knee against a low table. This time I couldn't stifle a cry of pain.

'Oh, so very sorry, Your Highness. Must be more careful, mustn't I? I won't get full price for damaged merchandise.'

If he wanted me to believe he planned to hold me for ransom, it didn't work. Whatever his plans were, I was sure they were more violent than that.

The door opened. 'In here!'

'Here' was presumably a bedroom, though the shutters were tightly closed and I could see almost nothing. The atmosphere was close and musty, and I thought I heard a scurrying that augured rats. I was thrown unceremoniously down on a surface that gave under me, with a creak of rusty springs. It smelled of mould and other things I didn't care to identify. The door was slammed shut and I heard something heavy moving across the floor outside. A chest or something, I guessed, pulled across the door in lieu of a lock. Then the very final slam of a door.

Ben had left, and I was well and truly imprisoned.

THIRTY-TWO

For a few minutes I simply lay there and allowed tears of self-pity to spill out. Then as I began to sniffle, and realized I had nothing suitable for blowing my nose, I told myself it was no fun to cry when one couldn't mop up. Besides, I would only add that well-known headache to all my other woes.

Anyway, self-pity was not only unattractive, it was inapt. This was all my fault. I couldn't blame anyone else for my predicament. I had been incredibly blind and stupid. So many pointers could have led me to this man as Ben. That little encounter in the church, for one, on the day I'd seemed to run into the man everywhere I went. He'd been so insistent with the vicar, so obviously looking for someone, and I'd forgotten the incident as soon as it was behind me. And even earlier today, I could have eluded him. The man had made me uneasy when he first showed up at the car. Always trust your instincts, runs the oft-repeated advice. Why on earth hadn't I simply locked the doors, called Alan, and waited for help?

Self-reproach was no more productive than tears. Here I was, and here I would almost certainly stay unless I could figure out a means of escape, so the first priority was some industrious thinking. What assets did I have, what resources that could get me out of this house?

I took inventory. Couldn't see much; very little light and no glasses. Could hear and, unfortunately, could smell and feel. One unpleasant feeling among the many that beset me was the increasingly urgent need for a bathroom. At my age, that is not a need that can be denied for very long. If I shouted to my tormentor, would he respond?

Well, no, even if he was still in the house, not if past performance was any guide. And I would all too obviously not be the first person to use this room for such a purpose.

The idea of removing my jeans was abhorrent, given what might be on the other side of that door. I could only imagine what he would do if he came in and found me half-naked. On the other hand, I couldn't even contemplate spending time in sodden and stinking clothes. Blood-soaked clothing was bad enough, but that was, as someone in a Dorothy Sayers novel once said, 'past prayin' for'.

So I sat on the edge of the bed, removed the necessary articles of clothing as quietly as I could, located a corner, and did what I had to do. Once more, as I leaned against the wall, I heard rustling. With a shudder, I got back into my clothes and back on to the bed, with my feet up. Of course I knew that rats are not like mice, scurrying around on the floor. They'll get up on a bed just as easily as a cat. It didn't matter. My instinctive response to any sort of rodent is to put my feet up.

All right. Most of my senses were in operating condition. And exactly how much good would that do me?

Not a lot, except perhaps defensively. I could hear Ben if he came back, and maybe blockade the door ... no, it opened out. But I could be ready for him.

Ready with what? My handy karate chop? My Uzi? Right.

All my possible weapons, my Swiss Army knife, my heavy handbag, my phone, were back in the car. I was in pain, I was bleeding in a dozen places, and (might as well face it) I was old.

The heck with the stiff upper lip. I lay back on the disgusting bed and let the tears flow. Eventually I slept.

I don't know how long I lay dozing, but when I came back to full consciousness, the room was totally dark. Nothing shone through the chinks in the shutters. I got up, wincing at the stiff joints and the aches that had developed while I slept, and made my way to where I presumed the window to be. I moved my fingers over the glass, very carefully in case it was broken, but there was only the smooth surface, and no light at all.

It must be really late, then. I tried to remember

when the sun set at this time of year. After nine, I was pretty sure, and on a sunny day the light lingered for quite a while after that.

No wonder I was hungry. And thirsty.

I wished I hadn't thought of that. Now, thinking about my thirst, it began to be all-consuming. I needed some water. I could imagine water, lovely cold water, flowing down a mountainside, cascading into a pool...

And of course the thought of all that water brought to the forefront another urgent need. That one at least I could satisfy.

Having done so, I lay drearily back on the bed, the springs clashing horribly, and tried to think. My head was aching, pounding so that I couldn't seem to make my brain work. Thump, thump, thump.

It is a symptom of my distraught frame of mind that it took several minutes for me to recognize two things. One was that the sound was external, not within my own body. The other was that the rhythm was very familiar.

Those rustling noises earlier might not have been rats. Certainly no rat was tapping out SOS on the wall.

I forgot my headache, my aches, my thirst. Here was human contact! And I was willing to bet I knew what human.

I tapped back, cautiously in case Ben had returned, though I wanted to shout for joy. I knew no Morse, had no idea how to signal 'OK, I've heard you'. But any response would convey the idea. I tapped three times, slowly. Paused. Three more times, slowly.

There was no sound from the other side of the wall, until the rustling began again. Was it just rats, after all?

No. There was a purposeful sound to the rustles. After a moment I realized, or at least I hoped, that the person on the other side had found something hard and was trying to dig through the wall that separated us.

How I wished I could see! I could help. I felt around, repelled by the smell of mould and decay all around me. The walls would almost certainly be crumbling, after all that neglect, if I could only lay my hands on...

Ah. My exploring hands had found a bedpost, and it was metal. I was in a cast-iron bed. Was it too much to suppose that it had knobs?

I slid my hand up the post, only to find a curve, and then a horizontal stretch. No knobs.

Well, then, slats! The mattress had to rest on something. It was lightweight, not exactly your high-class inner-spring. I pulled it and the disgusting bedding to the floor and reached under the springs, hoping that whatever was coming off on my fingers was only rust. After breaking a couple of fingernails and stabbing myself with the point of a spring that had come loose, I found a slat, and though it might be as decayed as everything else in the house, it had supported my weight. I pulled it out from under the springs, listened, and began to attack the wall where I thought the sound was coming from.

We were lucky. Evidently, at some relatively recent point in time, the one back room in this cottage had been made into two. This was no

300

wall of solid stone, but a flimsy partition of wood and drywall. I tried to be quiet, even though I was pretty sure Ben wasn't in the house, so progress was slow, but even gentle digs at the damp-damaged wall yielded results. I had soon created a hole big enough to put my hand in, and then I could pull away larger chunks of drywall.

The shock of touching something warm almost raised a scream, until I realized it was no rat, but a human hand.

By now I had few doubts. I put my face to the hole. 'Jo?' It was the merest breath of sound.

'Who are you?'

'Dorothy. Dorothy Martin. And you're Jo Carter. You can't imagine how glad I am to ... well, see you isn't exactly the word, is it?'

'Oh, *don't* make me laugh,' came the agonized whisper out of the darkness. A stifled cough or two followed.

'You have your medicine, don't you?' I asked anxiously.

'Yes. Wait a moment.' An interval. Then a clearer whisper. 'How did you know about the medicine?'

'Oh, we know quite a lot, Alan and I. And I'll tell you all about it when we get out of here. I don't want to talk too much now, because...' I trailed off as we heard the bang of a door. 'Quiet! He's back!'

'Well, ladies,' came the hated voice, full of geniality now. 'I do apologize for the primitive conditions. I expect you've been a bit cold, so I propose to take care of that.' There was a sound as of splashing water. What was he...?

Then my nose told me. Above all the other repellent smells rose, strong and penetrating, the smell of gasoline.

I heard a gasp. 'Petrol! He's going to...'

'Not if I can stop him, he's not,' I whispered back.

Too loudly. Footsteps neared the door. 'Oh, you think you can stop me, do you? One of those superwomen, are you? Think if you talk tough enough, you're going to grow balls? Sorry, bitch, it doesn't work that way. I'm told the smoke puts you out almost at once, and you never know another thing. I'd prefer a more painful death for both of you, but this has gone on long enough. Have to destroy the evidence. Oh, and never fear. I'll find that bitch Sarah and her bastard son, if it's the last thing I do. So you'll both have died for nothing. Night-night, sweethearts!'

I heard the click of a lighter, then another, and another.

The language this time surpassed all his earlier efforts. He finally stomped off, and I heard the nasty sound of a hard slap. 'Wake up, you useless turd! Matches! Give me your matches!'

Fred. Poor Fred, dragged into this mess simply by doing me a favour. 'Leave him alone!' I shouted. 'He isn't involved in this at all. Leave him *alone!*' I shoved desperately, with my bed slat, at where I assumed the door to be.

The door was of the same cheap construction as the wall. It splintered, than gave way completely, shoving the chest aside, and I was stand-

302

ing in the front room.

Ben turned to me with a roar of pure rage, matches in his hand. I screamed, and then several things seemed to happen at once. Ben slipped in a pool of gasoline and fell, hard. The chair where Fred was tied up fell over, and Fred was somehow out of it and at Ben's throat. And from outside came the most beautiful sound I've ever heard, the loud, frenzied barking of a dog. Watson! Watson, somehow escaped from whatever fate Ben had planned for him, and come to find his people.

I should let him in. I should help Fred disable Ben. I was too confused to know what to do first, but a cry from Jo roused me. 'What's happening? Help! Somebody get me out of here!'

Jo! She was the first order of business. I screamed back at her. 'I'm going to try to break down your door! I don't know where the key is!' And at the sound of my voice Watson solved one problem himself. He found the open shutter and leaped into the house.

Barking and jumping, alternately licking my hand and growling at the fight now raging on the floor, he added considerably to the confusion. I tried to look for something to use as a battering ram. Jo's door was old and solid; my bed slat wasn't going to make much headway against that.

Besides, I noted with despair, the hinges were on this side. The door opened out. What I needed was a lever of some kind, a good stout piece of metal to force between the door and the jamb...

A tyre iron!

303

Fred's car would have one. Someplace. What a frustrating thought! It would take too many precious minutes to get there, find it, and get back. Meanwhile Fred was losing his battle. He was older than Ben, and injured, and Ben was fighting, I saw with despair, with the strength born of madness.

The reek of gasoline, and the noise, was making me dizzy. I stumbled to the door for some air. I could get away, easily. But I couldn't leave Fred and Jo and my valiant dog to be vaporized when the house went up.

And then I opened the door and saw the car. Ben's car? It didn't matter. A car, with the boot open. That was where the gasoline came from. That was where I would find my crowbar.

I rummaged, tore another couple of nails, swore (forgetting all my good resolutions), and finally laid my hands on the tool kit and a small but serviceable tyre iron. I was back in the house with it in seconds and working at the door, tears streaming down my face from stress and the ever-stronger gasoline fumes. I didn't dare spare any attention for Fred and Ben. *Get us out!* The refrain pounded in my brain. *Get us out!*

The door began to give. 'Push!' I screamed. 'Jo, push on the door.'

She pushed, I pried, and she fell into the room just as Ben got to his feet, matches in hand. He shouted in triumph, and I gave Jo a shove. 'Run! I've got to help Fred!'

She didn't run. She bent over, grabbed Fred by one arm as I reached the other. Watson got a good grip of his foot, and we had dragged him

304

nearly to the door when Ben managed to strike flame from his match.

Inferno. Flames, choking smoke. Screams. I couldn't see, couldn't think, could react only with instinct. Somewhere there was freedom, air I could breathe, escape from this hell. Someone was nudging me. There was pain, sharper than the pain from the flames. I moved away from it, but it came again.

Dragging a weight with me, for an eternity of moments, I emerged into the sunlight and was struck to the ground by something heavy. Then came a blessed coolness on my face, and then welcome oblivion.

THIRTY-THREE

Hours later, I was half-lying on a couch in the lounge of the Holly Tree, Alan next to me with my hand firmly clasped in his. Ranged around the small room were Jo, Inspector Owen, Superintendent Davids, Paul Jones and his mother, Fred, and, of course, Watson. The dog was sound asleep after having devoured most of a steak. The rest of us were sipping the tipple of our choice and trying to sort things out. Gathered around the edges were our hostess, Pam, the two Irish ladies, who couldn't bear to miss anything, Penny Brannigan, the manicurist, and a woman I vaguely recognized, but couldn't put a name to.

305

The only thing that spoiled the party atmosphere was our appearance, four of us looking like *The Spirit of '76*. Jo, Fred, and I had superficial burns, in addition to the wounds Ben had inflicted. Watson had been burned a little, too, and had scratches on his nose, another little present from the villain of the piece. And the three humans, at least, were a bit dazed with the relief of still being alive.

'How did you find Paul and Sarah?' had been my first question when I was more or less sitting up and taking notice.

'I was stupid about that. It took far too long for me to think of ringing up Rose and Co. for Paul's mobile number, and then I had to leave several messages before Paul rang back. He'd forgotten to turn it on, which is, I suppose, why the police couldn't reach him.'

'And why did they leave the Ritz?'

Alan had shrugged. 'Couldn't bear the inactivity any more, from what I could gather. Had to be up and doing.'

Cabin fever, I'd thought. But in such a luxurious cabin!

'But how did you find me?' I asked now, taking a steadying gulp of my bourbon. 'I never got a chance to give you the coordinates. And I wasn't there any more, anyway.'

'You'd given me a rough idea, so I cruised around and looked for the car. Of course when you didn't answer the second time I called, I knew something had gone badly wrong. I was beginning to be feel a trifle panicky when my mobile rang.' He smiled at the woman I couldn't quite place. 'That's when Helen, here, came to the rescue.'

Helen Hoster, of course! 'But how ... !'

'You gave me your mobile number, remember?' she said. 'And I heard from one of Gillie's therapists that she'd seen a car around the old Blanchard place, and wondered about it. So I phoned you, only your husband answered, and he thought it was worth investigating, since the farm was near where you had said you were.'

Alan took up the tale. 'And when I found the car, and your phone and bag, and blood all over the place, with you nowhere in sight...' He in turn tilted his glass.

'Did you follow the dog biscuits?'

'Did I do what?'

'I left a trail ... never mind. It seemed a good idea at the time. So how *did* you find me, then?'

'It seemed logical that you might be at the old farm. It was the only habitation in sight, after all. And when I neared and heard a dog barking its head off, at a place that was supposed to be deserted, I got out and ran.'

He had already told me the rest of the story. How he found three of us lying just outside the burning farmhouse, Watson lying on top of me. How he found an old water butt in the yard and managed somehow to drench us all with its contents.

'Though in fact Watson had already managed to douse most of the flames, rolling on all of you,' he had said. 'That dog has more sense than many a human.'

'Well, you certainly turned up in the nick of

307

time,' I said now. 'That house was due to explode any minute, and we were awfully close to the doorway.'

'But what I can't understand is how *you* found the place, Dorothy,' said Jo. She was enjoying an abstemious glass of tonic water. We'd offered gin to go with it, but she said she'd seen enough families destroyed by drink to put her off alcohol for a lifetime. 'It was out in the middle of nowhere,' she went on, 'and you don't know the country around here.'

'Ah, but Fred does. He was the one who found it really. I just came along for the ride.'

A chorus of voices lauded Fred, who buried his red face in his beer. 'What I meant,' Jo's voice rose above the rest, 'was, how did you even have any idea where to begin looking?'

'I followed Brother Cadfael,' I said, and then snickered at the look on everyone's face. 'There is a wonderful book by Ellis Peters where Cadfael – he's a twelfth-century monk – anyway, he figures out what happened on the strength of a strand of hair from a horse's mane. And I found some blond hair at the shed where you ended up when you tried to run away, and decided it was from a palomino horse, and then...'

'Then she worked out where she would be if she were a horse, and went there, and there it was,' put in my loving husband.

'So you knew I'd escaped on a horse. Remarkable! More like Sherlock Holmes, I'd say. I nearly made it, too. I'd nicked that dreadful man's mobile—'

'Oh, so I was wrong there! I thought you'd

probably found one somebody had lost.'

'Well, in a way I did. The beast dropped his and didn't notice; he was too busy abusing me. So when he left me to go for my asthma inhaler, I stole the phone and one of his horses, got away as best I could, and made the nine-nine-nine call as soon as I thought I was far enough away. Unfortunately I hadn't got quite far enough.'

There was a depressed little silence. Alan cleared his throat. 'More of anything, anyone?' He gestured at a rather impressive array of bottles and at the remains of pizza, fish, chips, and Indian takeout that littered the room.

'However you did it, Mrs Martin...' Sarah began.

'Please. Dorothy.'

'However you did it, Dorothy, you've freed Jo. And us.' She raised her wine glass in a rather sober toast, and we responded in the same way.

For Ben would never abuse anyone again. Even if Alan had known that anyone was still inside the burning house, entering it had been out of the question. Part of me hoped that Ben had been right in his description of death by fire, that smoke inhalation induced a coma and there was no pain. Part of me doubted it. That fire had been so intense, and certainly I had experienced pain (though much of it was from the nips Watson had administered to get me moving). There was so little left of the man that his true identity might never be known, but I wasn't sure that mattered any more. And the worst part of me whispered that Ben deserved to die horribly. I had another sip of bourbon to drown that un-

309

worthy thought.

'There was good in him once,' said Sarah.

'No, there wasn't, Mum.' Paul had been silent until then, his arm around his mother. 'You only thought there was. He was a right sh— a right prat, all along.'

'Have you worked out, Mrs Martin, why poor old Symonds was killed?' asked Inspector Owen.

'I think so, and I think you have too.'

I looked at Jo, who was nodding in her chair. Her short grey hair had been combed in Casualty, but there had been no attempt at styling. Her dark pants and top were clean and neat, but had never been fashionable. Fashion wouldn't suit her sturdy, blocky body. And the scarf around her neck was purely for comfort.

'Yes,' said the inspector quietly, 'I agree. Mistaken identity. Ben thought he was Jo. Remember, Paul was pretty sure Ben had overheard Jo saying she was going up to see the Tower. He wanted to capture her, not kill her, but when she – as he thought – didn't answer him, that hair-trigger temper of his got the better of him and he gave Symonds a shove. I don't suppose we'll ever know whether he meant to push him over the edge, or just grab him, but we know the result.'

'And the poor man wouldn't have answered, of course. Ben was shouting for Jo, not Bill, and in any case, Symonds was nearly stone deaf.'

There was a little silence in respectful memory of a good man, undeservedly dead, a silence broken by one of the Irish ladies. 'Well,' she said, her voice full of self-satisfaction, 'we were the ones who called the police, weren't we, Barbara?'

'Indeed they did,' Pam agreed with a little sideways glance at Alan and me. 'When you all came in looking like the wrath of God, Barbara and Eileen thought some reinforcements would be a good idea.'

I was sure they had thought we were all dastardly criminals, and from the expression on his face, Alan did, too. 'They meant well,' I whispered to him, and he clasped my hand a little harder.

'But the real hero of the day,' I said, to change the subject, 'is Watson here. If he hadn't managed to get away when Ben caught Fred, and raised such an unholy ruckus later, Alan might not have been in time.'

The dog raised his head at the sound of his name, smiled at us, burped gently, and went back to sleep.

'It's going to break my heart to give him back now, if we ever do find out who his real owner is.'

'I can tell you that,' said Fred unexpectedly.

We all turned to him.

'Didn't want to say before. Wanted to be sure you'd be good to him.'

'Fred! He isn't yours, is he?'

'Nah. I've never had but Alsatians, and after old Bess died, I'd not got the heart for another dog. No, this dog belonged to Bill Symonds. He ran away when his master didn't come home. I reckernized him the minute I saw him. Reckon he was running over the hills, looking for a home. Reckon he's found one now.'

Alan and I looked at each other. 'I don't know what Sam and Emmy are going to say,' I said.

Alan smiled fondly at Watson. 'Sam and Emmy,' he said firmly, 'are going to have to lump it. Watson's a member of the family now.'

That seemed to be the last word. The party broke up, and Alan and I didn't try to detain them. We all needed a good, long night's sleep. The last one out the door was Penny. 'How long are you going to be in town, Dorothy?' she asked.

'Oh, we probably won't leave until tomorrow afternoon. I want to sleep late.'

'Good. I'm stopping by around noon, and I'll have a kit with me. You *really* need that manicure now!'

AUTHOR'S NOTE

Readers who know the lovely Cotswold village of Broadway will recognize the liberties I have taken with some of its geography. In general, the pleasant places and beautiful views I have described are real; the unpleasant ones are the product of my disordered imagination. The Holly Tree, though modelled very closely on an actual, charming guest house in Broadway, has been fictionalized to spare the delightful proprietors any embarrassment at the behaviour of some of their guests. The Arts Festival, on the other hand, is (except in timing and certain details) very much like the inaugural event I was fortunate enough to happen across some time ago.

The town of Upper Pinnock is entirely fictional. There was, in medieval times, a village called Pinnock, a few miles south of Broadway, but almost nothing now remains of it. My Upper Pinnock is in a slightly different location and endowed with a river, a large church, and a railway station, among other amenities.

I have anticipated, by months or years, the rebuilding of the Broadway railway station. The GWR is indeed planning to extend the Honey-

313

bourne line to Broadway, but the effort requires an enormous amount of money. If you are a steam train enthusiast and would like to contribute to the appeal, visit the line's website at www.gwsr.com.